THE SINGING WOOD

A College Story

Books by

FLORENCE CRANNELL MEANS

Penny for Luck
A Bowlful of Stars
A Candle in the Mist
Ranch and Ring
Dusky Day
Tangled Waters
The Singing Wood
Shuttered Windows
Adella Mary in Old New Mexico
At the End of Nowhere
Whispering Girl
Shadow Over Wide Ruin

DURING THE SUCCEEDING DAYS DUSKY WATCHED DAVID SNATCH ODD MOMENTS TO LABOR GRIMLY AT THE OCTAGONAL BENCH (*p.* 90)

The SINGING WOOD

A College Story

FLORENCE CRANNELL MEANS

Illustrated by
MANNING DE V. LEE

HOUGHTON MIFFLIN COMPANY · BOSTON
The Riverside Press Cambridge

The Riverside Press
CAMBRIDGE · MASSACHUSETTS
PRINTED IN THE U.S.A.

CONTENTS

ILLUSTRATIONS

I. THE DAY GROVE

'If you're going to start our junior year *this* way — !' Dusky protested, glaring down at her roommate. 'Are we supposed to be college students, or housekeepers? I ask you!'

Dusky, named Loduska Day, was tall and broad-shouldered like a boy. Her black-fringed blue eyes were startlingly light and alive in the deep warm russet of her face. She was boyish and positive, from her curly mop of black hair to the tips of her scuffed oxfords.

Yet, positive as she was, she knew she could not push this pliant little fair-haired roommate any further. There came a point where Mary Beth stuck fast.

'If you'd turn back the big rug and wipe up the outside edge with the dust mop *before* you use the sweeper —' Mary Beth suggested mildly. Already she had thrown the windows wide to the September breeze and lugged to the balcony a pair of small Chinese rugs and a dozen assorted cushions. Now she was beginning to empty the cupboard of its teacups and plates and glasses.

'As for turning back rugs,' Dusky declared, 'it's against my principles. Anyway, before the end of the semester. A lick and a promise is plenty when we've only been here two weeks.'

Mary Beth's mouth puckered to match her soft forehead. 'But, Dusky,' she said indulgently, 'with Open

House this very night? And you know some of the boys think it clever to investigate every corner.'

Dusky smiled at Mary Beth's precise speech. Even after two years in an American college her Chinese background popped out whenever she opened her mouth.

'I'll plant myself here and stay,' Dusky said. 'Nobody's going to go snooping around the internal arrangements of this room if I'm sitting spang in the middle.'

'Even Professor Davis sometimes runs his fingers over the tops of the doors to see if there's any dust,' Mary Beth continued, unmoved. She set a basin of soapsuds on the balcony floor as on a table, and stood at the window scrubbing the dishes and draining them on a clean newspaper.

With an exaggerated sigh Dusky flopped back the rug. She picked a dime and a half-dozen hairpins out of the dust and swooped an energetic mop around the concrete.

'These glasses will *not* come clear,' Mary Beth was sputtering softly. 'I cannot imagine why, unless —— Dusky, you haven't —?'

Dusky pushed the mop toward the window and peered at the glasses. 'I guess I had paint water in that one,' she said pleasantly. 'The other' — she sniffed — 'is turpentine. Don't be any more of a granny than you have to.'

'You have used the best tea towel for a paint rag, too,' Mary Beth accused her. 'It does seem as if ——'

Dusky flopped down the edges of the rug, snapped the sweeper cord into an outlet, and clattered the sweeper across the rug and onto the concrete. To make more certain of drowning Mary Beth's complaint, she sang in a throaty voice, somewhat off key,

> 'Down at the STATION,
> Early in the MORNING,
> See the little PUFFER BILLIES ——'

From the gay Mexican blanket on the bed sounded a plump small chuckle. A delectable four-year-old, Mexican to match the blanket, was nested there, with round-bladed scissors and an old magazine for entertainment. She pursed a rosy mouth and said, 'Poffer beelies! Seeng some more poffer beelies, Dosky!'

'Say please,' Dusky prompted automatically. 'And don't drop any scraps on the floor, Carmelita, or Mary Beth will just naturally throw you out of the window.'

Carmelita tucked her round chin down into her little brown neck, crowded her dimpled hands between her dimpled knees, and giggled. She was the youngest child of one of the campus gardeners. Now and then Dusky brought her home, either to make drawings of her black eyes and black silk curls, or just to have her around, like an engaging kitten.

Carmelita loved the visits. They always began with a Cashmere Bouquet bath. Carmelita's home baths were accomplished with yellow laundry soap, and the smell of yellow laundry soap was one of the many things Dusky detested. Carmelita loved the baths; she loved the South Suite; she loved the old magazines; and she loved Dusky. So she sometimes came uninvited, and sometimes, as today, not too welcome. But Carmelita, as Dusky admitted, was so completely adorable that one could not rebuff her.

> 'See the little PUFFER BILLIES
> All in a row!'

Dusky shouted obediently above the clatter of the sweeper.

> 'See the station master ——'

'Dibs on the Hoover, Dusky,' a voice shrieked from the door.

'It's yours this minute' — Dusky trundled the sweeper toward her with alacrity — 'And don't forget it's your turn to clean the bathroom, Maxine. It would be nice if you'd wash your stockings down in the laundry today — for once.'

Maxine was the third of the four suite-mates. Oddly enough assorted they were: Dusky, tanned and buoyant and positive, from Colorado; Mary Beth Masterson, small and fair and prim, born and reared in China, where her parents were missionaries; Maxine, all sweet curves and golden-brown waving hair and curling lashes and coquetry, from a crude little gold-mining town caught in a cleft of the California mountains; Kate Oliver ——

'Kate!' Maxine called. 'It's your turn to clean the bathroom, joy be.'

Kate strode through the connecting bathroom and looked shyly out at the busy group. Kate had come straight from a cattle ranch in Arizona. She was bigger than Dusky, and rangy as a colt. The paddy-green hair ribbon that ran through her chestnut ringlets looked strangely out of place, but since it was Freshman Week she had to wear it.

Dusky, who had dragged a box of paints from her closet and flopped down on the swept rug with it, looked up at her appreciatively, and made a frame of her hands, through which she studied Kate's flushing face.

'Your features are put together awfully well,' she commented frankly. 'I'm crazy about the way your eyes are set, and I always liked big mouths. Hair curls all over your head like a baby's, too. — But I just can't figure what colors I'd use for your skin. It's so transparent, and at the same time so tanned ——'

'You'll get used to her,' Maxine reassured Kate. 'When she makes passes like that, she means she wants to paint your picture. But she'll probably never get around to it. She's an art major, and they're all goofy. — Good land, what's this in the lavatory?' she broke off sharply.

'That? Nothing but wave-set,' Dusky explained nonchalantly. 'Spilled it when I was setting Caro Felton's hair. I'm not going to do any more hair, but she pestered me into it this time.' She jabbed her brush into the paint on her palette and worked swiftly, outlining a design already painted on the corner of the rug.

'My goodness,' Mary Beth remonstrated, returning to the cupboard with her hands full of clean dishes. 'Dusky, how many years are you going to work on those dragons, anyway?'

'Don't you want us to look neat?' Dusky grinned at her and went on outlining scales with black paint and touching up claws and forked tongue with vermilion. 'I'm just giving this one a shampoo and a facial. Though I'm thinking of doing a phoenix in the middle of the room, where it's getting to look so scrubby.'

'But not now! And be sure to put a chair over this one when it's done. Remember Carmelita rolled in the last one you repainted.'

'I'm doing this one because it can have the edge of the dresser over it to sort of keep off the callers tonight,' Dusky assented. 'And I'm using lots of turps, so it'll dry quick.'

'She's — *painting* — on the *rug?*' Kate asked wonderingly.

'Dusky will paint on anything. You can't stop her.' Maxine spoke with resignation. 'But this really was necessary. We were doing our second-hand bookcases and things in enamel when we were Frosh. One of the Green Valley paint shops was giving away samples, so we each got one: peacock blue and Chinese red and yellow and black. All we had to buy was one can of black, and now look at it!'

The furniture was glossy black, with edges and some top surfaces of exotic color.

'It's — different from anything else I ever saw, anyway,' Kate acknowledged.

'Oh, it's really artistic,' Maxine instructed her. 'You can count on Dusky for that. When I was a Frosh I couldn't quite see it, either. I was all set for pale pinks and blues. — Well, anyhow' — Maxine smoothed her slightly too plump waistline with an habitual gesture — 'Dusky spilled the can of Chinese red on the rug, and so she spread it out and made a Chinese dragon of it. And then, of course, she had to match up the other four corners. Lucky the rug is a flat weave, so she could. — Come along, Frosh, we've got to clean up our end of the dump. Do you think Luisa's going to bring those curtains today, as she promised?'

Absently Maxine dropped a chunk of butter toffee into Carmelita's eager mouth and turned the bag upside down over her own extended tongue to catch the last buttery, nutty crumb.

'Say thank you, Caramel,' Dusky admonished.

'S-k-you,' Carmelita responded, shaping her moist red mouth with difficulty over the bulge of the sweetmeat.

'I should hope so,' Dusky belatedly answered Maxine's question about the curtains. 'Maxine, I thought you were off candy. You've gained again, haven't you?'

'I hadn't had a speck of candy for a week,' Maxine defended herself. 'And it's going to be just too bad if we haven't any curtains for tonight.'

The big windows were bare, though the rest of the room was fast resettling itself. Mary Beth plumped the red and blue and yellow cretonne cushions down in the Chinese reed lounge chairs and placed one Chinese rug exactly straight in front of the bed, the second exactly straight between bed and dresser.

Chinese embroideries glowed on the walls, and they were augmented by a print or two and a decorative portrait by Dusky. Odds and ends of cinnabar and lacquer and brass stood on table and bookcase and cupboard. One door-bed had been turned on its end and trundled back into the closet for the day; the other, covered with Dusky's striped Mexican blanket and a flock of cushions, served as divan.

It was a gay room, except for the blankness of the many-paned windows. Last year the curtains had been plain monk's cloth. When they were taken down for summer vacation, Luisa, Carmelita's eldest sister, had suggested that Mama Vasquez would embroider them with bands of Mexican embroidery if the girls cared to buy the wool.

'Luisa will probably bring them when she comes after Carmelita,' Dusky said, a paint brush gyrating tipsily between her teeth.

'Mmm,' Maxine murmured doubtfully. 'Luisa. — Dusky, I can understand your liking to pet *any* kind of *baby*, but I just wonder if you aren't going to find it a little too much of a good thing if her seventeen-year-old sister gets to tagging around after you. You do have to draw the line somewhere.'

Dusky ground her teeth. Secretly she wished that the Luisas did not begin to use such whitewashings of powder, such splashings of rouge and mascara, as soon as they reached their teens. She wished they did not chew gum so loudly.

Still, her principles remained firm, and she demanded with scarcely any hesitation: 'You wouldn't have me snub Luisa because of her nationality, would you? Maxine, I think it's imbecile of you to draw such lines.' — She flopped back on her heels and jabbed the brush in Maxine's direction. — 'Anyhow, you don't have to be so superior about Mexico. It's a darned interesting country, and it's got a darned interesting background. I'd give my eyeteeth if I could get that exchange fellowship and spend a year at the University of Mexico. My word!'

'You do get more notions than anyone I ever saw,' Maxine observed amiably, drifting back toward her room.

Dusky thought it unnecessary to tell her that this particular notion had been born in a single flash — born of her defense of Luisa and Luisa's country. It was a good idea, though, and already growing rapidly. Dusky wondered that it had never occurred to her before.

'Well, of all the nerve!' Maxine called back. 'I didn't

see this gormy old paint brush. Why on earth did you have to stick a gormy old paint brush in the lavatory?'

'It isn't a gormy old paint brush. It's a new sable one and it cost three dollars. You wash three-dollar paint brushes reverently, with soap and water and prayer. I'll clean out your old lavatory when I'm through here.'

From the hall, muffled by the closed door but sifting through the open transom, came the sound of radios, tuned high, tuned low; girls' voices; a tap and shuffle of dance steps; a bang of doors; the clatter and hum of sweepers; feet pelting up and down stairs.

From the campus came the whirr and bang and rattle of rowdy campus automobiles; the birdlike whistle of a boy; laughter; the high and not unpleasant squeak of one of the watering units, which stood like a semaphore, sending out long twisting arms of water and twittering each time it turned.

Dusky sat back on her heels again: her posture had been that of a small child looking at funnies spread on the floor. She approved her dragon with a sharp nod, sprang to her feet, deposited paint box and palette on the closet floor, perched on the bed, and cut out another paper doll for Carmelita.

At the door sounded a hesitant double knock. A glossy head was thrust inside. Liquid brown eyes peered through heavily blackened lashes. Luisa edged in on high-heeled sandals.

Dusky's eyes dropped at once to the visitor's hands, and she brightened. Luisa was carrying a bulky newspapered package.

'My little sister here yet?' she asked unnecessarily, shifting her chewing-gum with an expert smack. 'Mama says I shall bring her right home.'

Dusky lifted the child out from the litter on the bed. She was so tiny for her age that it was hard not to treat her like a baby. She stretched imperious hands back toward a paper doll she had dropped, uttering small demanding grunts.

Mary Beth was unwrapping the curtains, and Luisa watched with pleased expectancy while Dusky shoved the desk over by a window and climbed onto it to hang a pair of them. She gazed bright-eyed down at the broad band of vivid colored crewel work.

'Luisa,' she said solemnly, 'it's absolutely absolute.' — Luisa giggled. — 'Tell your mother no design could be more beautiful for these rooms.' She pushed the brass rings even, leaped down, shoved the desk to the next window.

Mary Beth had been standing pucker-browed, breath held. 'It *is* lovely!' she admitted. 'It is — *lovely*.'

Buzz — buzz — buzz: Dusky's signal. She dashed to the speaking-tube, calling to Carmelita as she went, 'Dusky'll get you again just as soon as she can, Caramel! Good-bye, Luisa!'

Luisa edged out, her little sister astride her hip breathing gusty remonstrance through her negligible nose.

'Hello; Dusky Day speaking. — Oh, Poddie. — Right *now?* This *morning?'* — Her eyes swept the unfinished room protestingly. — 'My word, Paul, I don't see — They want to go toMORrow? You really mean tomorrow? — All right, then, I'll meet you as soon as I can make it. — Yes, over at the cottage as soon as I can make it.'

'My word!' she snorted, wheeling from the speaking-tube. 'Saturdays aren't what they're cracked up to be. And why in the world would Grandpa and Grandma Wilson take it into their heads to go back to Indiana now? I thought they were safely settled for the winter. And here it's almost eleven o'clock and they want us over there this minute. — This dress won't do to go off campus, will it?'

She was stripping off the pink print as she spoke, and reaching into the closet for a blue jersey. She went on talking from its muffling folds, emerging flushed and discomfited to fumble at the wrists of the long tight sleeves.

'Those snaps are off. You were going to sew them on last night,' Mary Beth reminded her untactfully. 'Don't you remember?'

'Well, I couldn't sew on snaps while I was double-dating with you and David and Paul, could I?' Dusky demanded righteously. David was Mary Beth's brother and Paul was Dusky's, and the four were known on the campus as the Brother-and-Sister Act. — 'Just sort of tack 'em on for me, Ma' Beth.'

Mary Beth reached for her tidy workbasket and a needle threaded with navy blue. 'I can't do it without scratching you if you keep wriggling and standing on one foot,' she said patiently.

'A hole in the heel!' Dusky groaned, coming down with a thud. 'Did you ever know it to fail? And holes in the heel are one thing I won't go outdoors in. Runs don't seem so sordid, but holes in heels —— Just a sec, Mary Beth, till I pull that stocking off.'

'Oh, honey, did you know there was a rip under your arm?'

'Where? Oh, my word! Well, I'll keep my arm down. I've got ten million things to do yet, and —— But when you've got an orange grove of your own — an orange grove of your own, Mary Beth!' she repeated, leaning over to shake her roommate ecstatically.

Mary Beth gurgled and rethreaded her needle. 'It's like sewing snaps on a — on an erupting volcano,' she scolded. 'But I don't wonder you feel that way about the grove. It is the most like a fairy tale of anything I ever knew.'

'Come, come, my pet!' Dusky grumbled. 'That's plenty good for this time. It'll last out the day, and that's all ——'

Mary Beth gripped her firmly with one hand and continued to push the needle in and pull it out. She clipped the thread precisely and fastened the cuffs.

'Thanks a lot, you fuss-budget,' said Dusky, 'and if anybody wants me, tell 'em I've gone to Alaska.'

'Don't forget to sign out,' Mary Beth placidly reminded her.

Dusky took the stairs with her long-legged rush, and scribbled on the blank that hung in the lower corridor: Dusky Day — Day Grove — Return Indefinite.

The Day Grove! she thought with pride, as her long strides carried her swiftly across the campus. It would have to have a better name than that, though, now that it was going to be really theirs. Garden of Hesperides? Bells of Saint Clemens?

The semaphore near Lawrence Hall went on twirling its bright streams and twittering with every twirl. Autumn sunshine burned upon the red-tiled white buildings of the university. The quad glistened with sprays of water like great milkweed silks that had settled on the bright green. Blackbirds fluted brittlely and mocking-birds scolded and whistled and piped.

Dusky sprang into the air, pulled a long flat pod of Saint John's Bread from a tree and chewed meditatively on its tough sweetness. She broke a varnished leaf from a hedge and sniffed its camphor fragrance. She half-consciously noted the ivy geraniums twining their pink blooms high overhead on the rough trunks of the palm trees.

She waved a hand at a boy, at a girl who walked alone.

'Hi, Cordelia!' Dusky shouted.

Cordelia Jacobs was the only Negro student at Highland, and she walked almost always alone, her lovely brown face somber.

Past Senior Bench strode Dusky, behind the sunning stateliness of the Administration Building, down the circular steps of the Greek theater bowl, across the diminishing autumn trickle of the Zanja, by an echoing footbridge to the gate of a small white cottage set in the shade of an orange grove; around the side of the cottage by a well worn path to the back door, where a venerable white rooster named Peter marched belligerently ahead of two equally elderly red hens who scuttled and pecked right and left.

Just inside the kitchen a boy was replacing the cover of a cooky-jar while another boy stood seriously by, cooky in hand: a slim boy little taller than Dusky, with a lock of brown hair falling over a broad brow and brown eyes as clear as brook water — Dusky's brother Paul; a straight young giant with wheat-colored hair — Mary Beth's brother David.

David was worth a look, with his mighty shoulders and his steady eyes and the smile that could so suddenly light his intent face; yet Dusky's glance was inclined to take him for granted as an adopted brother — an especially nice one, to be sure, and even more warmly close than Paul. David, on the contrary, looked at Dusky as if he were always surprised to find her just the kind of girl she was: surprised and delighted.

'Hi, Peter!' Dusky greeted the rooster, who followed her onto the porch. 'Hello, David and Paul. What on earth is up?'

'They decided they had to go back to Johnnie's wedding,' said Paul. 'Tomorrow, if they can make it. They want us to help them get off; and then to take possession, Madam, of house and grove!'

'My word!' gasped Dusky.

'Congratulations!' said David, his smile flashing. 'Be seeing you!' He swung away.

'Our own grove,' Paul muttered thickly. 'Gosh, I can't make it seem true.'

'I either,' Dusky agreed, reaching over to break off half his cooky. 'But if it should fall through — oh, wouldn't it be a blow!'

II. GRANDPA AND GRANDMA WILSON

Grandpa and Grandma Wilson were waiting for them in the dim sitting-room. Grandma was pottering around the towering walnut secretary. She took out a book and put it into the battered Gladstone bag that yawned on the floor, looked at it indecisively with tilted head, her soft pursed mouth making a thousand drawstring wrinkles, and then took it out of the bag and set it on its shelf again.

'We ain't going to cart much along, this time,' she explained, 'but it seems like there's *some* things ——'

Grandpa had the top drawer on his spread knees and was peering at the papers as he thumbed through them.

Grandpa and Grandma were nobody's grandparents and Dusky and Paul nobody's grandchildren. The mutual adoption had begun when Dusky and Maxine lay in the tangle of vines and shrubbery on the banks of the Zanja, in their freshman year, studying, and Grandpa and Grandma gave them oranges and cookies. It had been completed when Grandpa, defying his eighty years, had climbed into his trees to pick oranges, and had won a broken hip by his defiance.

Even now Dusky re-lived the evening when she had learned of the accident. She had been surprised by a For Sale sign gleaming at her in the moonlight, and running into the house she had found Grandma rocking desolately in the bay window, where Grandpa sat today.

The place was for sale because they couldn't manage to

take care of it, Grandma explained, dabbing at her eyes and biting her lower lip to master its trembling. 'It's time to irrigate tomorrow!' she had wailed suddenly, looking up at a blatantly pretty girl on a calendar beside the secretary. It was not the pretty girl that admonished Grandma, but the circled dates on the calendar pad: circles with wavering guide lines to the broad margin. 'Iragate!' the marginal notes commanded. 'Cultavate!'

After that night the adoption had been complete. The brother and sister had spent all their spare time in the grove and house. Paul had become vitally interested in the problems and possibilities of orange-growing. And when Grandpa and Grandma's only son, Johnnie, had come home from years of motor-selling abroad, and decided to marry and settle down in 'Indiany,' Grandpa and Grandma found Indiany tempting too, and offered grove and house to these adopted grandchildren of theirs.

The price and terms had been ridiculously low: two hundred dollars down and 'what you can manage a year' until twenty thousand dollars had been paid.

But while the offer had seemed even at first a piece of amazing fortune, a fairy-tale come true, it appeared more and more amazing as they inquired prices of established groves; more and more overwhelming as they learned costs of operation. Dusky said she felt as if she were in one of those nightmare dreams where you are trying to hang a million-dollar business on a ten-cent shoestring.

Paul had learned enough about groves to know that price and terms were an absurdity for a twenty-acre grove in full bearing — a kindly device of Grandpa's to give the young people some twenty thousand dollars and yet keep them independent. But he knew also that it was a gift to challenge all their industry and courage. Plenty of groves showed no profit at all; and a few years of insect pests and frosts, or a few more years of low prices for oranges, would make it hard to keep up even small payments.

'It's such an awfully big thing,' Paul had said, conferring with the old people. 'I realize that two young folks could go a lifetime and never have such an offer. And I really think I could make it pay a nice income. I never was so keen about any other kind of work, either. But — isn't it too big and dangerous for us to try to swing?'

Grandpa cleared his throat in embarrassment.

'Well, it's like this,' he explained: 'jest the minute they's a good year you'd ought to get a buyer easy for half the grove — ten acres. Twenty thousand would be cheap for ten acres, and if you was to dicker a mite you'd ought to get twenty-five. That would give you what folks calls a free ride for the other ten, and a five-thousand-dollar nest egg for a rainy day.'

'But why don't you — or Johnnie — ?' Dusky asked.

Grandpa pushed the suggestion from him with big, knuckly hands. 'I'm too old to be bothered. And we already turnt over propitty enough to Johnnie.'

When Dusky and Paul hesitated, their Aunt Phronsie had proffered the down payment. — Aunt Phronsie's investments had suffered and she could find two hundred dollars only by selling part of her beloved stamp collection, but she was charmed with the idea of retiring to her own orange grove, with her niece and nephew to help her operate it. For Aunt Phronsie was at loose ends. Even the freight-boat junketings around the world which had been her delight were no longer possible on her restricted income. She had been supplying for Highland professors on sabbatical leave, but those two years of teaching were at an end. The grove seemed a safe and lovely refuge.

But she had run into unexpected difficulties: Grandpa and Grandma Wilson speedily made it clear that their offer was to Paul and Dusky, not to miscellaneous relatives. Eventually, Paul and Dusky, poor though they were, scraped together the two hundred dollars, and the deal was made. Grandpa and Grandma stayed on, held by the inertia of age and ill-health.

'Aren't you afraid of your old bronchial colds if you go back just as winter is setting in?' Dusky asked today. 'You know what the doctors told you about another attack of pneumonia, Grandma. I can't see how you came to decide in such a rush.'

Grandma Wilson sat down shakily. 'Well, when it got closer and closer to Johnnie's wedding,' she said, 'we just commenced to feel like we'd got to be there. Johnnie'd ought to have his own folks at his wedding, seems like.'

'You know how the womenfolks is about weddings,' Grandpa said indulgently, tipping up his head to look at them through the spectacles that had slipped down on his nose. 'And I don't feel to blame her, this time. Me and Granmaw's mighty closet to the end of the road. We won't never see grandchild of ours, like enough,' he said with a bluffness that did not hide the wistfulness, 'but seeing our Johnnie hitched is next best. And we only just got time to make it.'

'Grandma, what clothes —?' Dusky inquired anxiously.

'I got my best gray satin, not wore a mite,' Grandma assured her. 'And I thought maybe I could find me a little toque all made of them rainbow-shiny duck-breast feathers, when I got to Indiany. I always did hanker for a toque all made of them feathers, and one all made of vi'lets. They seem to me the elegantest kind of hat.'

'You can have the both of 'em,' Grandpa promised grandly. 'We got to look neat for Johnnie's bride.'

'Oh, Johnnie's sent us her picture,' Grandma twittered, groping in the depths of the Gladstone bag and bringing to light a large photograph carefully clipped between pasteboards.

Paul and Dusky studied it with interest.

'Slick-looking girl,' Paul said.

'Oodles of style,' Dusky added.

She didn't think much of Johnnie, fifty-year-old bridegroom, who hadn't managed to spare time from Singapore and Shanghai and Tokyo to visit his lonesome old parents. Yet she felt a twinge of pity for him when she studied his expensive-looking fiancée, small mouth drooping and big eyes consciously lovely. Johnnie was going to step lively, if Dusky was any judge of faces.

Aunt Phronsie, coming in after a twist of the bell, admired the picture as non-committally as had her niece and nephew.

'What lovely hair!' she said, peering through her thick-lensed glasses. 'She's as pretty as a doll. What a beautiful bride she'll make!'

'And my land, we got to be quick if we're going to see her make one!' Grandma recollected herself, returning the photograph to its place and blinking round the room. 'Granpaw jest figgered it out that we got to ketch the afternoon train if we want to get to Indiany in time for the wedding.'

'The afternoon train? *This* afternoon? But can you possibly?' Aunt Phronsie frowned at the gaping bag, at Grandma's black alpaca dress with a blue checked apron firmly tied around its soft middle.

'*This* afternoon?' Dusky echoed.

Grandma Wilson sat down, folding and unfolding her hands. 'We ain't going to bother to pack, seeing it's you folks that will be here. We'll jest take our clothes and a few knicknacks it seems like I can't never leave behind.'

Grandpa tilted his glasses at them again. 'We kind of figger on getting Johnnie and his bride to come back with us later on when things has settled down,' he explained, 'and then we can clear out our personal belongings.'

Dusky's glance coasted round the staid room: Brussels carpet, sober secretary, walnut rocker, demure ladder-backed chairs, standing sewing-basket. 'But wouldn't Johnnie — ? People are using old walnut, and since this was yours ——'

'It wasn't ours. We bought it jest as it stands when we

took the place five-six years ago. Dear knows how long it had been here then. It wouldn't hardly be worth freightin' back, even if Johnnie wanted it. And I figger that girl of his is going to have things spandy new, every smidgin. No, it's yours, lock, stock, and barrel,' Grandpa finished.

'I'll sort of chuck some of our personal stuff into that old trunk off the upstairs chamber,' said Grandma, 'but I want you should feel perfectly free to go after anything you might want before we come back — if ever we *come* back.'

'If you could tell me what to chuck, I could help you chuck it,' offered Dusky, who had been poised ready to fly ever since she heard the fateful words, 'this afternoon.'

'Maybe I could be helping Grandpa,' Paul offered, lifting the desk drawer from the old man's knees and wedging it into place against its squeaky protests.

'I guess you know the grove pretty near as good as I do,' Grandpa said, taking off his glasses to rub his nose, and looking through the bay window with regretful fondness. 'And you won't go fur wrong if you jest foller the dates on the calendar.' He swung his head toward it without turning his eyes that way. He sighed heavily.

'Let me be getting some lunch,' offered Aunt Phronsie, starting toward the kitchen. At the door she paused, looking back at the old people. 'I can't feel quite easy about Paul and Dusky's accepting such an offer,' she murmured. Her cheeks were pink with the painful resolve to speak — pink and soft like peaches just losing their first freshness, Dusky thought. 'They wouldn't want to take advantage. Two hundred dollars down and — and as much as they can manage a year. Wouldn't a lawyer laugh at the terms? And at the price, too? Wouldn't he think they were imposing —?'

Grandpa's eyes could sharpen to steeliness, and they did now, glittering between drawn-down scraggly brows and gold-rimmed spectacles. 'Imposing on old fools in their second childhood?' he snapped. 'Well, they can jest think again. I don't claim I'd 'a' made them terms with anybody else, Miss Smith. You'd ought to know I wouldn't. But these young ones is another kittle of fish. They stood by us when Johnnie was gallivantin' off to the other side of the world and we needed help bad. And besides all that, I'm frank to say the market for orange groves ain't boomin'. I'd hate to think of them trees sufferin' whilst they waited for a buyer. As for the money, me and Granmaw's got a little annuity that's going to keep us without nothin' more. And Johnnie's makin' plenty for a young fellow, and, if he wasn't, we settled propitty back East on him anyways. He don't need them trees. No, siree bob!' Grandpa swore, smiting palm with fist, 'that bargain's already made and bound, and I'll get a lawyer to fix up the bill of sale soon's everything's simmered down and I got time to think.'

He settled back, easing his lame leg and breathing noisily. Aunt Phronsie escaped; they could hear her filling the teakettle and thumping it onto the stove. Grandma lifted a hand to her gray hair.

'I never thought to put it up on curlers last night,' she mourned. 'It looks witch-ed. Dusky, you s'pose you can crimp it on the iron?'

The next hours were topsy-turvy, Grandpa and Grandma moving with the deliberate slowness of the eighties and Dusky and Paul cutting ineffectual circles around them. Even luncheon was not restful. Grandma would pause with a spoonful of soup on its way to her mouth, and her eyes would narrow thoughtfully. 'I clean forgot Granpaw's cough sirup,' she would exclaim. 'Dusky, it's in the right-hand top corner of the kitchen safe. — Not the horse liniment!' — raising her voice as Dusky dashed to the kitchen — 'I guess the tonic's in the left-hand corner.'

And Grandpa lost interest in his bread and gravy and slapped one pocket after another, clucking: 'My far spectacles. They ain't here. My land, I'd be a gone gander ——'

Yet the hours did go racketing past; and Paul ran over to the dormitory to telephone for a taxi; and at length the young people had the old people settled in the green plush opulence of their Pullman, Grandma's hat over one eye and Grandpa's tie riding low under his gold collar-button.

'I rather have this satchel on the seat where it's handy,' Grandma told the porter, 'because I've got us a snack of supper in it and I don't aim to have Granpaw heaving any grips up on seats, lame as he is.'

She straightened her hat and smoothed her silk gloves and smiled tremulously at Dusky. 'You best go off right away,' she quavered. 'I can't rest easy for fear this train'll start and you'll get a leg broke. — But I can't never tell you ——' Her soft mouth shook and twisted and stopped her words.

Grandpa patted her with a big, venous old hand. 'Now, now, Granmaw. — But that's how we both feel, young ones. You been awful —— Good land!' he said pettishly, turning sidewise to drag a clean bandanna from his hip pocket. 'I'll tend to that contract of sale,' he said hoarsely, emerging from the blue folds. 'Though there's alluz the note I made of it, down in black and white, and signed by the both of us. Jest in case. So they ain't a thing to worry about. — You better go. You better go.' He blew his nose prodigiously and made pushing motions with his other hand. 'You better get off, young ones.'

The 'young ones' kissed Grandma's trembling upheld face, and Dusky kissed Grandpa in the blue-veined hollow of his temple, and Paul shook his hand hard, and they stumbled out of the car.

'Oh, I wish the train would start. I *wish* it would start!' Dusky muttered, jigging from one foot to the other while they stood gazing up at Grandma, who was frankly weeping, and at Grandpa, who was trying to tell them something with exaggerated lip motions.

'"The calendar," he's saying,' Dusky interpreted after moments of frowning concentration and a flurry of head-shakes. 'He means we should watch the irrigation dates and all that, of course.' She and Paul nodded vehement understanding.

The call 'Allll a-boarrrd!' cleft the waiting time with one sweeping stroke, and the cars jerked and buckled and slid away, while brother and sister ran alongside until the train gathered speed and pulled Grandpa and Grandma Wilson out of Green Valley's circle of life.

'I don't feel as if I'd ever see them again,' Dusky said solemnly, sniffing as they climbed onto the bus that took them back to Highland.

'Oh, slush!' Paul contradicted irritably. 'All the same,' he admitted, when they had captured seats, 'I think that's the way they feel about it themselves. A broken hip's a bad jolt, I guess, at his age. And Grandma's suffered as much from it as he has.'

Dusky jerked her mind away from the old people who were speeding farther and farther into the distance. 'We'll get back just barely in time for dinner,' she said, turning her wrist to consult her watch, 'and — my word! — won't I have to step on it tonight! I can't take a minute to run over to the cottage, and I want to awfully. Don't you think we ought to name the place, Pod? I thought of Garden of Hesperus, and the Golden Wood — out of that old fairy-tale — and Bells of Saint Clemens.'

'Bells of Saint Clemens?' protested Paul, who had been staring out of the window as if he too were finding it difficult not to follow two lonesome old people.

'Oh, you remember. In those English nursery songs Mother used to sing us. "Oranges and lemons, Say the bells of Saint Clemens."'

Paul snorted.

At Lawrence Hall again, Dusky found her room a perfection of cleanliness. Mary Beth always lifted everything from the tops of dresser, bookcase, cupboards, desk, and dusted every inch of the surfaces before replacing the bric-à-brac. Mary Beth also replaced that bric-à-brac in ruler-straight lines and angles. Dusky pushed vases and books into easier arrangement and loosened the masses of coral-red pyracantha and quaint lantana.

With a laugh at Mary Beth she pulled the pair of Chinese rugs cornerwise. Those rugs had come to be a symbol. During the girls' freshman year Mary Beth had placed them cornerwise and Dusky had jerked them straight.

'But they look prettier slanting!' Mary Beth had argued.

'Poppycock!' Dusky had scoffed. 'Furniture and rugs should never be placed diagonally unless there is a structural reason.'

For a long time she had jerked them straight after Mary Beth placed them cornerwise, and Mary Beth had taken the first opportunity — her soft chin set — to yank them cornerwise again.

But the passing months had knit a strong friendship between the two, so that Mary Beth had given in to Dusky's strange notions and Dusky granted indulgence to Mary Beth's old-fashioned ideas. Now Dusky jerked the rugs cornerwise and Mary Beth jerked them straight, and they held laughing battle over them.

'Anyway, our room does look lovely,' Mary Beth conceded, stooping to pull the rugs exactly parallel to the walls.

'How about Maxine and Kate's?'

'It's lovely, too. Maxine got Kate to have all her things dyed to harmonize.'

'That fierce orchid toilet set?' Dusky asked interestedly.

'Kate's going to keep them in her drawer.'

'Do you suppose I could get that gray ensemble-dress

whacked together before Open House begins?' — Dusky abstractedly changed the subject. 'I haven't a thing to wear.'

'Why don't you wear the apricot organdy? It's seven o'clock this minute.'

'But there isn't much to do on the dress.' — Dusky already had it out and was ripping the sleeves from the jacket, pinning them in place in the sleeveless dress, slipping into it with a squirm as the pins scratched, twisting her mouth and posing at curious angles before the mirror, like a slightly unbalanced mannequin. 'Look, Mary Beth, if you'll just pin here where it ought to be nipped in at the waistline —— That's right. And then like this: the scarf around the neck to make a sort of trick collar. — Now isn't that smart?'

She stripped it off, with pauses to disengage pins that had stuck through into her slip, and plumped down on the edge of her desk to stitch by hand, while Mary Beth scrubbed her round little self pink, and coiled her soft blonde hair into precise buns, and put a fine finish on her nails.

'Dusky!' she implored. 'It's quarter to eight!'

Rapid as was Dusky's needle and large as were her stitches, they had not been swift enough. 'I suppose I'll have to give up,' she admitted. 'If only I hadn't done the pockets I could have finished. Cute, aren't they? — made out of the ends of the scarf with the embroidery already on. — Oh, well, the apricot's probably better for tonight; it's such a warm evening.'

She hung the gray dress in the closet and wriggled into the apricot after the thickening hum and click and thud of heels downstairs told of the arrival of guests.

'It's probably better,' she nodded to the girl who faced her from the mirror. For the apricot organdy gave her cheeks a deeper apricot, and made her eyes flash more brilliantly blue under the densely cloudy darkness of her curly hair.

The girls received the procession of professors and professors' wives, of board members, of townspeople, of girls from other halls, of boys from the boys' halls across the quad. They joined the train that visited the other girls' halls and the boys'. They inspected Paul and David's room with critical interest and sisterly pride and scorn, and noted the exact location of their own pictures in the constellations thumb-tacked to the walls and to the panels that held the disappearing beds. They partook of punch and wafers in the Belton Hall living-room and listened to the program prepared by the Belton Hall boys.

Yet through all the gay evening Dusky's mind was pulling toward the grove, toward the small white house with jigsaw lace under its eaves.

Next morning she made time for a pilgrimage before church. It was strange to walk across the echoing little footbridge and up to the small white house and be thinking with every step, 'This is ours — ours!'

'It's a little too much like, "The king is dead; long live the king!"' Dusky thought; and her eyes were wet. Yet it wasn't as if Grandpa and Grandma hadn't been happy about their possessing it; really glad from their hearts, enjoying the giving of a kingly gift.

Dusky plucked the key from where it always hung, under the bougainvillea vine that swung its heavy mantle over one side of the porch, and unlocked the door and went in. The house met her with the faintly musty clean smell of old houses; greeted her with small creakings and groanings of emptiness as she walked through.

She paused in the sitting-room and thought how bright and pretty it could be, with sunny curtains and new paper and painted floor and scatter rugs and inviting new furniture. But that should not be until after the Wilsons had come back and packed the rest of their personal belongings — if they ever came.

One thing she could do: she could depose the smugly

smiling calendar girl from her place on the wall. She'd always wanted to. 'Wouldn't I love to smack your silly face?' she said aloud.

She made one long step toward the calendar. And then she stopped. The leaves for the preceding months had not been torn off, but turned back and held firmly with paper clips. The September leaf bore a reminder in Grandpa's angular hand, 'Iragate,' with a red line leading shakily to the eighth. Dusky's face grew soft at sight of it.

'No, sir!' she said, aloud again. 'The boys will want to make their own charts, but I'm going to leave this as it is. I'm going to leave things exactly as Grandma had them. Anyway for the present.'

She went on into the kitchen and mechanically lifted the lid of the cooky jar. No fancy cooky jar, this, with hollyhocks painted on its sides, but the proper kind of plain stoneware crock with a blurred blue numeral its only decoration. Of course there would be no cookies, she thought: Paul had probably got the last crumb yesterday. The breath of the jar told her otherwise as she lifted the chipped plate from its top. She peered in. Opulently the thick soft spicy disks rounded almost to the brim.

Dusky sniffed avidly: there were other fragrances than molasses. She lifted the top cookies and probed. Beneath were Grandma's prize rocks, lumpy with nuts and citron and raisins, hard with a hardness that would mellow to rich perfection.

Dusky put the plate back carefully and went out into the grove, munching first a molasses cooky, then a rock. She must write Grandma Wilson that very day.

The back dooryard was neat and bare, but plumbago bushes were bright blue with blossom, and a rose geranium reached almost to the cottage eaves. On each side and behind stretched the glossy avenues of the grove, deep green, hung with yellow fruit and an occasional waxy blossom, an off-bloom.

Dusky dropped a pinch of cooky for Peter, who loudly called his wives and then gobbled the morsel before they could arrive. She wiped the crumbs from her mouth and sniffed. The smells of California! Air saturated with fragrance, with sweet flower smells, with bracing herb smells.

And not only saturated with fragrance: drenched with song!

'My word!' Dusky murmured, 'I've been here at Highland more than two years and it seems to me I haven't stopped to notice what it was like!'

For the whole grove seemed to sing. It sang with color: vibrant orange and yellow and green, with the earth between the rows red-violet. It sang with motion, as mocking-birds careened from tree to ground, flickering keen gray and white, as leaves quivered, as palms along the roadway waved stately hands. It sang with fragrance. It sang with song!

'My word, my word!' Dusky repeated, 'if it isn't almost too lovely to stand. It's — why, there's the name for it, shouting at me all the time. It's the Singing Wood.'

III. ART SCHOOL

Art School was a new department in Highland University. It had not even a home among the other red-tiled white buildings, but was temporarily housed in a fine old residence of the sixties, facing the campus on the side opposite the Singing Wood: a massive stone house with cupolas and large verandas, sitting back among grounds stately with palms and lacy pepper trees.

It was stately inside, as well. Its spacious entrance hall was lighted by the skylight, three stories above, and by soft-toned old stained-glass windows, and was grand with mellow oak in curving staircase and high paneling.

Dusky went back to it that Monday morning with an eager appetite. Last week had been merely preparation; now she was actually beginning something long dreamed.

With Mary Beth pattering breathlessly behind her, she went leaping up those stairs. Into the upper hall, flooded with light. On up the narrower curve of the final flight, into the top story, which was the main studio.

Here had probably been the servants' quarters in the heyday of the mansion. Now easels stood everywhere, and odd corners were already occupied by still-life groups — bottles and teapots hobnobbing with eggplants and onions and squash, backed by carefully careless draperies of blue velvet or batik and fronted with boldly printed signs, 'Do *NOT* disturb.' All the usual casts stood around, hung around: masks of Beethoven and Shakespeare; a lion's head; an Apollo; a discus-thrower; arms; legs; hands; feet.

The sweet autumn air drifted through the windows and mingled with the breath of the studio: oil and turpentine and charcoal dust. Dusky jerked open the locker she shared with Mary Beth and pulled on her smock, sniffing, her eyes closed.

'My word, there's nothing else like it. It smells like Dad's studio in the barn, where I spent half my time. — Half my time in Dad's studio and half outdoors. — Mary Beth, I get darned lonesome for Dad and Mother; darned lonesome even for Pendleton.' Pendleton was the elderly fox terrier who had shared her childhood and was old in her youth.

Dusky thumped her drawing-board onto her easel and the easel into place in front of the hand and arm she had started. Hands were hard.

Mary Beth buttoned her little blue smock precisely and tied the black artist's bow at the neck: Mary Beth liked to have everything according to tradition. She, too, sat down, and squinted hopefully at a bas-relief of apples, trying to gauge the angles with her charcoal held off at arm's length, as Dusky did. Mary Beth maintained that she was taking the course as a cultural one. She had always liked to draw neat profiles of pretty girls, and to tint Christmas postcards with pale smooth washes of color. Perhaps she did not suspect that what she most wanted was to share these two hours with Dusky every morning. If she did suspect it, she took care not to probe the matter and make sure.

Other students eddied through this and the adjoining rooms. Art School had drawn some older artists, serious, purposeful, taking the opportunity to work under the excellent masters. It had drawn also a group of arty youths and maidens who desired to seem sophisticated, blasé, superior to the prevailing fresh-air wholesomeness of Highland. For Art School was not quite like the rest of the University, slightly removed though it was from the watchful eye of the campus.

Jane Andrews, one of the arty ones, slapped Dusky boyishly on the back, while Dusky glared. Jane was large and overwhelming, her hair cut mannishly and swept back from her forehead, leaving a falling lock that could be thrust back with an effective gesture. She clumped through the room in a stench of cigarettes.

After Jane strolled a smallish youth with indefinite features but a most determined bush of straw-colored curls. His name was Dorian White. — 'Though I don't believe it for a minute,' Dusky whispered aside to Mary Beth. 'Not any more than I believe that his curls came that way.'

A short stocky lad with scowling black eyes and a tousle of black hair as prodigious as Dorian's tousle of blond was Andrea Garramone. There were others whom Dusky catalogued with Dorian and Jane. There was a loose-jointed six-footer with pale hair. There was Michi Nasaki, a Japanese doll in American costume. And there was Dorcas Brenneman. That was good. Dorcas and Dusky disagreed — even fought — but with a fundamental friendliness.

The first time Dusky saw the pale-haired six-footer, she began at his shoes, which established themselves beside her after she had started to block in the hand and arm which were her first cast. Because Laban moved as softly as a cat, those shoes appeared without warning. They were incredibly large. Dusky stared unbelievingly at their great length, and then her eyes traveled up the trousers above them and on to a topknot that shone like a candle-flame in daylight. From the hair her eyes dropped to the face: it was preternaturally solemn and pale, with a few large golden freckles. His eyes were pale, too, and fringed with long light lashes.

'Laban Hitchcock is the name,' he said. 'Junior Transfer from Pasadena J.C. Nineteen. White. Unattached. Would be quite a tall boy if so much hadn't been turned up at the end,' he added, indicating the long feet that had drawn Dusky's fascinated gaze back to themselves.

By common consent Dorcas and Dusky, Mary Beth and Laban, had grouped themselves near the west windows, where they could breathe real air when the cigarette smoke lay across the room in blue filaments. They worked absorbedly this Monday morning, and Jane moved among them, knocking over easels, and patronized them largely.

'Come on down to Moulton's,' she invited Dusky. 'Just about time before the Maestro shows up.'

'Not any,' Dusky refused shortly. 'I'd rather draw.'

Jane h'mphed and moved on.

'Maestro!' Dusky grunted.

'I rather like it,' Mary Beth demurred. 'Though I thought it usually referred to a musician. But it seems to fit Professor Faunce.'

'It fits him so well he doesn't need it. — Her and her maestros!'

'What are you two chortling about?' Laban complained.

'Do *you* pronounce it *court*ling?' Dusky demanded.

'How else would you pronounce it?'

'Chortling, as in chuckle, of course,' Dusky snapped. 'It's a sort of cross between chuckle and snort, anyway. "Oh, frabjous day, Calloo, callay, he ——"'

'He courtled in his joy,' Laban completed it stubbornly.

'Chortled.'

'Courtled.'

'Chort —' Dusky bit the word off, only flashing defiant eyes at Laban, and applied herself so vigorously to her drawing that she snapped the charcoal short. She and Laban bent for it at the same instant and whacked their heads together.

'LABAN HITCHCOCK IS THE NAME,' HE SAID. 'JUNIOR TRANSFER FROM PASADENA J. C. NINETEEN. WHITE. UNATTACHED.'

'Courtled!' he whispered impishly. Her light blue eyes glared into his light gray ones with two inches of space between.

When she had righted herself she found Professor Faunce standing solidly behind her, arms folded across chest. She looked at him over her shoulder when she could stand the silence no longer. His eyes rounded, narrowed. His mouth pursed out. He pressed his nose flat with an unconscious fist. He nodded briskly.

'Lots of movement,' he commended, making a sweeping gesture with fingers bunched and long thumb extended. 'Who taught you?'

'My father.' — The color poured into Dusky's face.

'Do me the Apollo,' Professor Faunce said, and moved on to Mary Beth.

'Tight little lines,' he commiserated. 'Like wire. No movement. Break it up. Sweep it in.'

'All wrong,' he told Dorcas. 'Start over.'

Glancing at Laban's blank board, he went on to another group.

'Courtle,' Laban resumed conversationally.

'Chortle,' Dusky answered through her teeth, while she pinned new paper to her board.

'What'll you bet?'

'A copy of *Alice*.'

'Got one already. Make it the *Hunting of the Snark*.'

'Well, at any rate,' Dusky said, when Laban had gone leaping down the stairs at the beginning of the rest period, 'he knows *Alice in Wonderland*, which is more than you can say of most boys.'

'David used to read *Alice*,' Mary Beth reminded her. Mary Beth was acutely jealous for David.

'I suppose he'll get something to eat,' Dusky mused, watching Laban start his old car toward town. 'I'm so hungry I could chew my belt, like an Eskimo dog.'

'I know a trick worth two of that' — Dorcas slid into

the conversation — 'What-do-you-call-it — anyway, the Art Fraternity — are having a tea here this afternoon.'

'And so —?'

'Well, Wing Lee always makes too many sandwiches. He always has stacks left over and gives them to you if you're around. If we eat some beforehand it will come out just the same answer.'

'Wing Lee?' Mary Beth inquired.

Dorcas nodded. 'Wing Lee was the cook here when this was the old Brewer place. He stayed on as a general houseboy. I've known him forever: he's a million years old.' Dorcas spoke in staccato sentences. 'Come on.'

Silently they followed her. Down a back stair. Down another back stair. Into a huge clean kitchen with copper butler's sink and copper saucepans.

A small black-jacketed figure sprang up before them, soundless on cloth slippers. 'You go back plitty klick!' it bade them in a shrill singsong. 'Lookee sign say no admittee!'

He waved a long-nailed bronze hand toward a black-lettered placard: 'Students Not Admitted to Kitchen!' The hand hung in air as his eyes alighted on Dorcas. It dropped, and the face crinkled with pleasure. 'Missee Dawkee!' shrilled the voice.

'Umhum. And this is Dusky Day. And Mary Beth Masterson. We're starved, Wing Lee.'

Wing Lee was already padding across to the table, lifting a pile of delicate sandwiches from their linen towel.

'You eatem on stairs,' he ordered, thrusting the food into Dorcas's hands. 'Come back after tea maybe some more.'

Dorcas was delicately raising a sandwich lid. 'Mmmm!' she gloated. 'Avocado!'

'*Ngo ge ka ya tsoi chung Kwok!*' Mary Beth murmured, a small catch in her voice.

Wing Lee, rewrapping the packet of sandwiches, whirled and blinked.

'*Ngo ge ka ya tsoi chung Kwok!*' Mary Beth repeated.

Dusky and Dorcas retired to the stairs as to gallery seats, leaving the door ajar. While they munched Wing Lee's sandwiches, they watched and listened. Wing Lee's mouth was wide open and his eyebrows climbed toward his cropped hair. — 'He looks like a kid that sees Santa Claus!' Dorcas whispered.

His words stuttered with amazement, and so did his outspread hands. On a tall stool perched Mary Beth, hugging her knees like a little girl and answering his singing syllables with singing syllables. The two made a strange picture in the lofty room, clean and ordered as only a between-meals kitchen can be: the little old Chinese and the blonde young girl, tossing to and fro what seemed to their audience a mystic gibberish.

Suddenly Wing Lee's eyes passed Mary Beth and took in the other girls. Without pausing in his chant he skittered over to them, snatched their remaining sandwiches, pressed them on Mary Beth, and then, from a deep drawer in one of his work tables, drew a square of fruit cake, rich and dark, and presented it also to Mary Beth.

Dusky and Dorcas fled, laughing, up the stairs.

A few minutes later Mary Beth rejoined them, a small smile quirking her lips, her face flushed. 'I didn't know how homesick I was!' she murmured breathlessly, sitting down and taking up her charcoal to squint along it at a plaster apple.

'Homesick for *China?*'

Mary Beth compressed her lips and nodded vigorously.

'S'pose Lee's homesick, too?'

'Goodness, yes! He intended to go back to spend his last days, and he'd saved almost enough. But he says he made the mistake of putting his savings into Melican stocks instead of the lottery, and it is all gone. Now the best he can do is to send his bones back.'

'His bones?' Dusky questioned.

'Yes. They all do that. Am I really supposed to make this apple square, Dusky?'

'Like this,' Dusky advised, leaning over to block it in. 'And big, Ma'Beth, big! You're not doing place-cards.'

'There's only one other Chinese in Green Valley,' Mary Beth continued, contemplating Dusky's broad black lines without favor. 'He's the vegetable man. — There are always students, but this year only Jimmie Tang, and he's from Northern China, so that doesn't do Wing Lee much good.'

'I think this is an awfully interesting world,' said Dusky.

'But *I* was Lee's favorite before,' Dorcas observed pensively. 'You never know, when you introduce a man to another girl.'

'Oh. That reminds me.' Mary Beth took the square of cake from her blouse pocket and looked at it.

'I have a pretty clean palette knife,' Laban offered helpfully, peering around Dusky at the cake.

So Mary Beth divided it into four crumbly pieces. Two cherries, a chunk of citron, a nut, remained in her palm.

'Fate!' Laban intoned, leveling a long forefinger at the vestiges. 'The two cherries are — hm — Mary Beth and Dorcas; the — lemon — must be Dusky; the nut ——' He sighed and tucked it into his mouth. 'And I have an idea that this is the beginning of a very beautiful friendship.'

Dusky sniffed. 'Nut is absolutely correct,' she remarked scornfully. 'I only hope it isn't catching. I shouldn't care to study art in a psychopathic ward.'

IV. LUISA

SHARPLY as Dusky expressed her scorn of Laban's foolishness, she noticed that the art class hours swooped past more gayly when Laban was in droll mood than when he sat on his shoulder-blades staring sulkily at nothing. Today she banged her possessions into her half of the locker and raced blithely downstairs and over onto the campus, at ten. The period had left her bubbling with energy.

At ten she had an education class; and immediately after luncheon the history of art at Art School; and at two a course in Contemporary Novel with Miss Corinne; and from three to five on Wednesdays and Fridays composition and design at Art School again.

'This ought to keep my weight down without a lick of dieting,' she panted hopefully as she and Mary Beth dashed across the quad. 'My word, it's fun to be busy!'

There was such a thing, however, as being too busy to indulge in extras. She was not so pleased as usual, back in her room after class that day, to hear a soft thud on the door and see the knob wriggle ineffectually.

She opened the door, and Carmelita tumbled in, glancing backward and laughing excitedly while she banged the door shut. Carmelita had evidently run away. She was entrancing in a frankly single slip and a pair of torn sandals, and she swarmed up Dusky with assurance.

'Caramel,' Dusky said sternly, 'you are going home at

once if not sooner. Dusky is a busy woman with no time for life's lighter sides.'

Carmelita squealed and snuggled closer into Dusky's arms as steps sounded in the hall, but they heralded only Mary Beth.

'You are a nuisance,' Dusky went on, tossing the child on the bed and making corkscrew motions at her stomach. 'I shall march you straight home. — I have to go downtown and get a pair of decent hose, anyway, Mary Beth. It does seem strange that both you and Maxine should have such silly feet. Kate's are reasonable: I may in time be able to make use of Kate. — Now, Caramel! we'll see if we can't find an ice cream cone on the way. — I guess it isn't too warm for this jersey. It's the only dress I've got that's completely all right. It's even got snaps on the cuffs.' She approved of the snaps complacently, as if she were responsible for their presence.

'There's the rip under the sleeve,' Mary Beth reminded her, but Dusky was already out of the door, Carmelita riding her shoulders.

She stopped at a drugstore to buy the promised cone, and with it Carmelita strutted through the quiet streets, looking down her nose with the complacency of the rich at the children they passed. Presently they came to the section where the Vasquezes lived. It was a region where small dingy houses crouched behind rickety fences, and gates sagged on their hinges. It was also a region where blue plumbago and scarlet hibiscus and varicolored lantana painted rainbows on the dinginess.

The Vasquez abode bore an especially gorgeous mantle of flowering vines, and Mrs. Vasquez sat in their shelter on an old automobile seat: a small meal-sack of a woman, whose heavy black hair slid down into a knot at her swarthy neck.

She made round eyes of reproof at Carmelita. 'You will sit down pleass?' she invited Dusky, stretching her apron sidewise to dust the cracked leather seat beside her. 'Oh, the bad Carrrmelita! Again she have ron away! — Luisa, it iss Mees Dosky!'

Luisa came inquiringly to the door.

'I have to go downtown.' — Dusky refused the proffered seat with a smile.

'I, too, go downtown,' Luisa observed.

'Oh, fine!' said Dusky, 'we can go together.'

She would not admit to herself that she was anything but glad to walk beside Luisa's too-red lips, Luisa's too-clinging dress, Luisa's resounding gum. Restlessly, while she waited, she stepped into the side yard and admired the flowering maple that hung its gay bells against the house wall. At that point her eye was caught by a curious-looking cart in an open shed. Vestiges of blue paint lay like a bloom on its wooden sides and large wheels.

'Luisa!' Dusky called, 'this looks like an old Mexican cart!'

'Sure!' Luisa assented, coming out and staring at the familiar object as if she had never noticed it before. 'My grandfather bring it years ago, and it just stand. Since he die maybe we burn it up, get it out of the way.'

'Oh, no!' Dusky urged. 'It's so quaint.'

Luisa shrugged. 'You all ready?' she asked.

Dusky bowed to Mrs. Vasquez and waved at Carmelita. Carmelita sat erect at her mother's side, feet straight before her. She revolved the cone, watching it with eyes that crossed in the intensity of her enjoyment, and luxuriously diminished the ice cream with a small tongue that licked out like a flame.

Dusky found herself loitering in the dingy street. As soon as she emerged from its shelter she would begin to meet students. She would meet students like Caro Felton and Langston Trevor. Not that she liked either of those two. There was always feud between her and Caro, and Caro's condescension always stung. As for Langston

Trevor, while she despised his arrogance she was secretly attracted by it, too, coupled as it was with arrogant good looks. — Yes, Caro and Langston would be the kind of students she'd meet.

Not that it mattered, she told herself hotly. But she did wish her own nails were more nearly immaculate, since Luisa's were so shinily dingy. Dusky's hands were thoroughly scrubbed, but oil paint was the dickens to get out. And that abominable rip under her sleeve! She jerked her arm down convulsively.

They met Dorcas Brenneman on the first corner of Main Street. Dusky nodded to her, keeping up a vivacious chatter with Luisa.

'Where are you in school now, Luisa?' she asked, and hated herself for putting on the bright smile of a patron. Look! that smile seemed to say: This is a humble protégée of mine.

'Soph'more in high,' Luisa told her. 'Mama wants me to go on through and graduate, but I don't know. If I get a job in the orange packing-house —— And anyhow, I don't know what good it does me to go any more to the school. Most of my girl friends got married already without going past junior high.'

'Oh, but seventeen is too young to marry!' Dusky disapproved.

Luisa caught at her arm possessively. 'Lookit this dress in this window, Dusky! Would youse get it if you was me?'

Dusky itched to pull her arm away. She cleared her throat and said firmly, 'I think the dress looks awfully cheap, Luisa.' And to make up for the goody-goody sound of that, she added, 'Come on into Moulton's and have a milkshake with me, won't you?'

'Dusky?' Dusky whirled to look down into Miss Corinne's eyes, frosty blue under the triangular folds of their lids.

'There's room for you in my car, Dusky,' said Miss

Corinne, 'if you're starting back to the campus.' Her suave gray head in its suave hat nodded toward the suave coupé at the curb, where another teacher waited.

Dusky's brain rocked. Miss *Corinne* inviting her to ride. The professor she most dreaded and much admired. She'd make another trip downtown for the stockings, or telephone for them, or — anything rather than miss the opportunity.

Luisa's gum smacked loudly and Dusky sagged. For the moment she had forgotten Luisa.

'Thank you, Miss Corinne,' she said regretfully, 'but I can't go yet.'

She opened Moulton's door, Luisa hanging to her elbow. Hopefully she scanned the dimmer back end of the narrow room. Every seat seemed taken.

'Two places up here in the window!' a 'soda jerk' announced. Squealing delightedly Luisa climbed on one of the stools and Dusky perforce sat beside her.

'Two milkshakes!' Dusky snapped, and watched him concoct them. Insufferable idiot! his starched white cap sat the side of his oiled hair and he simpered at Luisa.

Luisa was whitening her whitened nose with a gray puff, deepening the deep red of her lips, flattening with expert palm the curls that lay in painted scallops on her cheeks. She turned toward the soda jerk the baby stare of a favorite movie star. He thumped down the two glasses and with a flourish presented the straws, their ends protruding from the tissue paper.

Dusky made herself take the milkshake slowly, its rich creaminess cloying to her. Moulton's milkshakes would stand alone, it was claimed, if emptied carefully enough from their glasses. Today Dusky did not feel equal to one. She was glad Luisa did not talk. Her brilliant brown eyes wandered to and fro and spent much time with the smirking youth behind the counter, while she pursued her drink to the last hissing intake.

'Gee, but that was swell, Dusky!' she said heartily, relinquishing her glass at last.

Everyone seemed to be scrutinizing the two girls as they slid from their stools — contemplating them over glass edges and straws. Dusky took her tickets to the cash register and clicked down the necessary coins.

'Don't you want to go to Davis's with me, Luisa?' she asked clearly. 'I've got some shopping to do.'

Luisa went to Davis's with Dusky for stockings. Dusky went to the Five-and-Ten with Luisa for perfume and diamond clips. Dusky tramped home with Luisa, spasmodically making talk. She tramped the rest of the way to the campus alone, still simmering.

Darn all snobbish collegiates, anyway! There wasn't one of that crowd in Moulton's that would have been caught dead in company with Luisa's rouge and gum and finger nails.

V. 'DEAR SISTERS!'

'I'M GOING to cut chapel!' Mary Beth announced placidly next morning. 'I think when you're in college it's a sort of duty to cut chapel occasionally. Can't you plan something interesting and pretty bad for us to do, Dusky, so I'll have something more to tell my grandchildren?'

Dusky kicked off her shoes and sent them spinning into the closet, stepped into another pair, wet a comb and dragged it through her hair, urged the cloudy waves into place with her palms. 'No, I can't, silly. Because this is one chapel I wouldn't miss. It's that Steiner man, and I want to hear what he has to say. His books are keen.'

Dusky had felt sore and disgusted during those intervening hours. It was not her fault that she hated to be conspicuous on the public street. It was not Luisa's fault that she made herself and any companion conspicuous. It was not even Luisa's mother's fault, since she had been brought up in an Indian village in Old Mexico and set down bewildered on the edge of 'American' civilization.

This new consideration of people's backgrounds and biases had really begun when Dusky reluctantly visited Maxine's family during her first Christmas in Highland. The stark tar paper and pine-box ugliness of the little gold-mining town of Torrence, climbing its slag-heaps below the jagged peaks; the devotion of plain Mr. and Mrs. Lennox to their pretty daughter Maxine and their spoiled fragile little Billie; Maxine's fierce desire to escape the gossiping pettiness of Torrence, with its loafers fringing the store-fronts and staring at everyone who clattered along the raised boardwalks under the rickety wooden canopies. Dusky had never again been able to despise Maxine. But she still found it annoying, this not being able to blame people whole-heartedly for their shortcomings. She reached forward to chapel, today, and to the chapel speaker, for help in her muddle.

Often chapel was too collegiate to please Dusky. The boy on one side of her sat on the end of his spine and chewed gum or dozed, and the girl on the other side of Paul — they were seated alphabetically — passed notes across Dusky and Paul to the sleeper. The boy in front of Dusky studied, and the girl next him read a novel.

Yet there was always the beauty of the building, its arcaded cloisters serene and its great chancel window showing the Sermon on the Mount. Almost always there was a master at the organ, sending sheer beauty of sound throbbing through the throng, singing over it, holding it together in a whole for ever so brief a while.

Today there was, besides, the vivid small man on the platform, his head tilted a little upward to send his voice out across the assemblage, his words, still edged with his native Carpathian accent, whimsical, incisive, stimulating.

He found all races likable and admirable; he had friends among all; he had foster children from several. He felt that life, that civilization, could not emerge into the full light until it had achieved world friendship and understanding. And he warned his hearers that it was not impossible for American civilization itself to pass out into the dark.

Dusky would not forget the challenge of his voice when he cried, 'We are too young to die! We have left nothing big enough, high enough! We are too young to die!'

Paul was scribbling feverishly on a flyleaf and she strained her eyes to read the lines:

'Youth has forsaken us. Laughter and boasting are done.

'Blindly we grope ——'

Paul found an outlet for his emotion in verse. Dusky sometimes thought it was more effectual than the outlet of painting. She rose rather dazed when chapel was dismissed, and made her way ahead of her brother between the seats and into the aisle.

All day her mind kept returning to the chapel talk. She gloomed toward Miss Corinne Smith as that teacher discoursed on the Brothers Karamazov, until Miss Corinne paused, set her long, transparent fingertips together, and inquired: 'Are you dissenting, Dusky Day? Or merely listening for the dinner bell? Suppose you share with the class those inner yearnings.'

Dusky said desperately: 'Life is so discouraging. Just when you think you're emerging into the full light of understanding, you find yourself in the dark again. How are you ever going to judge people? And how can you live with them without judging them? Don't you have to evaluate them — place them in some sort of scale?'

She hadn't the least idea what Miss Corinne had been saying, but it seemed as if this load of birdshot should hit some part of any discussion of the Russian novelists. Most of her classmates, in their curving rows of armchairs, accepted Dusky's remarks without surprise, patting discreet yawns or looking ahead in their texts or glancing at their watches. One or two twisted to look at her with mild interest or question. Miss Corinne's three-cornered eyes were amused.

'You go far afield,' she said, delicately acid. 'I do not object to my students' going far afield so long as they *go*. Thought seems to be regarded as a handicap on most campuses. — I do, however, rather prefer to have the subject under discussion used as the point of departure.' — Dusky felt herself flushing. — 'Apply your entirely valid echo of Doctor Steiner to the Brothers Karamazov, if you please, Dusky.'

Dusky rambled on lamely until the glad sound of the bell released her. She strode out, setting her heels down hard.

Tuesday was always sorority night, and Dusky was still gloomy when she came to the meeting, in Dorcas and Sally Lou's room, down the hall. Highland, while it forbade only the national fraternities, did not officially smile on even the locals; so there were few fraternity houses.

Dusky sat on the floor and leaned her head against Dorcas's startling black bedspread, studying with half-seeing eyes the few prints on the walls. Probably the Maxfield Parrish and the Rosa Bonheur were Sally Lou's, but it was astonishing that Dorcas should endure them. Queer how stupid people were about pictures, Dusky thought. But then, she considered intolerantly, how stupid they were about almost everything!

She came to her feet when the president asked for suggestions 'for the good of the order.'

'Madame President.'

'Dusky Day.'

'It seems to me that when we're starting a new year, with new initiates soon to come, and all that, we ought to be thinking of ways in which our sorority can really matter. Mostly we're so darn' collegiate. Thought seems to be regarded as a handicap on the campus. My word! would anyone think we came here with the faintest notion of developing our minds? If we'd think even during class, we'd get a lot out of college. Doctor Davis said that to me, once: that if we had to choose between studying *outside* class and really devoting our entire attention to the subject *in* class, he'd choose the latter. Do you disagree with that, Sally Lou?' she shot suddenly at Sally Lou, who was frowning at the ceiling.

Sally Lou jumped. ''Scuse me, Dusky,' she apologized, 'but I was just trying to remember who I've got a date with tomorrow night.' She giggled.

Dusky glowered around the room at the girls perched on desk and chairs and bed and floor.

'Another thing,' she went on, setting her feet more firmly and cocking her head, 'is this business of race tolerance. Didn't you think Doctor Steiner was perfectly swell? Didn't you, Dorky?'

'I cut chapel today,' Dorcas admitted.

'Anyway,' Dusky plowed ahead, 'I don't think we have any right to a college education if we haven't sense enough to see that race barriers are narrow and — and silly. I think we ought to make all peoples at home — Jimmie Tang and Michi Nasaki and Cordelia Jacobs and all.'

'Darling, why don't you join the International Club?' Sally Lou inquired seriously, frowning at a blemish on a pink finger nail. 'Isn't that what it's for — to give you a chance to be nice to those people? And then you don't get all tangled up. Nobody minds your being like that if you want to; not if you keep it sort of separate.'

'But it oughtn't to be separate!' Dusky cried. 'It ——'

She flopped back on the floor with a quirked eyebrow and a tightened mouth. Maxine was biting back a yawn. Jan was deepening her wave with automatic fingers. No one understood what Dusky meant: that people shouldn't be divided off in bins, as if brownness or yellowness or whiteness were their main attributes.

The meeting moved on to reports of committees. 'Report of entertainment committee,' the president announced. 'Dusky, has your committee worked out anything on those costumes?'

Dusky unkinked herself from her huddle and opened the knitting bag on her lap. 'You wanted suggestions about futuristic costuming,' she said rather coldly, 'and I have this wig to suggest.' She pushed back her hair and fitted over it the shining cap she had taken from the bag—'Also costumes something like this, made out of oil-cloth——' She held up crayon drawings of geometrically patterned suits in white and black.

The girls swirled round her, gurgling. 'Dusky, that's gorgeous! But what would it cost? Too much, wouldn't it?'—'Oh, I've got to try it on!'—'Where did you ever, ever find the elegant metal hair, Dusky? It looks like something out of ancient Greece or somewhere.'

'It's copper sponges,' Mary Beth told them with awe. 'You know—the kind they clean aluminum with.'

'Doesn't she have the most *mar*-velous i-*de*-as?' Jan asked the roomful.

'*Ideas!*' Dusky scoffed. 'What I want to know is, are you going to support any of the honest-to-goodness ideas? What about the race tolerance business, h'm? Going to back me up in that?'

'Oh, sure, Dusky!' they agreed devoutly, passing the richly barbaric glitter of the curled copper wig from hand to hand and posing in it before the mirror.

'Well, we'll see!' Dusky promised, her brows darkly bent. 'We'll jolly well see about that, dear sisters!'

VI. A GROVE–WARMING

THE 'Brother-and-Sister Act' were not having many double dates this fall. Paul and David were too busy in the grove, disking the ground between the trees and planting the winter cover crop and irrigating. Caring for twenty acres of oranges was a full-time job for one man, even though the specialized culture was done by hired crews.

Both boys had gone out for football as in the previous year. The mighty David should have made a good player, but his eighteen years in China had spoiled him for athletics. Last year he had even committed the classic crime of passing a crucial ball into the enemy's hands. As for Paul, he was so reedy that only his quickness of thought and movement made him a passable player.

Both were on the second string, and they were not wholly sorry that they must give up athletic activities as soon as this football season was over.

With the opening of the winter semester they would move over to the cottage, and Aunt Phronsie would keep house for them. Dusky was to stay on with Mary Beth in the dormitory. Aunt Phronsie felt that she still needed the adjustments of community living. Dusky protested, but Aunt Phronsie, in spite of her blurred edges, was a definite person at the core, and won her point.

'But I sort of hate to date with anyone else when Paul and David are working so hard in the grove,' Dusky said wistfully one day, covering the speaking tube with her hand and turning toward her suite-mates. 'It's Langston Trevor.'

'Well, good gosh, Dusky, snap him up!' Maxine advised, nibbling the jewel-like seeds of a pomegranate with her small white teeth. 'If I weren't engaged ——' She glanced complacently at the dazzle of her diamond.

Kate Oliver, still the shy freshman, watched Dusky with awe. Mary Beth folded her lips and studied. Dusky glowered at her and turned back to the speaking tube.

'I'm all tied up, Langston,' she apologized. — 'Well, maybe.'

'Since we can't go anywhere,' she said to the girls, 'I believe I'll give the cottage a going-over and have a party there Friday night. I'll ask' — she checked them on her fingers — 'you three and Sally Lou and Dorky and — I'll make some cookies, I believe,' she added, 'and perhaps some cake.'

'*You?*' Maxine hooted. 'Since when have you been so domestic?'

'Well, I can turn off as good a cooky as any of you. There's a lovely old cookbook over there.'

All four suite-mates were singularly unskilled in kitchen crafts. Dusky had scraped together many a meal at home when her mother was deep in her writing; but they were mostly tin can and paper bag meals: salmon salad and baked beans and canned spinach and sugared doughnuts from the bakery. Mary Beth had scarcely stepped foot in a kitchen: in China servants tumbled over each other. Maxine had never been permitted to get hot and tired over a stove or 'spoil her pretty hands' with dishwater; and Maxine's fiancé was of a sort to continue such indulgence. Kate ——

'I was always the boy,' Kate apologized humbly, 'on account of not having any brothers. I always help Dad with the chores and ride the fence and like that.'

Dusky stood with her chin in her hand, her brows bent on Kate, until Kate flushed and jerked down her skirt. Dusky extended a horizontal finger at arm's length and shut one eye at Kate; extended a diagonal finger. Kate, childlike for all her five feet eight, moved her shoulders uncomfortably and nibbled her lip.

'Don't fidget so. You're swell-looking,' Dusky informed her. 'Your eyelashes are as thick as mine and as long and curly as Maxine's. Do you braid them at night to keep them from tangling?'

'But your clothes are awful,' Maxine soothed her. 'That's why so few folks find out how you look. We'll have to do something about your clothes.'

'Go away!' Mary Beth commanded. 'You're both unspeakable.'

'I'm gone already.' — Dusky cantered downstairs, intent on the cottage.

The cottage was dusty and stale, though not disordered. Dusky flung wide the windows and doors and pushed the carpet-sweeper over the Brussels carpet so fast that it had scarcely time to gobble up the lint and the cooky crumbs. Dumping soap powder in the pail till she sneezed, she mopped with vigor. Sneezing and bumping baseboards and doors, she made so much noise that David came inquiringly from the grove.

'Scat!' Dusky ordered. 'No cookies.'

He stood with the sun on his tumbled fair hair and one hand high against the door jamb, gazing down at her with puzzled pleasure. When David looked like that, Dusky felt queer mothering impulses toward him, though at other times he seemed to turn her into a taken-care-of little girl.

'Maybe in an hour. Cookies, I mean,' she said, relenting.

She made newspaper highways on the moist linoleum, and then rummaged out Grandma Wilson's cookbook. It was a fat old cookbook, rebound in black oilcloth that had ripped loose, and crammed with yellow clippings and recipes in faded ink on envelopes and scraps of paper. It smelled spicy.

Dusky found the molasses cooky recipe and went to work. It was the right one, because Grandma had written in the margin, 'Good. A mite more shortning.'

The pantry disclosed no sour milk, but it did provide a few cans of the condensed kind. There was no 'shortning' except bacon drippings. Dusky sniffed at them: they had been in the little 'cooler' and seemed fresh. There were eggs 'put down' in water-glass. Soda — flour — ginger — cinnamon ——

She hunted out the pastry board and floured it; rolled out the sticky mass; cut beautiful rounds. The beautiful rounds ruffled and pleated perversely when she tried to slide the cake-turner under them. She scraped them all up and tried again, adding more flour.

It was nearly five when the first tins were in the oven, and Paul and David making repeated trips past the kitchen door.

'Smell good?' she asked cheerfully.

'They do and they don't,' Paul pondered, wrinkling his nose.

She opened the oven, pulled out a tin, slid the brown disks out on a platter. 'Look out! Hot!' she warned. They all took investigating bites, lips drawn back from teeth.

'Why — they do and they don't!' Dusky agreed, focusing startled eyes on the bitten scallop. 'Do you suppose it was not having sour milk? My word, how dumb of me! The soda didn't have any acid to work on, did it?'

Thrusting out thoughtful lips, she studied the pantry shelves. Finally she measured a few teaspoonsful of vinegar into the remaining dough, worked it through, added flour and spice, rolled it out again, cut the cookies, and shoved them into the oven. 'Spice covers a multitude of tastes,' she said comfortably.

The boys did not answer, and she looked around. They were sitting on the back steps, each with a tower of the unsuccessful cookies balanced on his knee, chewing slowly while Peter and the hens scuttled and clucked for the fallen crumbs.

'My word!'

'We're going to get filled up for once,' Paul explained thickly. 'In dining-hall — seems as if you eat plenty, but you're always so darn' starved you feel as if you'd cave in.'

Dusky had just time to turn out the gas, take out the tins that were in the oven, and run for the dining-hall. She carried one of the doctored cookies with her, though it was so hot that she had to pass it from hand to hand and take even more cautious bites than before. It was lighter than the others and of better flavor, though it still fell short of Grandma Wilson's.

Again after dinner she went to the cottage, carrying her books with her. On the way she stopped at Aunt Phronsie's small apartment.

'Could I borrow a quarter of a cup of shortening?' Dusky asked. 'And you don't happen to have some sour cream, do you? And some powdered sugar? And a stick of butter? There's a recipe for cup-cakes that the book calls foolproof, and I've got all the other ingredients.'

When she trotted along the woodsy Zanja path from Aunt Phronsie's apartment with her pat of butter and her sour cream and shortening in a basket on her arm, she felt like Red Ridinghood. It was fun, too, to be alone in her own little house in the midst of the Singing Wood. Much as she liked the gay communal life of the dormitory, being alone was sometimes like a drink of cool water.

She turned on the light, thumb-tacked to the wall above the table a chart which she must memorize, lighted the gas oven, washed her hands, rolled out the rest of the cookies.

Twilight drifted in at the open door: it was the gentlest hour of day. Dusky whistled tunelessly but joyfully, staring at the chart level with her eyes; squeaking the oven open; pulling out tins of cookies.

'Never-Fail Cake: that's the one for me,' she murmured. 'And this time I've got everything except the powdered sugar. Glory! you don't have to separate the yolks and whites, even. Ticklish job, that is. — Early Sumerian Period — about 5000 B.C. — Five thousand — five ——'

Carefully she measured five teaspoonfuls of soda into the flour.

'Early Sumerian Period — Let's see: a cup and a half of flour, a half teaspoon soda ——' She looked blankly at the sifter before her, and then scooped off all she could of the soda, finer and whiter than the flour. 'My word! Maybe I ought to get in the ingredients before I begin to study. I do hope I've left as much as a half teaspoonful in. — Moderate oven — Now what is a moderate oven, I'd like to know?' She held an experimental hand inside and drew it out with a burn across the wrist.

But the cakes were in at last, and out when the toothpick test satisfied Dusky. Grandma Wilson had left brown sugar, and Dusky used it instead of powdered for frosting — after she had pounded its lumps to a degree of smoothness — mixing it with melted butter.

She turned the cup-cake tins upside down and lifted cautiously, but nothing happened. She urged a cup-cake with a knife and half of it plumped out onto the plate. The other half remained pale and moist in its cup. Lucky the cakes had started out to be big ones!

Dusky pried out the dozen tops and proceeded to frost their ragged under-sides. The soft cake devoured the frosting greedily, and mingled its crumbs chummily with the sweet. Dusky mixed more frosting, using canned milk since the butter was gone.

Dubiously she surveyed the result, and scanned the pantry shelves. Shredded coconut! With a sigh of relief she scattered coconut lavishly over the frosting. Now the cakes looked almost professional, with all the breakage and the crumbs hidden. She stored eleven in two covered vegetable dishes and ate one. The brown-sugar-and-butter frosting was delicious, and the coconut only slightly hard between the teeth.

She was tired by the time the mess was cleared away. Funny how two hours of housework could exhaust you, when a ten-mile hike merely made you hungry! She'd dash over early tomorrow afternoon and make orange juice.

She slammed down the windows, locked the door, and went back to the dormitory, murmuring to herself, 'Early Sumerian Period — about 5000 B.C.' She assured Mrs. Forrester that she had been studying all evening, while she baked; and she really believed she had.

Next day she had squeezed out the juice of two dozen oranges and washed the yellow pulp from her nose and chin before the first of her guests arrived. Dusky was well pleased to see that it was Cordelia Jacobs.

'Oh, Cordelia,' she greeted her, 'don't you want to go out into the grove and see how pretty it is? Before the others come?'

'Is it the International Club — your party?' Cordelia asked, hanging her coat on the old-fashioned hall-tree in the old-fashioned hall.

'Um-um' — Dusky shook her head — 'just some of the kids. Come on, Cordelia, before anyone else gets here. — Now!' she cried expectantly, when they stood deep among the trees in one of the sweet aisles. 'I haven't told a soul but Paul, but I've named it the Singing Wood.'

Cordelia's closed face seemed to open, and she pulled a branch down before it to protect herself, a branch weighted with green-gold fruit.

'I — love things like this: beautiful places,' she admitted huskily. 'I think the name is sweet.'

'You are sweet, against that tree,' Dusky murmured.

Cordelia's face was as softly polished as rubbed old walnut. She was perfectly Negro in type, and Dusky noticed for the first time how compact, how well designed that type was, as if it had been skillfully cut from fine-grained wood, the head a perfect oval, nicely set on the smooth column of brown throat, the planes of lips and nose satisfying, like good, crisp carving.

'I'd love to paint you,' Dusky told her earnestly.

'As a barbaric primitive?' Cordelia asked coldly, her face closing.

'Anybody at home?' called Dorcas, before Dusky had time to answer. 'Or was this the wrong day for the party?'

Reluctantly Dusky led the way back to the cottage. 'You know Cordelia Jacobs, Dorky? Cordelia, you've met Dorcas Brenneman?'

That open, friendly moment had passed.

Mary Beth came, and Maxine and Kate; Caro Felton and Jan Cooper and Sally Lou. With Sally Lou's arrival, the misty uneasiness began to condense into chilly fog.

'Sally Lou,' said Dusky, 'you've met Cordelia Jacobs?'

'Cordelia is in one of my classes,' Sally Lou answered, unsmiling. Her eyes did not turn toward Cordelia.

'Are you planning to carry blankets out under the trees, as you said?' Mary Beth asked Dusky.

They spread the blankets there, and sat down. The grove was as lovely as it had been a half hour ago, its rich shade grateful in the warmth. Hidden insects added their deep hum to the bird songs; sunlight polka-dotted the ground and the blankets and the eight girls with gold. It should have been one of those hours when talk is light and easy and flowered with laughter; but it wasn't; it was one of those hours when talk is so brittle that every subject breaks off short under a weight of silence.

'This is a kind of grove-warming,' Dusky explained, beginning to feel that it needed warming, no matter how high the thermometer might stand. 'I'll tell you: everyone's got to contribute something to the — to the fun. Maxine, you'll whistle, won't you?'

'Sure. Anyone to accompany me?'

'If I had a mouth organ ——' Kate offered timidly.

Dusky scrambled to her feet. 'Grandpa Wilson used to play one. I'll see.'

She found the harmonica in its old place in the top drawer of the secretary. Kate cuddled it in her hands and looked inquiringly at Maxine.

'I've got one to the air of "America,"' said Maxine.

With a preliminary pipe or two, they swung into a tumble of bird songs, with 'America' running through them like a chain through beads. This was better. Dusky relaxed.

Dorcas gravely went through a tap dance, on the porch where they could see her. Jan got a ball of twine from the kitchen table drawer and did a complicated string trick.

'Cordelia?' asked Dusky.

Cordelia looked at her hands, folded tightly in her lap. Everyone looked at Cordelia's hands, long, square-tipped, with pale palms and nails.

Cordelia asked: 'Would you-all like a piece by Paul Laurence Dunbar?'

'That would be fine!' Dusky said heartily.

She felt uneasily that there was something faintly hostile in Cordelia's closed face, even when she was bidding good-night to the 'little brown baby wif spa'klin' eyes,' in the poem; but she recited well, and the applause was almost exaggerated, as if it were a relief to spat strenuous palms.

'Do another, Cordelia!' Dusky begged, and Cordelia, leaning against a tree trunk, said, 'Well — but you won't like this of Dunbar's so well. It isn't comedy. — It's called "Slow through the Dark."'

Her voice was deep and soft as she repeated it, and she gazed over their heads, never dropping her eyes to their faces:

> 'Slow moves the pageant of a climbing race;
> Their footsteps drag far, far below the height ——'

The constrained silence had thickened when she finished. Sally Lou and Caro Felton shook their heads when they were asked to do their stunts, and Mary Beth cleared her throat and said, 'It's too bad to drop from something so beautiful and — and sad, to anything funny. But I can't think of a thing except some old Chinese nursery rhymes my *amah* used to say to me.'

Touching her own fingers one by one, she recited the lines with delicious solemnity,

> 'This little cow eats grass,
> And this little cow eats hay,
> And this little cow drinks water,
> And this little cow runs away,
> And this little cow does nothing
> But lie around all day.
> We'll whip her!'

The patter of laughter froze like raindrops on ice.

'Mary Beth,' said Dusky, 'will you come and help me a minute? — Did you ever see such a stiff bunch?' she demanded, as they reached the safety of the kitchen. 'Every wheel creaks.'

'But, Dusky honey, didn't you *know* Sally Lou came from Alabama? I know she hasn't got much accent, but she always boasts, even, that she's Southern clear through, and unreconstructed.'

'What's that got to do with it? Didn't the Omegas all say they'd stand by the race friendship idea? Wasn't Sally Lou *there?* Didn't she holler with the rest? Well, then!'

'But I don't suppose she ever dreamed you'd ——' Mary Beth was mechanically arranging plates and glasses, her face solemn — 'And do you suppose this is so very — so very pleasant for Cordelia?'

Dusky whirled from the cupboard and flung out injured hands. 'Well, my word, what on earth do you think I'm doing this for?'

'I don't know,' Mary Beth said gravely.

In silence they finished assembling the miscellaneous plates, each with its glass of orange juice, its frosted cake, its cookies, and bore them to the jerkily talking group under the trees.

But at sight of the approaching food, Sally Lou sprang to her feet, trembling and pale. 'I'm — I'm sorry, Dusky,' she stammered, 'but I've got work to do. I'll have to be going. Good-bye, everybody.'

Caro Felton rose, too. 'I'll be running along with Sally Lou,' she said coolly. 'Thank you so much for asking us, Dusky.'

The other girls sat in a miserable silence, some looking at nothing, some watching the two girls go. Dusky, standing with a plate in each hand, noticed that her mouth was open. She closed it and walked deliberately across to Cordelia, offering her the first plate.

But Cordelia fended it from her with the long brown hands. Her lips were bitten in and her face had gone gray. She stood up, tried to speak, and then turned stiffly away. Stumbling, she, too, walked down a corridor of the grove. This time the others watched in complete stillness. On and on until the converging trees had taken her.

When at last she had disappeared, Dusky came to life. With all her might she sent plate, glass, cake, crashing against a tree trunk. Her eyes were blazing.

'Oh, Dusky honey!' Mary Beth remonstrated, '*we're* still here.'

Dorcas lifted ironic eyebrows and reached up to take the other plate, tilting dangerously, from Dusky's hand. 'Talk about grove-warmings!' she shivered. 'I'd call this a frost and a fire. But I'm hungry as the dickens. Let's see if Dusky's as good at cooking as she is at — other things.'

VII. A LITTLE OLD LADY

Dusky and Mary Beth sloshed home from church next day through the drenching wet of an early autumn rain. Dusky's hair curled higher and higher, and she spatted her galoshes vehemently in the sidewalk pools.

'Don't splash yourself so,' Mary Beth admonished. 'You'll be coughing harder than ever. I don't like your cold a bit, Dusky, it is so persistent.'

'Mmmm,' Dusky said absently. 'Mary Beth, I can't get Cordelia off my mind one minute. All day and all night she goes walking down the aisle of orange trees, getting smaller and farther and sadder like the end of a drama. And I kept saying "Slow through the Dark" while the preacher was preaching. I can't stand any more of it. I'm going over this afternoon and ask her to forgive me for putting her in such a position. I suppose it seems to her that I was criminally careless.'

She donned slicker and galoshes again and set out as soon as dinner was done. A half hour later she came home and silently hung her wet things in the bathroom. Mary Beth questioned her without words.

'Cordelia just stood there.' — Dusky dropped limply into one of the lounge chairs. — 'She didn't even ask me to sit down. I stood, and she stood, and she said: "That is quite all right. What else should *I* expect? Please don't give it another thought." But of course it isn't all right, and I can't stir her a single inch.'

'How much she must have suffered,' Mary Beth said, her soft small face crumpled with sympathy.

'Even where she lives ——' Dusky went on monotonously. 'The Davises let her have a room in their house. It's a sweet room. But — just imagine what it would feel like not to be *wanted* in the dorm!'

'I always thought they were light-hearted and kind of on the surface, colored people,' Maxine protested. 'Like in the stories about them.'

'Gosh,' Dusky said simply, 'you ought to try to apologize to Cordelia once. I believe she hates every one of us.'

'Did Sally Lou accept your apology any more graciously?' Mary Beth asked, looking out of the window.

'*Sally Lou?* What should I apologize to Sally Lou for?'

'Well, I imagine she feels as — as deeply insulted as Cordelia.'

'But she's got no right!' Dusky blazed. 'It was the white Southerners who were responsible ——'

'They weren't any worse than the Northerners,' said Mary Beth. 'Only they needed cheap labor worse. But, anyway, it wasn't Sally Lou, nor her parents, nor even her grandparents. Was it? They've just had to suffer for it. And even the actual slaveholders — well, almost everyone held a different view of it in those days.'

Mary Beth turned a page in the book she was reading, and Dusky sat staring at her gloomily. She was feeling that there were too many sides to everything and life was losing its old two-dimensional simplicity.

'When I go crawling to Sally Lou you can just figure the end of the world has come!' she ejaculated.

Mary Beth went on turning pages, and the rain went on raining, and Dusky went on sitting. The buzzer roused her.

'Dusky, this is Paul speaking. I just found a letter from Grandpa Wilson.'

'On Sunday?'

'It was in the cottage mailbox and nobody'd thought to look.'

'Is he all right?'

'Yes. — Can't you and Mary Beth come on over? I'll go and get Aunt Phronsie. Why not bring your paper bags along?'

'Well, all right,' Dusky agreed. 'But, Paul, wait a minute. Are Grandpa and Grandma ——'

Paul was gone.

Dusky and Mary Beth put on their slickers and galoshes once more, and stopped in the dining-hall for the paper bags of Sunday night supper.

'An apple, of course,' grumbled Dusky, feeling her bag as if it were a rather inferior Christmas stocking, while they paddled through the rain.

'And peanut butter sandwiches,' Mary Beth murmured, looking in the top of hers, 'and chocolate cake.'

'I hope Grandpa Wilson says that they got the bed-slippers all right,' Dusky went on irrelevently. 'It seemed queer they didn't write.'

Paul silently handed her the letter as soon as she and Mary Beth came into the sitting room.

'First get off those damp duds, Dusky,' David adjured her in his physician manner. She peeled them off, reading while she did so; and then she sat down abruptly and turned her face against the back of the old rocking chair.

The letter was in the cramped angular hand of an old man who seldom writes. It said:

Dear Dusky and Paul:

Must write you of the Sadness that has come to me. Ought to have written before but have been porely. Grandma went Home a week ago. We hadn't hardly got here when she took Cold, and it run into Pnumony.

Am terrible lonely for was married to Grandma

sixty-three years come Thanksgiving. If the good Lord's will, hope I can go to her without a weary Waiting.

Hope the Grove is going good and this finds you and your Aunt usually well.

Very Truly Yours,
ABIJAH WILSON

When the girls' first tears were dried, they sat looking at each other soberly, and at the little sitting-room.

'It looks like Grandma. Such a little old lady of a cottage,' Dusky thought aloud. 'If anybody tried to make it modern it would probably look like a great-grandmother smoking a cigarette. This way, it seems sort of a — sort of a memorial to Grandma.'

'Little old lady's right,' Paul agreed soberly. 'Probably they wouldn't call it old, back East; but in California seventy-five is some age, for an American house anyway. And this must be seventy-five.'

'I suppose it's sort of nondescript now,' Dusky continued, thrusting out her lower lip to blow a curling hair out of her eyes. 'It's not old or new either. Wouldn't it be nice to *underline* the oldness? Make it as consistently eighteen-fifty as is comfortable?'

'As for instance?' asked Aunt Phronsie, peering nearsightedly.

'Well — didn't they use matting on floors? And how would creamy matting be in this room, with those braided rugs Grandma had packed away in the storeroom? — This old Brussels will have to be replaced in a month anyway, with two great wild boys rampaging over it. And turkey red calico cushions and skirts on the chairs.'

'Skirts? And what on earth *is* turkey red?' Paul inquired.

'I never exactly knew,' Dusky admitted, 'but I'm sure it's what we need. And it will give a chance for soft cushions.'

'Would you work out an eighteen-fifty yard, too?' Aunt Phronsie asked.

'Well — I wonder. David said once that the Indians brought down this very water, ages ago. The Zanja, I mean.'

David nodded. 'Somewhere around 1819, when the Spanish padres were building that chain of missions along the whole coast.'

'Just imagine them,' Dusky cried, glowing with the romance of it. 'Coming right through this valley — right through *here!* The very same Temecula Indians that are in *Ramona.*' *Ramona* had been one of her earliest book loves.

'Or perhaps the Coachuillans,' Aunt Phronsie interpolated. Concerning historical data, Aunt Phronsie was never fuzzy even around the edges.

'And a little later the Americans coming in and starting orange groves and having the Mexicans work them,' David went on, his eyes on Dusky's eager, tear-stained face. 'And living here just about as they had in Mexico ——'

Dusky stopped him with clasped hands and an arrested gaze. 'That's it! Wouldn't it be appropriate to have a sort of Mexican court for our yard? Grandma was always fretting because the grass wouldn't grow with the men tramping across it.'

'A Mexican court and a Victorian house?' asked Paul.

'Well, I know it would be mixed, but so were the eighteen-fifties. On the San Berdoo road there's a place like that, the darlingest little old house sitting inside a high wall, with a flagged patio around a big palm, and a chinaberry tree and an outdoor fireplace and ——'

'Consider it done.' — Paul raised a resigned eyebrow and shook back the lock of brown hair that always tormented him. 'Only where do we get the flagging? And where do we get the time?'

'There's that little old tumbledown brick shed back in the grove. We can pull it to pieces and use those bricks instead of stones. They're a lovely color.'

'And the time? Or have you an idea that would stretch the usual twenty-four hours a day?'

'Well, we shouldn't be able to fix the court right now,' Dusky admitted.

'I'd like to do this room myself,' Aunt Phronsie offered.

All this while Mary Beth had been sitting quietly in Grandma's rocker, her round small face so registering every remark that no one had noticed any lack in her conversation. Now she said, eagerly: 'I could help a little bit, Miss Phronsie, if you and Dusky would let me. I loved Grandma Wilson, too. And I love the cottage.'

Dusky jumped up. 'Let's see this minute what Grandma had in the store closet and all,' she proposed. She blinked grimly, for she hated a display of emotion; but after all Grandma had been the nearest to a real grandmother that she had ever known. 'Grandma would have loved to have us fix it up old style and homey. Grandma *would*, wouldn't she, Pod?'

With that appeal, she bolted up the narrow stairs, to hide the tears that had started all over again, in spite of her.

VIII. FROZEN BUBBLES

THE girls had a feeling, comforting though not too logical, that they were doing something for Grandma Wilson when they snatched hours to work at the refurbishing of the cottage. Paul and David could take on no more than the load they already carried; but the girls poked dustily through Green Valley's two second-hand stores; and joined Aunt Phronsie in cutting and sewing, waxing, and polishing; and questioned the Vasquezes about the paving and equipping of a Mexican court. It was difficult to make the Vasquezes understand what they had in mind, and quite as difficult to understand what the Vasquezes had in mind: like a game of cross questions and silly answers.

It became evident that the Vasquezes were laboring over Dusky's strange ideas between whiles. One morning when she was setting out for her first class, Papa Vasquez accosted her. He detached himself from the watering whirligig with the squeak, which he had been making motions to oil, and put himself in her way, one foot extended, toe in air, and his limp felt hat twirling deferentially before his stomach.

'Mees Dusty,' he asked, grinning whitely and setting in motion a diminishing series of nods, 'you got it a minute, heh? — My Luisa, she say about a wall for your court. Why not 'dobe wall, heh? I make it the 'dobe bricks when I got nothing else to do. Got a lot pile' up in back yard.

What you say I build it a wall when I got it spare time, heh?'

'It would be great,' Dusky said regretfully, glancing at the chapel clock, 'if we had any money to spend, Mr. Vasquez. But we haven't. The wall's going to have to wait.'

'It don't got to wait, Mees Dusty.' He shrugged and grinned. 'I got it the 'dobe. I got it the spare time.'

'Oh, my word! But we couldn't — not unless there was something we could do for you in return ——'

'We-ell ——' Papa Vasquez twirled his hat faster, wriggled his elevated toe, blinked rapidly.

'*Is* there something we could do?'

'We-ell — the woman she would like it a picture of one of our keeds, for frame and hang on wall. Beeg!' — He measured off the dimensions of a giant picture — 'Colored!'

'Oh — why, I'd love that!' — Dusky mentally contrived more hours — 'Which one? Carmelita?'

He shook his head.

'Luisa? — Consuelo? — One of the boys?'

He cleared his throat. 'No, ma'am. Maria. The woman like to have it Maria.'

Dusky looked puzzled. 'Maria? I didn't know you had a Maria. Surely I never met her.'

His grin was a sober one. He crossed himself. 'No. Maria, she die long time ago. Before Carmelita born. Before Consuelo.'

'You have some small picture of her you want me to copy?'

'No, we got it no picture. That's the bad thing. That's why we like you to make us a picture.'

Dusky felt shocked laughter rising within her. 'B-but how —?'

Papa Vasquez was nodding reasonably. 'You talk it over with the woman. Maria so beeg like Carmelita. Got

Carmelita's eyes; mouth like Luisa; not any curls. The woman tell you. You do it, pleass?'

'Well, my maiden aunt, I never—! Well, yes, Mr. Vasquez, I'll do my best, but I can't promise how good——'

'All right, all right, all right. Then I breeng it load of 'dobe brick.'

When she ran over to the cottage that evening, Papa Vasquez was departing and a load of great dust-colored slabs lay in the back yard. The little Vasquez wagon swayed so shakily on crazy wheels behind a shambling horse that Dusky marveled at its carrying itself. It had carried, besides, the bricks, the pudgy little Mama Vasquez, who waved a benignant hand from the seat, Papa Vasquez, and Carmelita and Consuelo, shrieking farewells from the wagon-bed.

Dusky went, laughing, to watch Paul and David irrigate. The water-gates opened, the water carried the pink sunset down the zigzag furrows between the trees. Dusky stretched her arms as if to embrace the whole grove. 'Don't you love and adore it?' she asked.

Paul looked at her rather somberly. 'Do you think it would hurt to write Grandpa Wilson and ask him about the contract of sale? I'll feel a lot easier when I've got it in my fist.'

'Just a week or two, until he's had time to sort of get adjusted, poor old dear,' Dusky said pitifully. 'And we'll tell him about Papa Vasquez's wall and everything.'

The next Saturday noon found Dusky in the Vasquez parlor, sketch-pad on knee, jiggling uneasily on a spring that pushed up through the cracked leather of the davenport. Mama Vasquez sat at her left and Papa Vasquez leaned acrobatically over the davenport's right arm. The two little boys dashed in now and then, stared at the sketch-pad, giggled, and dashed out again. Carmelita, ten-year-old Consuelo, and Luisa were the models.

'Maria had the laugh jost like Carmelita,' Papa Vasquez contributed. 'Carmelita! Laugh for Mees Dusty!'

Carmelita coughed for Mees Dusty instead. Stoically she crowded herself down in her chair and cupped her hands over her face and coughed until her eyes filled with tears and she sagged limply.

'It isn't croup, is it?' Dusky asked in alarm.

Mama Vasquez shrugged, her face troubled. 'Not croup, I theenk. Very bad cold, mebbe? Nothing I do make no difference.'

'The hair also straight like on Consuelo and very shiny,' put in Papa Vasquez, who had been looking from the sketch-pad to his three daughters and back again. 'I cut heem with a bowl.'

Mama chuckled delightedly as Dusky roughed in Dutch-cut hair with her soft black pencil, leaving bright high-lights for the shininess.

'Look, Mama! the hair of Maria! Maybe you cut heem a little shorter, heh? So!' He traced a line across his corrugated brow with a stubby forefinger.

Mama Vasquez, feet planted wide and plump hands on knees, leaned over Dusky's shoulder, frowning with concentration. 'It iss not quite right the eyes,' she concluded, and shut her own, swaying backward and forward in deep thought. 'It iss the eyebrow!' she declared suddenly. 'Maria's eyebrow go so! And so!'

'This way?' asked Dusky, drawing.

Mama Vasquez shook her head.

'This way?'

Mama Vasquez laughed across at Papa Vasquez delightedly.

'Maria was never so fat like Carmelita,' Luisa offered, tiptoeing over to look at the pageful of sketches. 'And I remember she had a nose that went ——' She arched her pointed forefinger to an aquiline curve.

Papa Vasquez was studying his daughters. 'Very

brown, like Carmelita. But with the much red lips and sheeks like Luisa, though it come from the *in*side and not ——'

'Not painted on like this naughty Luisa!' Mama cried dramatically, fond reproachful eyes on her eldest.

Dusky stood up. 'I'll start the painting from these sketches,' she said, 'and bring it as soon as I can have the girls pose again.'

'Mebbe you like it some of my tortillas?' Mama Vasquez heaved herself up from the davenport and puffed out to the kitchen. She returned with a plate of appetizing-looking turnovers. 'I keep them warm in the oven,' she added.

Dusky went her way, sketch-pad clasped under one arm, while she ate the tortillas, filled with a meat mixture and fried. The food was delicious, and she was always hungry; she ate it to the last crumb, weeping over the pepper as she ate.

After luncheon she spread out her sketches and propped a large canvas-board before her. 'I had to get this picture started' — Dusky tried to keep the defensive note out of her voice — 'Papa Vasquez has already begun the wall. No *mañana* business about it this time! — And if I have this blocked in I can work on it in my spare time. Maybe Professor Faunce will even give me credit for it. — I think I'll sketch it on canvas-board and get the first color in.'

'What about your lessons?' Mary Beth asked accusingly. 'Didn't you say you were badly behind in Miss Corinne's course?'

'My word! and a quiz Monday! I wish I had my Oliver here: I can type a lot faster than I can write. — If that woman didn't scare me into a blue funk I'd get along better. And if I could read my notes a month after I wrote 'em.'

'And what are you going to wear to the tea?'

The Panhellenic Tea was one of the large formal events

of early fall. Held in the gracious living-room of Abbott Hall, it was an exercise of the combined talents and form of the four sororities, entertaining faculty women and any mothers who might be accessible, as well as students. This time Dusky, as vice-president of her sorority, would be in the receiving line.

She penciled an outline on the canvas-board. 'My gray dress!' she announced. 'It's exactly right.'

'But it isn't finished,' Mary Beth countered. 'And what about shoes?'

'I can finish it in ten minutes and press it in fifteen.' — Dusky had dropped her pencil and was boring her way into the gray dress, head first. 'Do you think it'll show through without a slip?' She established herself before the desk light and revolved.

'No, I guess not. It really is smart, Dusky. I don't comprehend how you do it.' She ran over and peered into the sleeves. 'There are some ravelings that show, Dusky honey. You'll turn in that raw seam and sew it, of course.'

Dusky pushed her gently away. 'I'll sew it with the scissors,' she said firmly. 'I'll be darned if I take another stitch on this. Being a lady, I have to give *some* thought to my shoes and stockings.'

The shoes were not encouraging. 'My best ones are out, being brown.'

'I told you brown wouldn't ——' Mary Beth's reminder died under Dusky's withering glance.

'My black ones — h'mph!' Dusky sent them flying back into the closet. 'The white gabardine — well, they just don't whiten any longer. Not since that last mud puddle. — My word! I'll paint them gray!'

'But they won't dry in time.'

'With lots of turps they will.' Dusky went scrabbling after paints and palette and mixed diligently, an eye to the dress.

'I think,' she murmured, when she had the shoes,

beautifully gray, on a newspaper on the window sill, 'that I'll just go ahead and cover this canvas, so that I can get along with Maria in the morning. I mustn't put the Vasquezes off. It's a bad example.'

'You're rationalizing,' Mary Beth accused, pinning back the curtains so that they should not blow against the shoes. In Dusky's vicinity rugs and draperies, cushions, dresses, wore varicolored dabs of paint. 'You *want* to paint; that's all.'

'All right. I want to paint. You want to study.' — Mary Beth opened her mouth — and closed it. — 'It's better to press my dress in the morning, anyway, when I can see well.' She ended the topic by squeezing pillows of fresh paint onto her palette and sweeping flesh tint on the canvas while Mary Beth eyed her with fascinated horror.

The next morning was a busy one. Dusky had forgotten that she was a member of a committee on decoration, and that the chairman was a figurehead. However, she borrowed Langston Trevor and his car, and they carried loads of palm branches and pepper boughs with their lacy leaves and trailing berries, and of sleeping hibiscus and aspidistra. The rooms were soon lovely with color and greenery, and Dusky had dashed back to Lawrence Hall with an hour to spare.

Mary Beth was all ready except her nails and her dress. In her blue and rose robe she sat soaking her fingertips in a bowl of soapsuds while she studied outlines for a sociology quiz. She looked up, her face sober. That was because Dusky had borrowed Langston and his car.

'I suppose you're like all the other girls, and think him devastating,' she said coldly. 'All because of his money.'

'Goodness!' Dusky deprecated. 'I don't like him because he has money, Ma'Beth, but it's a lot of fun to be with somebody who doesn't have to think about money at all. — And it's a rest,' she went on thoughtfully, 'to bang around a little with somebody that hasn't two serious thoughts to rub against each other. I do get fed up with noble ideals.'

Mary Beth's mouth tightened on shocked remonstrance.

'Slowpoke!' Dusky gibed good-naturedly, turning the talk from its dangerous ground. 'You waste so much time, Mary Beth. I'll dip into the tub and be out and dressed in five minutes.'

Mary Beth's glance rested meaningly on Dusky's nails, rainbowed with Maria.

'Oh, I have a system on that,' bragged Dusky. 'But — that reminds me of gloves. I'll have to rub some cleaner on. I suppose it wouldn't do to roll them under at the wrists and pretend it was because of shaking hands? — Oh, well, maybe not.'

She scrubbed vigorously with cleaning fluid and hung the gloves from the ring of a window shade. The bathroom door slammed, the water ran noisily, there were splashings and bursts of tuneless song, and presently there was Dusky, standing on one foot to pull on a sheer stocking.

'Did you know your hose had a run?' Mary Beth inquired, looking up from a faintly pink nail.

Dusky groaned loudly. 'It *can't* have. Not my best pair.' Sputtering, she rummaged through a dresser drawer, and breathed relief. 'See, Mary Beth, when this is sort of shaded by my dress *any*one would think it was just a trick of the light, that little difference in color. Now all I have to do is press my dress.'

A few minutes before the designated hour, the two girls stepped into the porch of Abbott Hall. Dusky flamed out of the soft gray of her dress, and Mary Beth, in Alice blue, was like a sweet pea beside a Talisman rose. 'You do look lovely, Dusky,' she said warmly, 'and everything looks perfectly all right. Of course there's a smell of benzine from your gloves ——'

'Oh, well, I don't mind; nobody will be sure it isn't from yours,' Dusky said airily.

Mary Beth looked startled, but she had no time to express her sense of life's injustices. In the alcove the girls who were to receive were already assembling. As Mary Beth and Dusky approached them, a peculiarly violent and full-bodied sneeze resounded from the group.

'Caro Felton!' Dusky murmured. 'I'd know her sneeze in Calcutta. — Not so much noise, young ladies!' she called with gay malice. 'Sneezes should be seen and not ——'

She broke off with a horrified gasp. Caroline Felton was not in the group; and Miss Corinne Smith was covering her aristocratic nose for another spasm. Dusky's thoughts scrambled over each other. There should be some brilliant way out of the *contretemps*, but she couldn't find it. She only said, in a subdued voice: 'I beg your pardon, Miss Smith; I thought it was Caro. She has the most prodigious sneeze in captivity. — My word!' she whispered to Mary Beth, 'what a help *that* was!'

It was a 'help,' too, when Dusky found herself next Miss Corinne in the receiving line. The lady was gracious, but the blue eyes under her triangular lids held more than their usual amusement. Now, too, the fumes of benzine seemed to rise from Dusky's gloves in choking clouds, and there was not the least hope that anyone would think Miss Corinne's gloves responsible. Dusky glanced nervously from her hands to her feet. What more likely than that the gray paint was rubbing off?

Miss Corinne's eyes followed hers. 'A lovely shade, Dusky!' she commented. 'And how marvelously they match your frock.'

The first of the guests was sailing down the line, and Miss Corinne turned to her with a bow, and introduced Dusky. Dusky congratulated herself on the interruption. She had been on the point of telling Miss Corinne that she had painted the pumps and that the stockings were not mates and that she had made the dress out of last year's suit. The guest had saved her from her own garrulity. It was really time that she became more adult, more reserved. You did not need to tell people about your makeshifts, especially people like Miss Corinne. Dusky set one gray shoe slightly in advance of the other, like Miss Corinne's. In that pose the difference in stockings was safer from detection, too. Unconsciously she assumed Miss Corinne's autocratic arch of chin.

Miss Corinne, whose oxidized silver head was just on a level with Dusky's nose, reached up and deftly twitched at Dusky's shoulder-seam. 'A basting, my dear,' she murmured, dropping a long thread to the floor and turning to another guest.

Dusky was content with the world. The long living-room was lovely. Mary Beth was pouring tea at the nearest table, and now and again she caught Dusky's eye between eddying gowns and gloves, and her serene smile spoke satisfaction with the afternoon and with Dusky. Someone was playing the piano charmingly — The Omegas were well turned out today, and those Etas, who thought themselves the only smart sorority at Highland, couldn't turn up their noses at them this time — People blew in little gusts along the line, attractive people —— Here came a fresh batch, and the president's wife was among them — Dusky's hand went out to touch hers, and Dusky bowed an urbane Miss Corinne bow with the proper addition of girlish deference ——

But what was the sudden coolness descending from her shoulder? She glanced down. Her arm was bare from shoulder to elbow, and her whole sleeve was draped around her forearm.

'Mrs. Faber, may I present Miss Day?' 'How do you do, Mrs. Faber?' 'Mrs. Phillips, may I present Miss Day?' 'How do you do, Mrs. Phillips?' 'Mrs. ——'

Dusky straightened her spine and went on bowing, shaking hands, murmuring names, with never another look at the sleeve that had come out of its armhole. Not until the whole group had passed did she slip out of line and dash up to a friendly dormitory room where she could baste herself together again, fastening the last stitches with vigor.

Miss Corinne made room for her when she returned. 'My dear,' she murmured, with an inspecting scrutiny of the armhole, 'I'll be more discreet about bastings. I do beg your pardon. And —' she rippled with laughter — 'how I admire your poise!'

Poise! Dusky felt like a small girl grown suddenly oversize and all hands and feet. Miss Corinne's gaze was sharpening with thought.

'Dusky,' she said, 'I noticed you downtown with a young Mexican girl, earlier in the fall. And this other protégée of yours, the enormous-eyed infant —— You are interested in the Mexican people?'

Dusky found voice. 'Oh, very much so.'

'Have you ever considered,' Miss Corinne went on, 'applying for the graduate fellowship in the National University of Mexico? Rather a new fellowship, but interesting, I should think, if one were interested.'

'I've — barely thought of it,' Dusky said breathlessly. 'It would be much too marvelous to come true.'

'Miss Lancaster, this is Miss Day ——'

Dusky continued to bow and murmur, but the rest of the afternoon passed in a mist of eddying color and restrained fragrance, of smiles and vague words and the odor of clean kid gloves. Even the catastrophe of the sleeve was forgotten.

Mexico City! Miss Corinne's words, touching her fleeting dreams, had suddenly solidified them, as if glamorous bubbles had become jewels.

Mexico City!

IX. 'COME LAY A BRICK!'

'COME lay a brick, drink an orange, eat a cooky with Paul and Dusky Day,' the invitations ran. 'Open House — Court — Grove: Saturday, Two to Five. P.S. Wear galoshes or rubber boots.'

Before those invitations went out, late October had cooled and freshened Green Valley. Day after day Papa Vasquez had creaked and rattled to the grove in his rickety wagon; evening after evening he had spent in laying adobe bricks. The wall was up, and most of it covered with the outer plaster of adobe on which its long life depended. The sun-dried, straw-tough clay slabs would last for centuries if the rain was kept out of their seams.

Aunt Phronsie had moved into the cottage, and she and Dusky had completed its present alterations in a final spurt of energy. Dusky had squeezed gallons of orange juice and baked hundreds of cookies, cookies which had almost the softness, the rich fullness of flavor, of Grandma Wilson's. The boys' principal contribution had been the leveling of the ground in the court, and the spreading it, under direction of Papa Vasquez, with a deep layer of rich adobe mud.

That Saturday at two everything was ready and the guests began to come. Rubber boots had been pulled over clean junior cords or dirty senior ones or more formal serges; they even appeared grotesquely under smart skirts and traily dresses. Girls shuffled in large rubbers and marched in trimly zippered galoshes.

All were marched to the court first of all, and set to work laying the rich-toned old bricks according to the pattern Papa Vasquez had started, bedding them firmly in the thick adobe.

Jan teetered tipsily on an insecure brick, gathering up her frilly frock in one hand and holding a brick in pink-tipped fingers while she waited for someone to lay it for her. Dorcas, miniature in fisherman's boots, darted to and fro, placing her bricks with speed and precision. Kate clumped in arctics and slapped the bricks into the adobe with such force that it spattered the squealing Jan. The boys divided their masterful attention between girls and flagging.

Around the chinaberry tree, around a single clattering fan palm, around a clump of strawberry guava bushes, circular openings had been staked out with sticks and strings, and Papa Vasquez had neatly bordered one with edgewise bricks as a guide for the others. The paving closely hugged the well, however, a well with a rusty pump.

'Why not a wellsweep or at least a wheel?' queried a guest.

'I like the old pump,' Dusky countered. 'I never had seen a pump used before, and it looks so real.'

The chinaberry's heavy umbrella of shade had been thinned by autumn, unlike the usual California trees, which are evergreen. Its depleted foliage showed clots of mistletoe, but it was still able to spread a lovely shadow pattern over half the court; and the palm would weave its interlacing points all winter long. Already, inspired by the mellow brick and the shadows, Paul had started a poem—

> 'Mellowed to mauve and rose and bronze and blue,
> Gilt by the sun; patterned in curious weaves
> With purple pencilings of shadow leaves ——'

For, even smeared with the adobe as it was now, that swiftly laid flagging was beautiful.

'Now!' cried Dusky, when it was all in place, 'line up for a grand march, please! Kate, you lead!'

The guests boiled over in a laughing, chattering confusion, and settled back into a double line as Kate cuddled the harmonica to her lips and struck up 'The Campbells Are Coming!' She strode ahead, face flushed, eyes shining, and behind her, oversize rubbers spatted and boots clumped, pressing the bricks more securely into their adobe foundation. Jan, stepping gingerly, slipped on a smear of clay and waved violently to and fro while her partner waved with her. Dorcas took delight in flipping the mud far and wide. Langston Trevor and Caro Felton tap-danced airily with a jaunty fling of feet. And the clay squeezed up reluctantly between the bricks as those bricks settled down to a bed where they might rest for a generation.

After a dozen circuits of the court, Dusky took her place before a patch of fresh adobe plaster, prepared the night before in a protected corner of the wall, and stopped each guest to sign his name there with a homemade stylus. When they had all 'signed the wall,' she led the way into the cottage itself.

The cottage itself was enchanting. The chairs were at once prim and gay, some with deep soft cushions and full skirts of the turkey-red calico, some in flounces of glazed chintz.

Mary Beth had thought Dusky stubborn not to use chintz for the curtains also, but Dusky had insisted on Dutch half-curtains of dotted Swiss. Hanging in the bay window, with a tasseled bag of the Swiss on the bottom of his shining brass cage, sang a yellow canary named Pidge.

Grandma Wilson's round braided rugs brightened the cream-colored matting, soft with a deep padding of straw. The new wallpaper would have to await another day or year; but Dusky had found a wool-worked motto in Grandma's bedroom, and had given it the place of honor; and a pile of rumpled old magazines, time-browned and spotted, had given further adornment to the walls. The magazines were Peterson's, not Godey's; but they held similar colored plates of wasp-waisted ladies with festooned balloons for skirts and tilted saucers for hats; of doll-sized children with waists as pinched and festoonings as elaborate as their elders'. Dusky had framed a group of these in narrow black frames from the ten-cent store.

But even now she did not dispossess the smirking calendar girl from her post beside the secretary.

The store closet had yielded a candle-mould, which hung in a corner, and a bellows which wished for a fireplace, and a footstool that waited primly before a chintz-skirted chair. Second-hand stores had added an oval walnut table, another prim little chair like one of the Peterson ladies sitting with hands at sides, and a hanging lamp fringed with prisms, which now hid a large electric bulb under its etched-glass shade. The shed which had given the bricks for the court had uncovered the strangest of little heaters. It was a stove that played at being a fireplace, holding out a laplike fender for toasting chilly toes, and grinning from a whole row of grotesque little cast-iron faces.

The kitchen had had to content itself with a coat of old-fashioned yellow paint on the worn linoleum — paint which was to prove a delusion and a snare — and fresh yellow curtains at the four-paned windows. And on the oven door Aunt Phronsie had lettered primly an old proverb: 'If the oven scorch the inquiring hand the heat is excessive.'

Flushed and happy the hostesses flitted about, showing their house and explaining the watercolor drawing Dusky had made of the court as it was eventually to be, and serving the refreshments. They could not spare much thought for the guests who had not come; but —

'Sally Lou really did stay away,' Dusky hissed at Mary Beth; 'and so did Cordelia. Luisa isn't here, either, and that does seem strange.'

'Michi and Jimmie Tang are trying not to glare at each other,' Mary Beth murmured back. 'I can't blame Jimmie so much. Those Japanese ——'

'You're as bad as Sally Lou!' Dusky rebuked her. — 'Yes, that's the way the court's going to look *some* day,' she interrupted herself to answer a question at her elbow. 'Those glorious sky-blue morning glories over the wall, and a blue wooden gate. — Yes, we're going to paint on the gate, "Bienvenido seas!" and it means "Thou art welcome!"'

'And a fireplace and a breakfast table and benches,' chanted Mary Beth. 'And a circular seat around the chinaberry tree.'

'And a Mexican cart for local color,' added Dorcas, looking past Dusky and the drawing.

'A Mexican cart?' Dusky questioned; and then she looked, too, and dashed outdoors with her guests to answer the squeal of cart wheels.

Luisa and another Mexican girl and two Mexican youths were pulling it. Luisa, laughing, came to a stop, pushed back her flying hair, and froze with embarrassment. The boys ducked little bows and turned to go. Dusky stopped them, gazing delightedly at the dim blue of the old cart.

'Luisa, you don't mean it's for us?'

'Sure it is. We got no use for it, and we think maybe it look good with your Spanish court.'

'Oh, it's priceless! We'll stand it just outside the gate, and chain it so nobody'll swipe it. — But what are those gorgeous pots? Not for us, too?'

Luisa nodded, smacking her gum. 'My oncle is the man who make the pottery out at the Asistencia — that old Mission they fix up,' she explained. 'Look, they have little rough places, those potteries.'

But the jars, though slightly imperfect, were beautifully shaped and their burnt orange would go with the Mexican blue of the gate-to-be.

'They're wonderful!' Dusky assured her. 'And what is this funny case they're in?'

It was a large rectangular cage, neatly made of withes.

Luisa shrugged. 'Only a box to hold them. The kind they all the time send things in from Mexico. Just throw it away or burn it.'

'I should say not!' Dusky cried. 'It shall sit beside our well and be another piece of local color.'

Surrounded by the college girls whom she envied and resented, and enjoying the new experience of having them admire her possessions, Luisa showed sharp self-consciousness. She giggled and laughed with her companions, who were even more ill at ease than she. While the two girls giggled, the boys pushed at each other and combed their black hair, sleek with pomatum.

Relentlessly Dusky herded them all indoors, where she served them refreshments and showed them the high points of the cottage. They were difficult to entertain. The boys stared past everything into vacancy, and Luisa's and Refugio's sidelong eyes estimated the other girls' dresses, shoes, hair. Their interest was caught, however, when Dusky, with an orange crayon, sketched the two jars, one on each side of the blue wooden gate.

'Oh, lookit!' Luisa urged, nudging her companions, 'those are the potteries just exactly! And lookit the Spanish saying on the gate. Dusky, why don't you plant gourd vines to grow over the wall, too? Then you get gourds to use for dippers at the well, and gourds for bird houses.'

'Bird houses?'

'On a tall pole I have seen them, two or three gourds hanging from the top, and the birds building nests inside.'

'That court grows every minute!' Dusky exclaimed. 'Don't go, Luisa! Not till we try some more snapshots. We want you and your friends in these. I mean to send the whole lot to Grandpa Wilson.'

She grouped the crowd around the new old cart and the

jars that stood like sentinels beside the gateway, and used the last of her second roll of film.

'There wasn't a single snap where someone didn't manage to move or get a silly smirk or scowl,' she concluded, 'but by using the lot of them Grandpa Wilson ought to get a good idea of what we've been doing. — And somehow I want to get them developed quick — quick. Oh, there's Laban Hitchcock! Laban, you might take them downtown right away.'

Laban, who had only just sauntered up, said plaintively, 'If you'll feed me first, Dusky. I'm pretty weak.'

'I don't know whether there's anything left,' Dusky told him severely. 'Why should you be so swanky and Eastern, anyway, and amble in at half-past four when all the work is done?'

'Because I woke up at twenty-five after four,' Laban told her, following her into the cottage and into the kitchen, where she piled a plate with remnants.

When he had consumed it all and compared the adage on the oven door with the parallel rows of burns on Dusky's arms, he cranked up his old car and roared away with the cutout open, taking the two rolls of film to the kodak store. The other guests began to drift away, gingerly carrying their muddy galoshes. The official opening of the Singing Wood was successfully over.

Monday afternoon Laban brought Dusky the fifteen prints, and she mailed the best ones to Grandpa Wilson next day. He never received them. Coming over to the grove on Friday, Dusky saw the tin flag raised on the mailbox, and reached in to feel along its floor.

Two letters lay there, one from home and one from Indianapolis. The letter from home said that they were well but lonesome. Mother was hard at work on a new book — the best she had ever written, Father considered it, and sure to find a wild welcome from the publishers. Father had been to Denver to a meeting of the Philatelic Society and had got a marvelous bargain in early American stamps ('I bet that means he wears his same old overcoat another year,' Dusky exclaimed, 'the one with the moth-holes down the back'). Classes were going on as well as usual, though each new generation of students was more feather-brained and bull-headed than the last. Pendleton was well. Father was following Paul and Dusky's request and feeding him only once a day, in the morning, but Mother did get absent-minded and give him supper, so he wasn't noticeably thinner. — 'I bet she feeds him half her tidbits at the table, too,' Dusky chuckled as she read.

When she had quite finished, she opened the Indianapolis letter, realizing as she did so that it was addressed in unfamiliar handwriting.

Aunt Phronsie was waiting for her on the porch. 'Bad news, Dusky?' she asked anxiously.

Dusky lowered the letter and scowled, biting her lip. 'I'm beginning to think life isn't so hot,' she muttered, 'with such a lot of dying in it.'

She shoved the letter blindly into Aunt Phronsie's reaching hand. 'Grandpa Wilson — now he's gone, too.'

X. WHOOPS, MY DEAR WALRUS!

The autumn days marched past, warm and bright, but streaked, for Dusky, with sun and shadow. She expressed it otherwise.

'Life's an awful lot like bacon,' she said abruptly at the breakfast table one morning. 'For every streak of fat there's a streak of lean.'

'You're getting to be a streak of lean yourself' — Mary Beth studied her anxiously over the cereal she was serving —'Your cold may be different, but it isn't the least bit better, and you cough half the night.'

'I was thinking about life, not about me; and I wish to goodness you'd put cotton in your ears when you go to bed. — But here I insult Miss Corinne, of all people, and lose the sleeve out of my dress just as Mrs. Prexy heaves in sight, and then Corinne ups and suggests that I apply for the Mexican fellowship, and gives me a swell mark in her next quiz ——'

'You sat up till three in the morning, cramming for it.'

'Irrelevant and immaterial. I've sat up till four, and one glance from Miss Corinne —! But this time I thought the worst had already happened, and I sailed along without fear.'

'What are some of the lean streaks?' Dorcas inquired, poking her cereal with the tip of her spoon. 'This oatmeal's mine.'

'Well, my darn' cough. And Grandpa Wilson —— As for the fat streaks, look at the way our court's coming out, like a dream. On the other hand, I'm getting so I want to run and hide whenever I see a letter. Paul buzzed me after you went to sleep last night, Ma'Beth. He'd had a letter from Johnnie Wilson's lawyer.'

'From Johnnie Wilson's lawyer?' Mary Beth echoed.

Dusky nodded and laid down her spoon. 'He says, to put it in a few words, that they've been through Grandpa Wilson's papers and they don't find anything relating to this property. They say that Grandpa Wilson never went into details with Johnnie about our arrangements, the time being broken by Grandma's illness and death. And they ask us to let them know exactly the terms of the agreement, and to send them a record of the deed.'

'Well,' said Dorcas, frowning at her half-eaten cereal, 'isn't that all right?'

'We haven't any deed, and it worries me. Grandpa made a note of the agreement; he told us so the last thing; and I can't see why they don't find it.'

'But of course you can write and explain just how it was,' Mary Beth soothed her. 'They'll have to look more carefully. It might have been on a sheet of tablet paper, even; you know how Grandpa and Grandma were about writing on all kind of scraps.'

Dusky gloomed at her. 'It sounds so fishy when you put it down, the way Grandpa sold it to us — or gave it to us. But he *did*, and it *is* ours, and I love it horribly. And wouldn't it be the limit if we were to get it all fixed up and then have Johnnie — and that Mrs. Johnnie — come along and enjoy what we've planted? That's out of the Bible, Ma'Beth.'

Mary Beth looked dubious. 'I wouldn't quite recognize it. Have an egg, Dusky?'

'Hold on!' Dusky begged. 'Slow up, won't you?'

'Eat a while and let someone else take over the talking,'

Dorcas advised, 'or we'll be here as long as the faculty table, which heaven forbid.'

'I think we should bring it up in sorority meeting, though,' Mary Beth suggested. 'Our eating. It must be detrimental to the digestion to eat so rapidly.'

The girls did eat as if they were about to rush to a train. One tableful after another finished, rose, shoved in its chairs, and scurried away, leaving the faculty table in the center to continue at its leisure. The room was a bedlam of shoving chairs, clinking silver, talk, and laughter, with the Head Resident's bell slicing off the noise now and then to make space for announcement or reproof.

'Don't talk about slowing down!' Dusky protested, swallowing a last bit of toast and egg. 'Don't you wish they'd cut out the boiled eggs? A boiled egg is *not* piquant. — And they take so long. We're practically never on time at art school as it is.'

When they rushed breathless into the familiar disorder, the familiar oil-and-turpentine flavor, this morning, Laban was already there. He disentwined his yards of arms and legs and bowed before Dusky, handing her a book, a large plump book with a pinafored little girl and a white rabbit on its cover. She looked at it blankly.

'According to the misguided Webster,' Laban said sadly, 'the word is chortle, as in chuckle.'

'My word! I never gave it another thought.'

'I noticed that. But my ingrown conscience ——'

'It's a good edition. Look at it, Ma'Beth.'

Mary Beth turned the pages pleasurably. 'Ours is in China,' she said, 'and I grew up on it. "The time has come, the Walrus said, To talk of many things — "'

'"Of shoes — and ships — and sealing-wax,"' Dusky went on seriously, '"and cabbages — and kings."'

'"'But wait a bit,' the Oysters cried"'—Laban draped himself around Mary Beth's easel and declaimed, '"'For some of us are out of breath, And all of us are fat!'" That's me,' he whimpered. 'I choose to be an oyster. You be the Carpenter, Mary Beth, and Dusky can be the Walrus. Then we'll read it as it had oughta be read.'

'Don't be silly,' said Dusky, settling her smock and hitching her easel around toward the model stand.

'Now, Sister!' Laban chided.

'I'm no sister of yours.'

'You're a bold girl, that's what you are,' Laban declared, 'offering not to be my sister when I never even asked you to be anything else yet.'

Dusky snorted an unwilling laugh which worked itself into a cough, and then drew a trapezoid for the head and shoulders of the old man model.

'So I'll be an oyster' — Laban returned to the subject — 'And Mary Beth really should be Alice, since we are going into this thing seriously. She never has found out what America is all about. It's still Wonderland for her.'

Mary Beth chuckled, and Dusky looked at her questioningly. Dusky had a sort of humor, but Mary Beth's was of another pattern, and so was Laban's. Dusky could never put her finger on it.

'I'd rather be the White Queen,' Mary Beth objected. 'I always felt so sorry for her.'

'Mustn't stick in your hairpins so tight, then. But that reminds me: I'll be the White Knight.' — Laban made a great business of rubbing his large hands together. — 'Nobody can beat me at tumbling off horses; except that I've never been on one.'

'I think I'll be the Frog Footman,' Dorcas contributed, drawing swiftly. 'Dusky, you've got to be something, for the honor of the Painty Four.'

'Walrus, then,' Dusky said resignedly, 'just to get rid of you. You're all so silly. People don't talk like this.'

'Jane is the Duchess, I think maybe,' Laban cogitated, surveying his fellow students. 'But we'd better not let on to her.'

'Michi — well, she's just Michi,' Dorcas decided.

'And Dorian and Andrea might be Tweedledum and Tweedledee,' Mary Beth added.

'I'd like to see them tear their hair,' Dusky grunted. 'Some good in that.'

By the time the old model had lighted his rank-smelling pipe and the students had scattered for the short nine o'clock recess, the Wonderland Quartet was an established affair and Laban and Dorcas, White Knight and Frog Footman, were inventing an elaborate interpretive dance on the model stand.

Dusky sat blinking at her portrait. She was tired. This queer cough was getting her down. She should hurry, for she wanted to try the Beaux Arts problem this time, having paid her three-dollar entrance fee, and she should finish this painting and have a little spare time for the problem. But she was glad when Mary Beth ascended from the lower regions and slipped a sandwich into her lap.

'Thank heaven they have so many teas!' Dusky said.

'And here's a note Mr. Vasquez handed to Wing Lee' — Mary Beth handed her a wad of grayish paper.

'A note?' Dusky unfolded it. It was a sheet of ruled notebook paper, with punch-holes along one edge. 'Oh, from Luisa.' — She read rapidly, and thrust the page at Mary Beth. 'My word, Ma'Beth, what's going to happen next? Oh, my word, do you suppose ——?'

The note said: 'Dear Dusky, I am so sorry, we have just found out that Carmelita's cold is the hooping cough. The doctor says she have it all the time, even if she have never hoop before. Mama wonder if maybe your cold might of turn into hooping cough too. We are so sorry if it is. Yours truly, Luisa Vasquez.'

'Oh, no!' Mary Beth cried. 'You must have had whooping cough when you were little, Dusky. Everybody does.'

'I had measles and German measles and Liberty measles

and chicken pox and scarlet fever and mumps — or one mump —' Dusky counted with an inturned look, 'but —'

A racking cough interrupted her. She covered her face with her handkerchief and rocked to and fro in the spasm, until her eyes swam and her lungs ached for air — fought for air in one prolonged and unmistakable 'whoooop!'

'My word!' she gasped weakly, 'it can't be!'

'My word, Sister Walrus, it is,' Laban contradicted her blandly. 'Come along. Let me take you to Nurse Morris before they mob you up here. The way you've been broadcasting germs ——'

At the Infirmary, cool and white under its palm trees, Dusky went through revolt and defeat at the hands of the nurse. The nurse was cool and white herself, and starched. She had a pale yellow silk fluff of hair under the impudent white petal of her cap, and under the fluff of hair distrait eyes that would not be coaxed.

Yes, without doubt Dusky had been having whooping cough for some weeks. Why hadn't she come to the Infirmary for treatment of her 'cold,' as she was supposed to? Miss Morris put the question with her characteristic flavor, slightly acid, slightly sweet, well chilled, like limeade.

Yes, without doubt Dusky had already infected large numbers of people, but that was no reason for her infecting more.

Yes, without doubt Dusky must be immured until the contagious period was past: two more weeks, at least. She was run down, anyway. Miss Morris pinched off the words severely, scrutinizing Dusky.

'Stick out your tongue,' she ordered. 'Hmph! — Give me your wrist. — Hmph. — And no great husky girl like you has any business with white ears. You'll take a rest.'

Dusky murmured rebelliously.

'Unless you want to be sent home in a box,' the nurse ended gruesomely.

'My word!' Dusky bleated, and subsided.

XI. THE WALRUS CAGED

COULD she stay at the cottage with Aunt Phronsie? Dusky petitioned Miss Morris.

'Yes, I believe that can be arranged,' Nurse Morris admitted grudgingly.

Laban, who had waited in his nondescript car, sitting on his shoulders with one leg hooked over the right hand door, took her to the grove and promised to bring her painting things. Aunt Phronsie, pried loose from her book in the sunshine, heard the story, sympathized, and went in to rearrange her room for her niece's accommodation.

Dusky dropped down on the brick flagging with her head against the chinaberry trunk and took a long breath. 'Two weeks!' she murmured, looking up through the thinning leaves to the soft blue of the autumn sky. 'I can use 'em!' She slid down and lay flat on the sun-warmed bricks.

An occasional tardy orange blossom gave fragrance; an occasional bee buzzed contentedly; the usual mocking birds whistled and scolded; the grove, seen above Papa Vasquez's wall, was a Golden as well as a Singing Wood; the world outside the wall was muted and dimmed yet comfortably near; Dusky lay and soaked up sunshine.

'By rights,' drawled Laban, ambling through the gateway with his arms precariously piled, one thumb hooked through the handle of a vast tin paint kit and the other through the hole of a painty palette, 'by rights, being I yam who I am, I should tumble in. But you might sue me for the wasted paint.'

Dusky sat up and blinked at him. 'Isn't it awful how much paint costs?' she said sleepily.

'And I've got the darned stuff all over my best junior cords,' he grumbled, scowling ferociously from the palette to the smudges of color on the creamy corduroy.

Dusky still blinked.

'You're very welcome,' he drawled again, 'very, very, very, very welcome, my dear Walrus. That's Aliceish, too, so you needn't look so snooty. I was just thinking I'd better drift around here and build a bench around your tree so you won't catch your death of cold lying on the ground with whooping cough. Besides, you're such a grateful cuss that I can't bear it not to be working my fingers to the bone for you,' he said vindictively. He had dropped the paint kit on one of his astounding feet while he talked, and was hopping around nursing the foot in both hands.

Dusky laughed and immediately whooped.

'Wait — wait — wait — wait!' begged Laban, vaulting the wall. 'People have been known to take it twice. — Oh, hello, David. I was just telling Dusky I'd have to build that bench around her tree, if she's going to do nothing but drape herself over the scenery.'

'I'm going to build that bench myself,' David assured him, his square jaw jutting more squarely. 'Thanks all the same, Hitchcock.'

'Oh, don't mention it, Masterson. It's all right with me so long as I get it done. Good-bye, Masterson. Good-bye, Day!' and with an elaborate wink at Dusky Laban loped out to his car.

During the succeeding days Dusky watched David snatch odd moments to labor grimly at the octagonal bench. Paul was especially busy with quizzes, all his professors having chosen the same time to give hard ones; but Jimmie Tang came pattering over beside David, and helped him, with much violent knotting of brows and embarrassed giggling. The design had seemed simple, but neither boy had handled carpenter's tools, and for them the wood was amazingly perverse.

'It reminds me of sewing sleeves in dresses,' Dusky observed. 'I always get the right sleeve in the left armhole first, and the front in the back next. But it's going to be great, David, and I'm glad Laban got you to do it.'

'Got me to do it?'

'Of course. *He* wouldn't have pounded a nail in a million years. He never does anything he doesn't want to do.'

Eventually the seat was to be painted blue, but Dusky spent blissful hours lounging on it and carving her initials so that it would look 'real' when it was painted. The cough had worn her down until the days of stillness and healing air were anything but wearisome, especially since she had pleasant occupation and as much company as she cared for.

She read contemporary novelists, sitting or lying in the sun and sucking oranges. She made sketches of grove and cottage and court, and of San Berdoo, sapphire and rose at sunset; and of the chapel, white against its purple loom; and of the Greek theater, directly across the Zanja. And she finished Maria's portrait.

Luisa brought Carmelita and Consuelo to the grove after school, and Papa Vasquez stopped on his way home from work at five, to potter around his wall and assist with criticism, and then take the little girls home.

Sometimes Michi and Mary Beth, who were of those who had had whooping cough, came and watched the portrait, too, though not together. Mary Beth was only coolly friendly to Michi. She had been in Shanghai when Chinese and Japanese were at war, and she was partisan.

When the two girls happened to visit Dusky at the same time, they sat one on each side of her and paid scant attention to each other.

'You could make it just the least little bit prettier, Dusky,' Mary Beth suggested, as Dusky absorbedly laid on color. 'I know it's — it's wonderful, but ——'

Dusky frowned. 'Prettier! Prettiness is so piffling, Mary Beth: so unimportant.'

'It isn't unimportant to Mrs. Vasquez.'

'That's the way art is always being throttled,' Dusky grunted. But she deepened the melancholy black of those composite eyes, and added a picturesque fling to the black hair. 'There!' she scoffed, 'I suppose you like it better since it looks more like a magazine cover.'

'Mama Vasquez will,' Mary Beth assented contentedly.

Michi, who had sat very still on her heels, moved fluidly to Dusky's side. 'You handle it so charmingly, the paint,' she said. Her English was wholly American except for being a shade more correct than the average. 'I like your shadows, the edges crisp and yet not hard.'

Papa Vasquez took his stand beside her, too, in his characteristic pose, one foot stretched before him with the sole presented to view; his hat twirling; his incredibly weathered face cut by the shine of white teeth.

'Does it look like Maria, Mr. Vasquez?' Dusky asked him. 'I think I've done all I can to it.'

'Oh, sure it look like Maria!' praised Papa Vasquez. 'It *iss* Maria: she jost a leetle changed.'

He gazed at the portrait with shining eyes. 'That leetle Maria, she very loving leetle child,' he said huskily. 'We get it beeg gold frame with flowers on it, next payday. — And how you like it I build a fireplace like you draw it in the picture you make of the court?'

The court was growing with unexpected speed toward the likeness of their dreams, and Dusky was getting over the whooping cough and on tiptoe for school again. The only discordant note in the Singing Wood was the one that came from Johnnie's lawyer. That note was non-committal as to the extraordinary terms of sale which Paul had described to him, but was quite clear as to two points: the most careful examination of Grandpa Wilson's effects had disclosed no agreement of sale; therefore such an agreement must be found in the Wilson cottage if the sale was to be admitted valid.

This chilly communication came at the onset of the rains. All night the rain beat down, and next morning it was still sweeping past the windows in gray sheets. The furrows in the grove were dull silver; every hollow in the courtyard was a pool; the tree trunk was clean black. Dusky looked out at it while she dried the breakfast dishes.

'I'd like to try painting it,' she said to Aunt Phronsie, 'but there are other things I ought to be doing. At noon I'm going to send a note to Cordelia Jacobs and ask her if she can't come over and tell me what I need for Education. She's in that class, and maybe it'll give me a chance to make up with her. — And this morning I'm going over this house with a fine-tooth comb and see if I can't find Grandpa Wilson's agreement of sale.'

'You don't suppose the Wilson son could be — anything but honest about it?' Aunt Phronsie questioned anxiously, setting a soapy cream pitcher carefully off the edge of the drainboard. 'You don't suppose he's found it and is ——'

Dusky swooped to catch the china as it fell. 'No-o, I don't. But I feel pretty sure they'd never give us the benefit of the doubt if the old agreement didn't turn up. That Mrs. Johnnie —!'

Dusky and Paul and Aunt Phronsie had all searched the cottage before, but today Dusky started at the top and worked down with a consistent thoroughness, an increasing speed, and a diminishing accompaniment of off-key song.

Long before noon she had ransacked two trunks in the

storeroom ('though they seem silly places to look'), the dresser drawers into which Dusky had packed the Wilson knickknacks ('though they seem even sillier'), the secretary drawers, which had already been turned out three times. Looking crossly at that secretary, when she had edged and shuffled the old drawers back into place, she moved decisively upon it and took out all the books; took out the neatly folded newspapers Grandma had always kept on the shelves; shook them; replaced them; held every book by its lids and spanked it; replaced them also.

'I swear it is — not — in — that — desk,' she declared, falling into the chintz-skirted sewing-chair and stretching her feet wearily before her. Almost automatically she emptied Grandma Wilson's work-basket into her lap. They had kept it there, on its little standard, because it made them feel as if Grandma had only pulled her crocheted shawl round her shoulders and stepped out to feed Peter and the hens.

Buttons. Scissors. Tape measure. Thread. Needle-book. Cards of hooks and eyes. A poem clipped from a newspaper. That was all.

'Not a thing?' Aunt Phronsie inquired, and shook her head in answer to her own query.

'Not a thing. And all the while I have that maddening feeling that I could just stick out my hand and *touch* it.'

'Probably one always has that feeling.' — Aunt Phronsie was gently matter-of-fact, longing to get back to her book. 'I don't see how it could be in this room, after its thorough renovation.'

Dusky jumped up energetically. 'Well, I'm going to try one more place and call it a day. I'm going through Grandma's kitchen table drawer again. Her cookbook, too. She was always putting down recipes on envelopes. She might have picked up the agreement of sale and used the back of it.'

Aunt Phronsie laid her book face down on the work-basket — with a lingering look at the last paragraph — and joined her. 'That,' she commended Dusky, 'sounds hopeful. I'll help.'

They spread a newspaper on the table and dumped out the contents of the drawer. They relined the drawer with paper and replaced the miscellany piece by piece, turning over each scrap of paper and viewing it front and back. Dusky sat down with the fat old cookbook and examined every loose leaf between its lids. She even slipped it out of its partly ripped oilcloth cover to see that nothing had chanced to lodge inside.

Finally she slapped the book back into the drawer and banged the drawer shut.

'Any luck?' demanded Paul, breezing in at the back door, cool and wet.

'Oh, hush!' Dusky snapped.

XII. CORDELIA

All afternoon it rained. Dusky built a fire in the stove that played it was a fireplace, and the gay little sitting-room was gayer than ever by contrast with the steady downpour past the windows. Warmth and dampness brewed an atmosphere of long-ago from old books and old wood; and even the Chinese matting, new though it was, smelled comfortably old.

Dusky curled up in the biggest of the cushioned chairs before the fire, with a tower of books and notebooks on the floor beside her and a plate of cookies sitting askew on the work-basket. Aunt Phronsie was moving about the kitchen, baking something spicy and humming an unending tune that ran aimlessly from one fragment of song into another. The rain kept up a monotonous accompaniment.

Through the crackle and the hum and the patter cut the sharp jangle of the doorbell. Dusky had expected it, and leaped to answer. In yellow rain cape and tight cap Cordelia stood at the door.

'Have you had whooping cough?' Dusky greeted her.

'Yes,' Cordelia assented, eyes cold, voice crisp.

'Would you — would you *mind* coming in, then?' Dusky's words stumbled as if her welcome had stubbed its toe against Cordelia's stiffness.

Cordelia glanced significantly at her wrist watch — 'I might be able to give you five minutes!' the gesture seemed to say — and bent to take off her galoshes.

A wave of anger pushed the blood up to Dusky's eyes, and a wave of hurt sucked it down again, leaving her shaken and empty feeling. She was *mad*, she told herself, grinding her teeth together. What if Cordelia had had her feelings hurt? Didn't she have sense enough to know that Dusky hadn't meant it to come out that way? Couldn't she ever quit being cold and reproachful?

All the time she was taking Cordelia's cape and cap and hanging them up on the old-fashioned hall-rack, and ushering her into the sitting-room, with meaningless words about the weather. And presently the two were seated before the open stove.

Cordelia began with businesslike promptness. 'I inquired of Professor Andrews exactly how far we should have gone by the end of next week. Knowing that, I thought I could give you all the information required without a second visit.'

Dusky caught her lower lip hard between her teeth. Another wave of hurt, prickling in her nose and throat! She bent her head lower above the book Cordelia spread on her knees.

'Through the twentieth chapter of the text, he said, and with these books for collateral reading.' She handed Dusky a list of titles — 'He said if you made good general reports on both the collateral reading and the text he would excuse you from extra examinations.'

Dusky sat perfectly still. Her eyes were on the list of titles, but unseeingly. Cordelia sat still, too, as if waiting for her to speak. Pidge, the canary, chirruped, and the rain drummed on the soggy ground below the window, and Peter, the rooster, crowed hoarsely from his haven on the back porch. Still Dusky couldn't get enough command of herself to speak.

She simply *couldn't* humiliate herself before this cruel — this arrogant — this —— She fumbled angrily for words; fumbled wretchedly for a handkerchief. She could find neither, and had to sniff, most inelegantly. Even then one of those large tears that story-book heroines are always shedding splashed on the open book.

That was too much. Rudely Dusky slammed the book shut, her face screwed with crying.

'Do you enjoy humiliating people?' she stormed, her words stumbling over each other. 'Do you like making me miserable? Well, I certainly am. I hope you're happy about it.'

She glared through her tears at Cordelia, and Cordelia glared back, her own eyes growing wet. Then, surprisingly, Cordelia began to laugh.

'I'm — sorry,' she said weakly, after a minute.

'I don't see anything to laugh about,' Dusky grumbled, wiping her eyes with the back of her hand.

'Human beings are — so funny,' Cordelia said.

Dusky stared at her. She was thinking that those waves of hurt she had been experiencing must be commonplace to Cordelia: that day in and day out she had had to endure the sense of people's dislike, their contempt — full measure of what Dusky had been feeling for ten minutes.

'Oh, Dusky, isn't it queer how everybody is always hurting everybody else?' Cordelia burst out, her long hands unconsciously twisting together against her breast. '*We* didn't ask to be colored. And why does the littlest, littlest Negro child have to start with a burden on its back that it can't ever throw off — not ever — in a world that was made for white folks? No matter how good or how bright or how hard-working — no matter anything! — if my skin is dark and my hair kinky I must expect nothing better than the life of a — of a servant. Why should the stupidest, naughtiest white child have more chance than I? *Why?*'

Cordelia's words had rushed out, low-pitched, burning. She stopped as abruptly as if she had tripped over them, and reopened the poor mishandled book.

'Forget I said all that. Please,' she said in a different tone.

'Never!' Dusky vowed. 'Cordelia, will you be really my friend?'

They shook hands, Dusky gripping hard, as she always did; and stood staring through opposite angles of the bay window into the rain. Pidge, pleased by their nearness, burst into song, his little yellow throat swelling as if he were gargling a marble.

'Won't you have a cooky?' invited Dusky, turning back with her face normal once more. 'And — Cordelia, do come to dinner tomorrow night. I'm so lonesome. Just Aunt Phronsie and Paul and David and me,' she added hastily.

'I'd love to,' Cordelia said solemnly.

XIII. DUSKY LENDS A HAND

THE days before Thanksgiving were thrilled through with excitement as if an electric current had been turned on in Highland. Wednesday night was the occasion of the biggest athletic event of the year, the game with Citrus. Tuesday saw the mountain of brush and rubbish gathered on the field for the traditional bonfire.

Last year Paul had served on the bonfire committee, and he had conceived the idea of going to the city highway department and the telephone company for fuel. Both organizations had been glad to dispose of old poles and tree trimmings and other rubbish, and even to haul them to the field without charge. This year's committee had borrowed the idea. The result was a most imposing structure, a peak with Citrus in effigy on the summit, a figure with a vast tissue paper lemon for a head.

As usual, a guard of Highland men watched the wood all night Wednesday, lest Citrus scouts dart in and touch it off.

Next afternoon the town, even the Zanja Road, was alive with Citrus cars, with Highland cars, placarded, decorated, shouting. All that evening the life of the place seemed to be drained off into the football field.

Dusky drove Aunt Phronsie to the game, against her protests at leaving Dusky alone. She had discovered that Aunt Phronsie loved football, even though she did not quite know what it was all about. Her vagueness seemed livened by its swift excitement.

The evening was clear and edged with cold. Dusky put on her coat and sat on the farthest corner of the adobe wall. Here she could see the brightness of the sky above the floodlighted field, could hear the noise of the game and of the crowd, sifting to her across the campus.

Steady whirr of cars, blat of horns, blare of loud-speakers, rhythm of cheering, roar of applause, tootling of bands — on and on, maddeningly. Dusky went back to the house after cookies, and guiltily cut a wedge of one of the mince pies she had helped bake. She read a little. She returned to her wall.

Wild and continued cheering told her that the game was over. A ruddy glare lighted all the treetops. The whole student body would be doing a serpentine across the field, either in triumph or in gallant defeat. — Now the cars began to start, and rushed roaring through the town. Dusky hugged her knees and waited, shaking with excitement, until Aunt Phronsie came trotting across the bridge.

'How was it?' Dusky demanded.

'Seven to six!'

'But who won?' Dusky demanded, shaking Aunt Phronsie's tweed arm till the flashlight's beam danced a jig.

'Oh, dear!' said Aunt Phronsie, settling her glasses, 'if we could only have made the kick. — You are so excitable, child! Citrus won, I'm sorry to say, but it seems it was extremely close.'

Paul and David had planned to devote themselves to the grove the minute training was over, but on Friday morning an urgent summons took Highland men up to the mountain campus. A fire had started in the underbrush.

They had scarcely gone when Dusky clambered into her coveralls. 'Aunt Phronsie,' she said, 'I'm going to help the boys out. It's high time those Valencias were picked, and I don't see why I shouldn't pick part of them.'

Aunt Phronsie slid Pidge's cage over a newspaper on the kitchen table and set his bathtub carefully in at his door. 'Do you know how?' she asked.

'Well, I suppose you just — pick,' Dusky argued.

'There's something about being careful ——'

'Oh, of course you mustn't bruise them. How can you, when you have one of those postman sack doodads slung over your shoulder?'

'Wouldn't it be better to wait and have the boys show you?'

'They've worked so hard. I'd love to lend a hand.'

Dusky assembled her equipment with a rush: ladder, picking sack, long-handled clipper, field boxes. It was a fine morning with a high fog that added exhilaration, and the Singing Wood was as lovely as ever. Dusky worked impetuously, her speed increasing. Dusky was quick in almost anything she undertook.

Before long, however, it grew very tiring. Her arms and back ached from handling the unaccustomed clipper; and shortly before noon she made a discovery that dulled the fine zest of morning.

Yellowing leaves made her slow her work and look closely, picking samples marked by the sickly color and by certain pinhead objects on their surfaces. She went slowly into the cottage with them when Aunt Phronsie summoned her to luncheon.

Ordinarily she and Aunt Phronsie enjoyed lunching together. Aunt Phronsie loved to prop a book beside her plate and read as she ate, and Dusky had learned the trick from her. Both had developed a technique, and could read through the meal without depositing food on the tablecloth or their dresses. Today, however, Dusky grimly studied the wall beyond Aunt Phronsie's shoulder, and excusing herself hurriedly, rushed back to the grove and picked till dinnertime.

Saturday's picking was still harder, for every muscle seemed bruised and stiffened. Dusky gritted her teeth and dared those muscles to stop her. Doggedly she picked from breakfast to lunch time, from lunch to dinner. And at dinner the boys came in, grimy and burned. The fire had been quickly quelled, they said, and they were so hungry they could eat an ox apiece.

Not until they had emptied the table did Dusky show them her leaf samples. 'What *are* those pesky little shells?' she asked. 'Do they have anything to do with the leaves' turning so yellow?'

Paul blew an explosive 'whoof!' through his pursed lips. 'Oh, well,' he conceded, 'the fates is ag'in' us.'

'What are they?' Dusky repeated.

'Citricola scale, aren't they, Dave?'

'You know a lot more about it than I do. But I don't see what else.'

'And that means —?'

'Fumigating!' The word exploded with disgust.

'And *that* means —?'

'Scads of our hard-earned cash. And *that* means that we've got to get the picking done as fast as we can, though goodness knows the market's not much inducement. We'll not make millions *this* year.'

'I wonder if Johnnie's going to be satisfied with the payment we can make?' Dusky asked worriedly, scratching at a scale with a stained forefinger.

'I know the answer to that one,' Paul assured her.

'Dusky, how did you happen to notice all this?' David asked.

Dusky's face turned up in all its lines. 'I'll show you!'

The boys followed her and her flashlight out into the grove. Dramatically she pointed to the field boxes, piled with fruit.

'Well, I'll be —— Who did it?' Paul exclaimed, stooping stiffly to pick up a yellow globe.

Dusky slapped her chest with a theatrical palm.

'Gosh!' said Paul.

'Are you overpowered, or what?' Dusky inquired uncertainly.

'*And* what!' — Paul poked feebly at the contents of the nearest box.

'Hush up, Paul. Now, maybe —' David temporized, examining an orange himself.

'No maybe about it,' Paul ejaculated. 'I'm only glad my dear sister isn't twins.'

'My word! am I an infant or an imbecile, that you can't explain anything to me? Listen, Paul ——'

'Listen yourself,' her brother growled, disregarding David's restraining nudge. 'You'd do a lot better to keep out of things you don't understand, Dusky. I know you meant well, but all you've done is to give us a few hundred pounds of culls. We can't market half those oranges, except as juicers.'

'Culls! Can't *market* them?' Dusky stared down at his burned, cross face incredulously, by the light of her torch.

'Look.' He held up an orange and pointed to the stem end.

'Well?' she asked belligerently.

'You've cut it so short that you've broken the skin. Oh, I know it isn't much; but the least scratch on the skin of an orange starts decay. That's why they have to be clipped with a little bump of stem to spare if they're to be marketable.' He subsided limply on the ground among the heaped boxes. 'I'm glad this is all.'

Every one of Dusky's aches, forgotten awhile, tuned up a loud chorus of complaint. She had fallen from the ladder once, skinning her knee so that it was stiffly raw; and her right arm felt as if it had pulled out of its socket, and her neck creaked on a strained cord that ran aching into her shoulder.

'It isn't all,' she announced. 'There's a lot more packed in the shed. Forty more boxes.'

'Well, you're a good one,' Paul said heavily after a moment's blank silence. 'I should think when we are as hard pressed as we are, you might ——'

'What about the Ford, Paul?' David asked in an ominous voice.

'Well, but — my gosh, Dave, that Ford is nothing at all ——'

'What Ford?' Dusky demanded.

'Ours,' Paul said meekly. 'Now wait a minute, Dusk. What would *you* do if you had a chance to get one for fourteen dollars? Fourteen dollars won't make or break us. — We don't get it till the middle of the month, but I paid five dollars down to bind the bargain.'

XIV. JUICE

DUSKY went aching and miserable to bed that Saturday night, and lay, aching and miserable, passing the situation in review.

If they could have sent Johnnie a really good payment this fall he would have been more likely to take their word for the agreement of sale. Because, Dusky argued with herself, no son of Grandpa and Grandma Wilson could be utterly hard-boiled; and besides there wasn't any boom in orange groves, with the market what it had been lately.

At the best it would have been difficult to send a good payment. Fumigation would give their profit one sharp slash; and now she had had to add her mite to cutting it still more.

Juicers! Those beautiful big oranges! And juicers sold for almost nothing at all. Not that the number she had picked would make a great difference: it was the principle of the thing. It was humiliating to take the rôle of a blunderer, spoiling everything she touched. If only she could turn those juicers to a profit —— All night a stream of oranges jostled through her mind.

Monday morning she picked properly, to prove that she could. Monday afternoon she painted posters. Monday evening, when Luisa rode over with Papa Vasquez, who was laying up a delectable open fireplace with niches for pottery and pans, she enlisted Luisa's help.

Tuesday afternoon she squeezed her damaged fruit, using Grandma Wilson's old-style reamer, which had to be emptied and cleared of clogging pulp after every three oranges. She squeezed and strained, squeezed and strained; and when Luisa came after school with two dozen half-pint paper cartons, Dusky was ready to fill them.

First, however, she sent Luisa over to Lawrence Hall with posters and thumb-tacks and a note to Mrs. Forrester.

The posters bore cartoons of a globular girl and one built on the design of a feather, and their caption ran:

Milk Shakes Made Me What I Am;
Orange Juice Will Make Me What I Want to Be!
Fresh Daily from
The Singing Wood.
Delivered at Your Door
Eight Cents a Glass, No More!

While Luisa was tacking up the posters, Aunt Phronsie helped Dusky letter her cartons, 'Compliments of Dusky Day,' fill them, and pack them into the market-basket. Luisa was to deliver one each to two dozen girls in Dusky's dormitory.

Dusky walked with her to Lawrence Hall and on to the Infirmary, where Miss Morris had a fire crackling in the grate and the bright curtains drawn. A line of students waited their turn for throat-paintings, temperature-takings, iodine. Laban rolled pale eyes at her above the thermometer clenched between his teeth.

'Hi, Wawus!' he rumbled.

'Keep your lips firmly closed around the thermometer, Mr. Hitchcock,' the nurse ordered, 'though I know it's a lot to ask. — Sally Lou, if you would stick to the diet I gave you you would be perfectly all right. Oh yes, without doubt you stick to it at the table; but what do you eat in your room? And at Moulton's? — Dusky Day, have you quite done coughing? Very well; you may go back to Lawrence Hall tonight.'

Dusky emerged from the bright busy waiting-room with her slip in her hand, released from quarantine. Laban loped beside her.

'What seems to be the matter with *you?*' Dusky asked him.

'Going into a decline. Don't want to move. Don't want to eat more than six meals a day. Ache.'

'Got any fever?'

'She *says* not. The crazy woman told me to try walking six miles a day and going in for basketball. Me. — Baked any cookies lately, Dusky? Would you take a shot at me if you found me in a few of your orange trees?'

Dusky laughed in spite of herself. 'I can't be bothered with you tonight, and Paul and David ate the last of the cookies yesterday. But you can come over when I've got a bushel of oranges to squeeze out by hand. That'll be in a day or two.'

It was good to get back to classes next day — good to get back to the dormitory that night. Mary Beth greeted her with a spotless room. Even Dusky's half of the desk and the dresser were in perfect order. The tops of everything were dusted, and ornaments lined up as if with a foot-rule. Dusky felt better when she had pulled the Chinese rugs cornerwise, dumped a ragged armload of books on her desk, and draped her suede jacket across the bed.

She put up one more poster. She tacked it at the entrance to the dining-hall, by consent of Mrs. Randall, the Head Resident in charge. It said:

Addition and Subtraction:
What is the Difference Between
a Milkshake a Day
and an
Orange Juice a Day

Try it a month, and you will find it
ADDS $1.20 to your spending money,
SUBTRACTS four pounds from your avoirdupois,
MULTIPLIES your scholastic A's,
DIVIDES in half your dateless days.

Place your order for a month's supply, delivered before breakfast six days a week, $1.25 a month, cash in advance; 40¢ a week; 8¢ a day. Sign here.
(Arithmetic approximate)

A sharpened pencil swung on a string beside it.

Dusky found a dozen names signed to the poster when she lined up with her schoolmates for dinner that night. The hall was always crowded at dinner time, for by that hour the most earnestly reducing girls had given up the struggle for the day, and everyone had pressed into the lobby to wait for the welcome clang of the bell. Girls leaned limply against walls, stood on solidly braced feet, jigged exuberantly from knot to knot, pressed back against the walls to let the faculty pass through when the bell at last shrilled its invitation.

Girls called greetings to the returning Dusky; asked all the details of the new orange venture twice over; admired her initiative; patronized her commercialism.

'But Caro Felton can be as snooty as she likes,' Dusky whispered to Mary Beth. 'I bet there are twenty names signed this minute. If I get them by the month that would be twelve dollars itself. Do you realize that?'

'I realize that it's going to be extremely wearisome to extract all that juice, Dusky.'

'Oh, well, I don't have to squeeze them tonight,' Dusky said comfortably, weaving in and out of the mob that swept into the dining-room as soon as the faculty was seated. 'Do you smell Swiss steak? California cows should be entirely composed of Swiss steak. My word, but it's good to be back.'

Sorority meeting that night was like a welcome home to the released captive. Even Sally Lou was amiable. And after the meeting there was a feed, with the inner-toasted tuna sandwiches which Dusky loved and Sally concocted divinely: hot and of a mingled crispness and softness, and sweetness of white fish luscious with mayonnaise. Dusky also loved the persimmons, big as two fists and flame-red and ripely soft.

'I've inhaled three,' she sighed at length, wiping the scarlet juice from her forehead. 'It's been a memorable evening, and tomorrow I begin being a poor working girl.'

Next night, being Wednesday, came the weekly sing; and Dusky couldn't miss the weekly sing, working girl or no working girl. She signed out before going with the others to the Ad Building steps, where they huddled in coats and jackets and rammed chilly fingers into pockets and sang lustily. The moon was full, and flooded the campus, lighting the chapel to its loveliest translucent whiteness.

When they had sung the last song, Dusky rose with the crowd, stiff from sitting in the evening chill, and started toward the Greek theater and the Zanja. Laban detached himself from a pillar where he had twined, and ambled down the steps with her.

'Good-night, Hitchcock!' David said pointedly from the other side.

'Good-night yourself and see how you like it, Masterson,' drawled Laban. 'The Walrus invited me.'

'I forgot. He's going to help squeeze oranges,' Dusky explained. 'I've got to do about — let's see: three times twenty-six is seventy-eight, isn't it?'

'So am I going to help,' David replied evenly, and grasped Dusky's other elbow.

Dusky pulled away from both of them and went leaping down the circular steps of the theater in the moonlight. 'You needn't walk me, like a doll,' she told them over her shoulder. 'But I'd just as soon you'd both help. You can do three dozen apiece and I'll manage the rest.'

Grandma Wilson had left a large stock of the tie-around-the-waist kind of aprons, and the three were soon shielded by the blue and white checks, worn bib-fashion. Dusky washed oranges, and Laban sat at the table with his long legs thrust sidewise and cut oranges, while David clutched oranges firmly and screwed them around the reamer. Laban was pleasantly talkative and David folded his mouth straight and glared at the reamer.

Aunt Phronsie stood considering the exhausted orange halves and then gathered them up and began to cut them into narrow strips. 'Candied orange peel!' she explained.

'We might sell little bags as a side line,' Dusky said thoughtfully, urging juice through the clogged meshes of a strainer. 'And another thing that should sell like hot cakes is cubes of sugar soaked in orange juice and dried for afternoon teas. If it wouldn't dissolve.'

'The girl will never come to any good,' Laban observed, stretching a little nearer the horizontal and closing his eyes. 'She has too many ideas. And she doesn't know whether she is a college student or a factory.' He opened his eyes, disregarding David's angry flush — 'If your business keeps on growing, how much would you pay a good live energetic boy — like me — for this cutting job?'

'She's going to get an electric extractor,' David said grimly. 'A slightly used one at a bargain down at Rude's.'

'That will eliminate your job, but not mine,' Laban said, closing his eyes again.

'I think perhaps this extractor takes the whole fruit,' David countered, breathing hard.

Dusky was really tired by the time the twenty-eight waxed paper cartons were filled. The boys carried them over to Lawrence Hall for her, and she set the market-baskets outside her window on the balcony just as the outer door closed at ten, shucked off her clothes, and tumbled into bed to read the next chapter of the Education text.

Mary Beth brushed her silver-gold web of hair and braided it tight; scrubbed herself to a cool pinkness. Maxine wandered through and perched on Dusky's bed, her hair bound back with gauze bands, her face shining with cream. She massaged the cream in with devotional thoroughness, wiped it off with a tissue borrowed from Dusky's drawer, patted in another kind and scent. Dusky looked up at her with sleepy superiority over the top of her book.

'I verily believe you use an hour every night on your skin and nails and hair,' she scoffed. She was thinking to herself that Maxine had stopped chewing gum and wearing silly sandals and hanging on her escorts' arms; but was that all the good it did her to be rescued from her mining town?

Maxine looked down at her with glistening superiority over her massaging pink fingers. 'I must be well-groomed if I'm to keep up with Farraday,' she condescended, glancing at the platinum-set diamond complacently. 'An hour isn't much. Jan's roommate puts two hours onto her face every night of this world.'

'And fifteen minutes into her brain,' Dusky countered.

'There's a happy medium,' coaxed Mary Beth. 'You did say you were going to brush your hair and put cream on your face and hands every night this year, Dusky. — And your elbows, where they're so calloused.'

'I will tomorrow,' Dusky promised sleepily. She stretched luxuriously, wiggling her feet to make Maxine get off. 'Mmm, but bed feels good. I wish I didn't have to do this chapter.'

She woke under a small cold trickle of water. The room was gray with November daylight and Maxine was dripping a washcloth over her face.

Dusky had not heard of her electric juice extractor until the night before, but she went downtown and bought it that afternoon. Laban took her in his rickety car: he said he wouldn't have bothered, except that he knew it would give David such pleasure. Dusky laughed absently at that: she was figuring whether it was really wise to make the investment. She could pay for it from one month's profits, though, she thought; and it was really going to be impossible to squeeze all those oranges by hand every single night.

She stopped at the Vasquezes', too, and arranged with Consuelo to come and deliver the juice to all the customers in the three halls every morning between half-past six and quarter to seven. Delivery service raised the dignity of the project; Dusky had dreaded the peddling.

Finally she had Laban drop her at the Student Store, in the basement of the Ad Building, and take her extractor on to the cottage for her, which he did not without grumbling.

The store was a cubbyhole of a place, stocked with an amazing miscellany, from postage stamps to jeweled Highland bracelets, from ice cream cones to textbooks. A few boys usually sat on the counter eating sandwiches and swinging their feet. A girl or two usually dawdled over notepaper or kodak film. Dusky went into consultation with the student manager and arranged to sell a few containers of juice a day on commission, as well as bags of candied peel.

She set her extractor going that evening and had the juice ready in a half hour. Well content, she carried it over to the dormitory and settled down to an evening of intensive study.

But she had no more than opened her books when the door began to be assailed by student knocks. There was Jan Cooper: 'Dusky, the juice really didn't taste like the sample.' 'Say, did you use another kind of oranges for this second batch? — I wish you wouldn't.' And Dorcas, always outspoken, 'That orange juice was the dickens this morning, Dusky.'

They did agree to try it another day or two, but they seemed to think their agreement a distinct concession.

Dusky looked blankly at Mary Beth. 'My word, wouldn't I be in a fix if they canceled? But I know this batch is first class. It's fine. Try it and see.' She divided a carton with Mary Beth, who agreed that it was good. The oranges were large, full-flavored Valencias; certainly their juice should be of the best.

Nevertheless, Dusky slept restlessly, trying to figure her financial status if her customers went back on their bargain. And at the breakfast table Dorcas said: 'There's still something funny about the juice, Dusk. Not so funny as what you get in cans. But not so hot, at that.'

As soon as Dusky had eaten a sketchy and savorless breakfast, she pounded upstairs to her room, with Mary Beth at her heels. There had been an extra carton, and Dusky had not yet drunk it: her appetite for orange juice had flagged.

Now she pried open the lid with a nail file and took an indignant sip; savored it; puckered her brow. Mary Beth was watching her with held breath.

'It really doesn't taste so very good, Mary Beth!' Dusky admitted in a bewildered voice. 'It really tastes sort of thin and flat.'

She went into a deep study.

'I know!' she cried. 'A refrigerator! It stands to reason that if it's kept ice cold ——'

'Grandpa and Grandma Wilson didn't have a refrigerator?'

'No. Just one of those California "coolers." But if they had had,' Dusky swept on grandly, 'it wouldn't have been the kind *we* need. It's plain as anything. Aunt Phronsie can buy food in quantities, and the thing will pay for itself in no time. She's been having an awful time keeping those boys filled up, but she can get milk by the gallon and ——'

'What kind of refrigerator are you considering?' Mary Beth asked in a frightened voice.

'No one that's modern would think of anything but an automatic one, electric or gas,' Dusky said dogmatically. 'I'm going downtown at noon and see what terms I can get.'

'Hadn't you better — talk it over with Paul?'

Dusky shook her head. 'I've got to hurry or I'll be losing all my clients.'

She came home triumphant. 'Luckiest thing!' she declared. 'Family moving away and wanting to get rid of a practically-as-good-as-new electric refrigerator! I had to pay cash, but I can just scrape it out, and it will soon make up for itself. And huge! My word!'

It had been delivered and connected when Dusky and Mary Beth ran over to the cottage that evening. Aunt Phronsie was hovering over it in apprehensive delight. The whole side of the yellow-floor, rag-rug kitchen was gleaming white and shining nickel, like an Automat barging into a farmhouse. The mechanism clicked along cheerfully, for it was not one of the late silent models, and Pidge was jigging on his perch in a fury of song, trying to outdo it.

'Huge! But I had no idea ——' Mary Beth gasped.

'It had to be large, to take in all the cartons and the supplies of food besides,' Dusky said defensively, opening and closing doors very fast, and sliding trays of ice cubes in and out.

'It must have cost a fortune.' — Aunt Phronsie sounded dazed.

'It was a bargain,' Dusky said firmly. 'And it will be well worth what it cost to have my juice kept in good condition.' She swathed her gray dress in an apron and set the extractor going.

Next morning she took one of the extra cartons from Consuelo's full basket and smiled at the little girl. Consuelo grinned back happily. She was to have fifty cents a week for her services, and a daily quart of orange juice. Dusky secretly gloated over that daily quart poured into the Vasquez children.

Now she tasted the liquid with eager expectancy. It was ice cold, but —

'Ma'Beth,' she cried incredulously, 'it's just as thin and flat as it was without the refrigerator!'

XV. THE MYSTERY SOLVED

Dusky worked furiously in painting class that morning. She had shied away from Dorcas, who opened and shut her mouth as if starting to comment on flat orange juice and then relenting. Several had not relented. Dusky had found Caro Felton's name and a few others crossed off the list in the dining-hall lobby.

So Dusky vented her uneasiness on her portrait of Wing Lee, who had been persuaded to pose. At rest periods he trotted around the room, weaving between easels, hands folded into sleeves. Before Dusky's he paused, and his startled eyes sought a mirror.

'Gleen?' he sputtered. 'Lee's face allee samee gleen?'

'It's the shadows,' Dusky reassured him listlessly. 'The shadows look green. To me.'

He passed on, clucking doubtfully, to Mary Beth. As far as drawing was concerned, Mary Beth was in, but not of, the circle. She was still drawing casts, with tight, fine, unbroken lines and smooth hard shading.

'Plitty!' Wing Lee commended. 'Missee Mellibet plenty fine ahtis.'

Mary Beth flickered a sober smile at him.

'Missee Mellibet not feel so good? Hungly, mebbeso?'

She shook her head, with a chanted syllable of thanks, and Wing Lee stood with tucked-in hands and shook his head, too.

'What's the matter with *you*, Mary Beth?' Dusky asked under her breath when a tap of the gong sent Wing Lee back to the model stand. Gingerly he seated himself and jerked his head an inch this way, an inch that, an inch up, an inch down, according to directions, while his eyes clung to the cast at which he had been told to look.

'You've no idea what a difficult time the missionaries are having,' Mary Beth said reluctantly. 'I — I wish we didn't have to be a burden on Father and Mother. Of course David has that trust fund for his medical training, but ——'

Dusky understood. *But* there was nothing at all for the little extras. *But* there was not enough so that Mary Beth could wear stockings without mended runs — and Mary Beth had never brought herself to accept the anklets that were such a saving. *But* there weren't any spare dimes to let Mary Beth drop into Moulton's for a milkshake with the other girls, or into the Circle for one of its famous walnut-date sundaes. *But* any date of David's that cost money must be viciously pinched out of his allowance. *But* he had never been able to send Dusky a corsage bouquet before a party, or do any such gay frivolous things. — And yet Mary Beth had a stiff pride that would not let her admit it, and a Chinese background that would not let her try to make money herself.

Sometimes that enraged Dusky. It did today. She slammed on more of the green shadow.

'As for me,' she said quite audibly, 'the only thing that really troubles me is *money*. If we could make a fair payment, there'd be more chance of saving the grove, I should think, till we could get a buyer for half of it. I shouldn't wonder if Johnnie thinks we're nothing but a pair of schemers, trying to wangle him out of the grove. And *I* do want the grove more and more.' — She'd forgot her pique at Mary Beth's Chinese pride. — 'You could spend next summer at the cottage, Ma'Beth, and if the market was better Dave could have more of a real job there, and — But everything I do seems wrong. Mary Beth, what *do* you suppose is the matter with the juice?'

Mary Beth sat considering her. Mary Beth could never do two things at once: her fingers stopped, she said, when her brain began. Dusky was doing something still more startling to her canvas, and her voice had risen. Laban laid down his brush and rubbed his nose with the back of his hand, leaving a stripe of cadmium yellow.

'You'll have to let the people take the refrigerator back, won't you, Dusky?' Mary Beth inquired.

'They're gone, and it's all paid for,' Dusky said dismally.

'Juice flat-tasting, Walrus?' Laban asked.

Dusky stared. 'Somebody been telling you?'

He waved his head slightly, eyes half closed. 'Didn't have to be told. Orange juice oxidizes, or something. If I could figger a way to keep the fresh fruit taste in it, some cannery would pay me so much that I could sit down and rest myself forever.'

'For heaven's sake, why didn't you say so?' Dusky cried, turning bright purple.

'It wouldn't have done a lick of good. You're the kind that has to be shown, my dear Walrus. You'll have to squeedge the juice in the morning, and I knew you wouldn't cotton to that. Why should I put myself in the way of being slammed down by bringing the bad news?'

Dusky glared at him.

'Your Aunt Phronsie would do it, Dusky,' Mary Beth suggested.

Dusky shook her head. 'I can get Mrs. Forrester to let me go over in the morning at six,' she planned, dabbing on clear color while Mary Beth watched in alarm. 'My word, but I love to sleep that last half hour. But I can't let somebody else suffer for my boners,' she added virtuously.

'You're awful annoying, Dusky,' Laban said, scowling.

'I never supposed I'd put up with such a demon of energy. A fellow can't get his rest.'

Dusky suspended her brush. '*You* put up with *me?* My aunt! Ask anybody if it isn't the other way around.'

Laban's long face became seraphic and his hair a saint's nimbus. 'I call you to witness, White Queen — Frog Footman!' he adjured them. 'She says she puts up with me. It's the modern way of saying yes.'

'Cheese it!' Jane hissed from the other side of the room. 'Here comes the maestro.'

Glare at Laban as she might, however, and long to get a firm hold on his coat collar and shake, Dusky had to admit that he had saved her juice enterprise from flat failure.

'Of course I'd have found out sooner or later,' she said, 'but it might not have been soon enough to save the Business.'

The Business was really saved. It was growing. Every morning the alarm clock under Dusky's pillow beat a six o'clock tattoo on her incredulous ear; every morning she waked herself under the cold shower, scrambled into her clothes, scuttled through the chilly gray to the sleeping cottage, set the pale green porcelain and shiny chromium of the extractor to work on her oranges. Every morning she carried a load of filled cartons to Lawrence Hall, and Consuelo another load. Every morning the small girl, in an orange-hued dress Dusky had bought her and an orange headband Dusky had made, trotted through the halls and set down the cartons before the doors marked with small orange seals.

Dusky added marmalade to the products sold at the Student Store. She made new posters, suggesting marmalade and orange peel for 'the folks at home' for Christmas. Aunt Phronsie had plenty of time, she insisted, to make the marmalade and crystallize the peel.

By this time the boys had finished picking. They would sell most of the crop, though the price was pitifully low.

'But I might need it all for juice and other things,' Dusky remonstrated, pride seeping audibly through the protest.

'You can always buy culls very cheap,' said Paul, 'and we need cash right away for that payment, to sort of hold Johnnie off. And before that comes the pesky fumigation.'

'Does the fumigation cost an immense amount?' asked Mary Beth, large-eyed.

'It does. Twenty acres — fifty cents a tree. Mighty close to one — thousand — dollars. It's going to gouge our orange receipts so deep that we'll hardly have the nerve to send Johnnie what's left. I'll hold my breath till we hear from him.'

XVI. OMEGA FORMAL

AGAIN the crowded school calendar did the Brother-and-Sister Act a service by leaving them little time for worry. Christmas was approaching, and immediately before the holidays the Omegas were to have a party, a formal dinner at a Palm Springs hotel, fifty miles away in the desert. As Dusky caustically observed, nothing was swanky unless it cost twice as much as you could afford.

Dusky was chairman of the entertainment committee. She had begun with no idea except the copper wigs she had planned for the sorority's indefinitely postponed play. The feature sprung from those wigs, like Minerva from the head of Zeus, and the performers she chose, together with Dusky herself, worked out the details behind closed doors. The whole stunt was kept secret from the rest of the sorority, who were allowed to see only the costumes, which they had to make out of black and white oilcloth, and the bizarre coiffures, which they had also to put together according to Dusky's sample.

The performers were three of the sorority's trained dancers, Jan and two others, and Maxine, and Dorcas, who was an accomplished pianist. For those five the two weeks were a wild scramble; and for Dusky the 'number' spattered itself across all twenty-four hours of every day.

It spattered her art classes. Professor Faunce, whistling in a whisper behind Dusky's easel, conceded, 'You have good movement in this sketch. Go on with your canvas and paint as well as you've drawn. *This* is nice. And *this!*' — He made sweeping movements of the hand, held stiff like an Egyptian sculpture — 'They all swing in toward your focal point as they should. And these —' He touched with his maulstick the numerous sketches on the margin — 'Our model being hanged? Or what?'

Dusky colored darkly and rubbed a wad of kneaded rubber over the nearest sketch, a head dropped limply forward on the chest. There were others: figures with all their limbs falling loosely this way and that; and a bird of amazing design, perhaps a hybrid of the parakeet and the Mexican quetzal.

And when Professor Faunce had retreated to his den, Laban inquired irritably, 'Are you falling to pieces, Dusky Day?'

'Oh, I'm just trying to see how far they'll really go,' murmured Dusky, who had been dropping her own head and flapping her hands, a speculative gleam in her eyes.

Dorcas had been watching her as if hypnotized. Now she jumped up, humming a jerky tune, and kept time to her music with head and hands and stiffly raised and lowered knees.

'Have you all gone off your heads?' Laban growled.

'It's just our sorority Formal,' Mary Beth explained.

'Girls can spend more time and energy over the most useless things,' Laban observed, his lip curling. 'Fifty white Leghorn hens cackling after one grasshopper. No wonder they never accomplish anything worth while.'

It was one of his ill-tempered days. Dusky, stealing a glance at his bitter face, wondered whether he really minded not being asked to some of the sorority doings. But — there was David. Next time she didn't know but she'd choose a girls' college. Boys complicated everything.

The program 'spattered' Dusky's other classes, as well as art. A half dozen times Miss Corinne caught her bemused and plunged a sudden keen question into her misty mind. Once Dusky was penciling another grotesque sketch on a book margin. Once she was figuring out the mechanics of Maxine's harness, while her eyes fastened themselves on Miss Corinne's face.

'Dusky Day,' said Miss Corinne that time, 'your rapt attention suggests unutterable thoughts. Please discuss the subject for the benefit of the class.'

So far as Dusky knew, the subject might have been Timbuctu or skylarks. She could only moisten her lips and reply, 'I do not feel that I have anything of sufficient value, Miss Smith.'

Miss Smith stopped her as she left the classroom. Miss Smith's transparent fingertips were fitted together in her characteristic gesture, and her cool eyes studied Dusky under their triangular lids. 'A suggestion, Dusky. If you could train that rapt gaze to shift from me when I cease speaking, and focus on the person beginning to speak, it would deceive the very elect. The left-over effect is what betrays you.'

Dusky had never been quite so much in awe of Miss Corinne since the episode of the sleeve. She laughed sheepishly. 'It deceives everyone but you; and you've caught me out — how many times? I really did think I was grown up enough — a college junior! — to keep outside activities outside.'

Miss Corinne still regarded her thoughtfully. 'Another suggestion, Dusky. Since you have applied for the Mexican fellowship, why not relate all your courses to that end? Let's talk of that before the new semester.'

Synchronized and related courses. Mexico. Dusky walked home in a whirl. College was beginning to look so much bigger than it used to: so much more a part of life. Silly to let yourself scatter so. Yet how could she help wondering whether the oilcloth costumes would come right apart at the crucial moment? And whether the act was going to look smart and professional or pretentious and homemade?

And whether the only formal dress she possessed would 'deceive the very elect,' now that she had dyed it black and added wing sleeves and subtracted most of the back? And whether the soiled white satin sandals she had picked up on a grab-bag counter for fifteen cents and painted silver would look alluring or merely smell painty? And whether the fillet of silver leaves for her short black curls would make the whole costume appear as sophisticated as she hoped?

The time did come when all these questions were to be answered. The evening arrived, in a final rush of Omega manicures and the combing out of tight varnished Omega waves and a grand Omega descent to cars waiting in the early December dark. Dusky and her troupe crowded into three cars, with escorts and costumes and stage properties, and led the way, screwing down windows to let in the grateful air, screwing them up, hastily, to keep hair from blowing, just as all the other cars were doing.

A few minutes ahead of the others they reached the group of hotels and summer homes set among the palms in the shadow of San Jacinto; and they had the last arrangements made when dinner was ready to serve.

Dinner was imposing, and the guests suave and elegant young men and women, transformed for a few hours from their familiar rough and tumble campus identities. The beauty of it receded before Dusky's eyes, however, and she could scarcely taste food or conversation in her anxiety for the entertainment of the evening to be over.

When at length two screens were drawn away from the orchestra platform, her hands were clammy-cold and her face burning.

Three French puppets and a dazzling bird stood revealed in front of another screen done in vermilion. The puppets' cheeks were painted with disks of red, their mouths made into scarlet buttons, their eyes rounded with mascara; their mesh of silver strings disappeared over the top of the screen. The bird, which had evolved from the parakeet-quetzal hybrid, was a gorgeously colored shape of wall-board, large enough to hide Maxine, who wore it like a shield, her mouth behind its open beak.

Dorcas, dressed like the puppets in geometric white and black, and like them coiffured with flashing copper, struck into the sharply marked rhythm of a dance. From the bird's beak came a fluting, chirping song. The puppets danced.

In perfect time they lifted stiff hands, dropped them; lifted their feet in angular motion, dropped them; lifted and dropped their heads. Dusky watched with held breath.

She had contrived lead weights on the ends of the silver strings. They hung out of sight behind the screen, and when the hands lifted, the strings attached to them were drawn down by the weights, giving the illusion that the strings had pulled up the hands. There was always the danger that the weights might swing and tangle. Dusky willed them to keep straight.

Maxine, behind her bird figure, might work herself out of the harness of straps that held it in place. Dusky willed the straps to hold firm!

Once white elbows did sprout from the yellow wings of the bird, and an extra pair of feet leaped from beneath his scarlet breast. Once, too, the bird song hesitated, and Dusky heard Maxine hiss 'Your weights are stuck. Hold still.' Jan held still, until the weights evidently untwisted.

Even with these small defects, the total effect was excellent, and applause stormed up and down the table like breakers on a beach. The puppets gave an encore. The screens were pushed in front of them. Dusky let out her held breath.

Now she could enjoy the remainder of the evening;

could talk with David, who had had to work through dinner alone as far as Dusky was concerned.

When they started home across the desert some hours later, the automobiles by common consent turned first to Palm Canyon. A winding fissure in the desert, spilled full of old palm trees, it was mysterious even in daylight, and heavy with the feeling of tropic jungles, far north as it was of all other self-planted palms. Now a full moon shone down through the lace of fan leaves grotesquely high overhead; gilded the shaggy skirts of dead leaves that clothed the tall trunks to the ground; made jungles of the twisting path through whose shadows the boys and girls wound their way in one long double line. It was a stranger grand march even than the rubber-boot parade in the Mexican court.

Canyon and palms still belonged to the Temecula Indians — Ramona's Indians. 'Can't you picture them?' Dusky murmured to David. 'Buckskin braves and maidens slipping through these shadowy aisles once on a time?'

'And padres in brown robes with crosses gleaming,' David assented. His fair hair was what gleamed in the moonlight now, and the white expanse of his dress shirt. Dusky had never before noticed how good looking he was; but even his good looks were not half so nice as his way of understanding her fancies. Betweentimes she often forgot that way of his.

'I feel so happy,' she sighed contentedly, when they were back in the car, one of a procession speeding smoothly toward Highland. 'I feel as if everything were bound to come out all right for us — for us all. Johnnie will be decent, or that old sales agreement will turn up. The orange grove will do well, and the market will be higher next year, and I'll be awarded the Mexican fellowship, and you'll go steaming through medical school, and then ——'

'*And then!*' said David. 'Dusky, there's a lot in "And then."'

'I do believe Johnnie'll be decent, don't you?' Dusky turned the subject hastily. She didn't trust that moon. 'Especially when the market's so low and there's so little demand for groves. Because he certainly wouldn't want to come out here and run it, I should think.'

'No.' David's tone was so lacking in assurance that Dusky looked at him in quick alarm.

'There's something else! I never get good and happy that something doesn't come along and smash me down!'

'It may not be anything at all, Dusky; and it may even be to your advantage. We thought there was no use in worrying you. Paul and I were nosing around making inquiries about the value of groves, and we stumbled onto this piece of news. It's this: the university has been taking options on some of the land along the Zanja here.'

'Options? What for?'

'Well, if times get better they're going to need more ground — for the new arts building, for instance.'

Dusky nodded, her eyes wide on David. 'Right where our little old cottage stands, just back of the Greek theater — that would be a natural place. But, David, that would be fine! We could sell half the grove, and move the cottage. Or maybe they could take the half right up to the court,' she added excitedly.

David looked down at her. In the moonlight she could see his expression, the patience about his wide mouth, the kindness in his steady eyes, unwilling to hurt her.

'But they may have written to Johnnie's lawyer,' he said, 'and the idea of that option and a good price in a few years — well, it would make the grove a lot more attractive to Johnnie.'

'And to that slick-looking bride of his,' Dusky added mournfully.

XVII. LIMOUSINES AND SMOKESTACKS

On the first day of the Christmas holidays Paul drove the new Ford to the cottage and honked loudly. Dusky and Mary Beth ran out at once and looked up at it — far up — from all sides.

It was a Model T sedan of Nineteen Twenty-Five, but it did not resemble a dusty unblacked shoe run over at the heels, as did most of the Early American models on the campus. It shone smartly black and stood with head in air and its silver snout of a radiator cap turned up complacently.

'Oh, isn't it going to be fun to have a car!' Dusky caroled.

'Be ashamed to ride in it, Ma'Beth?' asked Paul, his gaze passing his sister by.

'Oh, indeed not!'

'She has the Chinese reverence for age,' Dusky explained. 'But we can go so many more places now. My word! if I should win the Mexican fellowship we could all drive to Mexico City on the new highway! — if we kept the grove and had any money.'

'Gas costs plenty,' Paul reminded her.

'Not near so much as railroad tickets. And I've got an idea ——'

'Hold everything!' Paul groaned, clapping a hand to his brow.

'Why don't we run a taxi line and charge ten cents flat to town? Or two for fifteen? That would cut under the regular lines, and the kids wouldn't care how the car looked. It ought to keep us in gas.'

'Your ideas sound great, Dusky, but so many of them have a kick-back,' Paul complained.

'It should have a name,' Aunt Phronsie suggested, undoing the tidy wire loop that fastened the back door.

'What about Limb?' Dusky offered. She was mentally lettering a 'For Hire' sign for the corner of the windshield and she thought naming cars rather childish. But Aunt Phronsie ought to have her fun: old people had so little. 'Short for Limb of Satan,' Dusky explained indulgently.

'And short *of* limousine,' Aunt Phronsie took her up.

'*Short* enough, anyway!' Paul grunted. 'Looks as if it were standing on its hind wheels ——'

'Like Pendleton sitting up to beg!' Dusky interpolated.

'But I've seen a lot of swank cars that didn't perform as well. All its life it's been pampered like a pet horse.'

'Look how they've covered the seats and backs with blanketing!' Mary Beth pointed out admiringly. 'So neat and clean!'

'Why don't you three girls pile in and see how she runs?' Paul invited Mary Beth. 'Hi, Dave! Come and take a spin!'

It was like riding in a float in a parade, high above the world. And slowly: though the Limb rolled smoothly along, thirty miles an hour seemed to be its maximum speed. That slowness, its new owners decided, was an advantage, since it gave so many hours to the dollar.

'The old man hated like everything to give it up,' Paul told them. 'Said he wouldn't, if it hadn't been for the young folks, but they kicked up such a row over it every time they came home that he and Liddy got worn down. He said, "You just watch out there's plenty of gas in her or she's li'ble to balk on the hills. And if she kind of sputters and quits on you," he says, "it's like enough the distributor. Outside of that, she's a dandy. Fourteen dollars!" — Seems fourteen dollars was all the dealer would allow him on it, and he said he was afraid some junkman would get her. — I'd swear there were tears in his eyes when I drove off.'

'Let's stop and get some hot dogs and go for a picnic out Turtle Dove Pass,' Dusky suggested, sitting forward between Aunt Phronsie and David.

'It would take six hot dogs to make any impression on me!' Paul declared. 'What are you? A millionaire? Anyway, Dave and I have got work to do, you carefree kid.'

'Can't it wait?'

'No, it can't. We've got to drag out four hundred heaters and stand them in rows in the grove, in case of frost.'

'Just five miles farther,' she coaxed, 'where those lovely low houses sit on the hill. And I'll help with your old smudge-pots to make up.'

'There's a law against calling them smudge-pots,' David warned, smiling down at her. 'They're heaters. We don't smudge orchards. We heat them.'

'What do you mean?'

'Well, smudge — that suggests something black and unpleasant,' he explained. 'You should know by this time that there's nothing black or unpleasant in California.'

'Why do we have to wash our curtains after the orchards have been heated, then?' Dusky inquired.

'Because the imaginations of your heart are evil,' David answered.

Before noon, Dusky and Paul and David were loading a push-cart with heaters that looked like four-foot stove-pipes sticking out of five-gallon tubs. They whistled and sang at their work, for the first ride in their own car had inspirited them, and the weather, bright and cool, was the sort that made grove work pleasant.

Only ten acres of the Singing Wood's twenty needed the ranks of heaters. Those ten were on a level, while the other ten rose from them in gradual ascent. The cold air flowed like a sheet of water down that slight incline into the low-lying portion. It was often necessary to heat that chilly pool, but the slope drew warmth from surrounding orchards — 'mooched' from them, Dusky said — and rarely, if ever, required heat of its own.

Dusky swung blue-denimed legs from the push-cart and watched the boys setting the heaters in line. 'I have an idea!' she shouted at them. 'If the university should want to buy part of this tract for the fine arts building, they'd want the level part, and we'd get rid of most of the need of smudging!' She beamed at them, her face russet-red from exercise and her hair a wild tumble of black curls.

'*Heating*,' corrected David, grinning at her as he pushed back his damp hair with a crooked elbow.

'Yes,' scoffed Paul. 'Yes, everything's going to work out as if it had been cut and fitted — Tailor-Made for the Days. Everything's always fine and dandy ——'

He broke off, for Dusky, with a shriek, had plunged at one of the nearest heaters and jabbed her finger through the metal of its smokestack.

'Hi! what you doing?' he roared.

'Will — you — look? It's a shell, about as solid as paper. I tell you, it's com-*plete*-ly rusted out!'

Already the boys were cantering along the row they had just placed, inspecting the reddish stacks. Stunned to silence, they dashed back to the storage shed, Dusky trailing them, and swiftly poked here and there, examining a hundred heaters. Like a trio of consulting doctors, they faced each other.

'About one in three,' Paul croaked.

'Weren't they looked after?' Dusky asked.

Paul nodded shortly. 'Grandpa Wilson cleaned them and dipped them in sludge or something as soon as the frost season was past. — We missed last year, but — they only last a few seasons at best.'

With her cleanest finger Dusky prodded a hole in an orange and absently sucked the juice. 'My word! I used to think oranges were clear gain, and when Grandpa Wilson said these twenty acres yielded nearly eight thousand boxes in a good season, I hadn't a doubt we'd get rich if we worked hard enough.'

'They never remember to say that each boxful costs you a dollar before it's even picked.'

'If you have good luck,' David supplemented.

'Which we don't. Scale, smudging, smokestacks — How much can we pay Johnnie this time, Paul?'

'Maybe two hundred dollars.'

'Two *hun*-dred *dol*-lars?' Dusky stared at him incredulously over her orange. 'Why, that wouldn't pay taxes.'

'Fruitlands haven't been paying taxes, some of them,' Paul replied gloomily, 'but if you can hold on and keep them up in good shape, they're bound to come back.'

'But I thought we could make a real payment — with all that juice and marmalade and orange peel —' Dusky's words trailed off and she contemplated the fruit in her hand with disgust.

'Well, there was the refrigerator and the extractor,' Paul reminded her.

'Done with long ago. And there was the Limb,' she reminded him.

'And you have to keep a reserve in case of smudging,' he added.

'How much does smudging cost?'

'Around a dollar an acre ——'

'Well, why fuss about a dollar an acre, with only ten acres to heat?' Dusky protested.

'A dollar an acre an *hour*. Which might tot up to a hundred and twenty dollars a night.'

A slender, wavering bugle note sounded from the cottage. With one accord the three started toward it, their faces brightening.

'Well, lots of winters there isn't any smudging weather at all!' Dusky said hopefully, rubbing her sticky, rusty hands on a snatched handful of leaves. 'And, Paul, I've wondered if we couldn't make a lot by keeping bees. The bee is a most interesting animal, and orange-blossom honey ——'

'Beekeeping is a science in itself. And anyway, all such contrivances wouldn't be a drop in the bucket if we had to fumigate and spray and smudge and then see prices drop besides. My gosh, Dusky, you talk in pennies when an orange grower has to think in dollars.'

They glared at each other heartily.

'What is it that smells so good?' David interposed tactfully. 'I could eat an elephant, well-broiled, I could.'

'Potatoes warmed up with onions,' Dusky analyzed, sniffing the breeze, 'and hamburger. And I fixed an experimental dessert ——'

'I suppose it was an idea you had,' Paul groaned.

Dusky did not bother to reply, for they had reached the back door, and Peter and the hens were cackling and fluttering before Paul's clapped hands, and the sputter and the smell of cooking food were an urgent summons.

Potatoes, flaked fine with a sedulous spoon as they heated in the skillet, so that each morsel was brown and savory; hamburgers well seasoned and oniony; johnny-cake that steamed richly as it was broken; and finally the experimental dessert, an orange ice, frozen in the refrigerator.

'Wish all your ideas were as good as this one, Dusk!' Paul complimented her.

'And it scarcely costs anything at all,' she said happily,

tasting a spoonful. 'It would have been better if it had been beaten a few more times while it was freezing. Don't you suppose we could have an Orange Bar, and sell this, and orange and cider half-and-half, and maybe mulled orange juice, heated and spiced? And — I wonder how a dipper of ice cream would be in a glass of juice?'

'It would be curdled,' Paul answered shortly. 'Dusky, you're hopeless. Now listen: we've — got to — stick — to — oranges! — and just keep hoping that there isn't any smudging weather this year.' — He swallowed the last drop of ice in his dish. — 'That was a mighty small helping,' he added expectantly.

XVIII. THE SMOKE OF BATTLE

As December passed, it began to seem that Paul's wish might come true: that this might be a smudgeless winter. Day followed balmy day throughout the holidays. School began again, and the campus blossomed with light dresses and bright sweaters. At the end of the week, the Gamma Chis were to hold a stag up at one of the farther mountain lakes, and on Thursday Paul and David were still debating whether or not they should run the risk of attending it.

'If it should frost once this winter it would be while we were gone,' Paul declared, as the Brother-and-Sister Act walked across the quad from chapel in the sun.

'How can you imagine such a thing as frost?' — Dusky pushed back the damp curls that clung to her forehead — 'Of course you must go. You've both worked like the dickens this year, and it'll be great to get up into the hills. It *couldn't* frost. Oh, it might if this were Colorado, but Colorado's more unexpected than California.'

'Well, maybe we'll take the chance,' Paul conceded.

Next morning Dusky woke to the steady beat of rain, muffled by the sogginess of wet grass outside the windows. And when classes were over that afternoon, the Gamma Chis set out, in heavy sweaters and caps and tall boots, skis bound to their car tops. This rain would mean snow in the mountains.

All day it rained. The sidewalks were pools, the lawns marshes.

'I always marvel at how *wet* rain is, in California,' Dusky said, racing in from her three-to-five class at art school and shaking her hat so vigorously that it made a dark spatter on the rug.

'I don't see why you wear that felt hat instead of an umbrella.' — Mary Beth looked up from her book abstractedly — 'It's wet through.'

'A reblocking system of mine,' Dusky explained, spreading a newspaper on the bed and turning a piece of pottery upside down on it. 'Observe!' She fitted the hat crown over the pottery, slid a pile of magazines under the brim on one side, let the other side droop. 'When it's dry it will be as good as new. Rain has its uses. — I'm afraid it's clearing, though, and I wish it wouldn't. Bad weather's such a help in studying, and I need to cram for that Education quiz next Monday.'

'Well, we haven't any dates tonight,' Mary Beth said, covering a yawn with both hands.

'If it turns out a beautiful moonlight evening, though — well, Laban might give us a buzz, or even Langston Trevor; or the kids might want to walk downtown and get a hot chocolate; or over to the cottage and do a mulled orange juice. While if it rains —!' Dusky kicked her sodden shoes into the closet, stepped into blue kid slippers, and thumped a large book open on her desk.

'*If* it rains? What do you mean? Isn't it raining cats and dogs?' Maxine asked, poking her head in. 'Say, Kate's got the swellest box from home: sugared doughnuts, homemade, and a big chocolate cake, only all the icing's come off on the wrappings; and listen: a roast chicken!'

'Woman,' Dusky threatened, 'belay there! Whatever befalls I'm going to absorb this textbook. I'm no Betty Co-Ed, to waste my hours on midnight feeds.'

Maxine, advancing into the room, waved a doughnut under Dusky's nose. It was a large fried cake, its crisp brownness visible through the thick white layer of sweetness, and its odor such as only homemade fried cakes can boast. Dusky gulped.

'Kate is — is new at Highland,' she conceded. 'I suppose we ought to have one feed, if she wants it.'

The weather did clear during the night, and the next day was bright and edged with coolness. It was the usual sort of Saturday, Lawrence Hall filled with girls clattering down to the steamy soapy laundry, taking turns at the tubs with their silk underthings, taking turns at the ironing boards to press, shampooing, manicuring. Dusky had to go downtown to bargain for several gross of orange juice cartons. She had to study feverishly betweenwhiles. She had to stop at the Vasquezes' to see whether Carmelita was sick again, and, once there and finding Carmelita well, she had to try Mama Vasquez's tamales, succulent and nutty of flavor, and searing her throat all the way down.

At dinner that night Michi stopped her. 'I wondered whether you would be my guest at the International Club tonight?' she invited. 'We are to have a special program in the Y rooms — Miss Mueller will tell of the Youth Movement in Germany, and I do a little dance.'

'Mary Beth and I?'

'Yes, certainly, if Mary Beth cares to.'

Mary Beth was afraid she needed the evening for study. She was afraid she'd have to spend the time balancing her accounts, since she was three treasurers and a secretary. She was afraid that she had nothing to wear. She was afraid she ought to wash her hair and set the wave. She ——

'Pshaw!' Dusky said with indulgent scorn, brushing her hair with swift, careless strokes. 'All those excuses are piffle, and you know it. If Jimmie Tang can work in the same club with Michi and Jiro, I should think you could be broad-minded enough to forget the squabbles between China and Japan. It's *ve*-ry *nar*-row —' She italicized her words with spats of the brush — 'and *ab*-solutely un-*Chris*-tian, and ——'

'Would that blue Shantung dress be all right to wear?' Mary Beth asked meekly. 'And, Dusky, help me remember that I'm putting the Y money here in this cinnabar handkerchief box. And the money in the cloisonné vase is Delta Alpha.'

Dusky, her head and shoulders out of the window, grinned back approvingly. 'Atta girl! It's really cold,' she reported, 'but it's beginning to cloud up, and I think that makes it safe — keeps it from frosting. I wish the boys were home, though.'

The Y rooms were inviting that night. All the folding chairs had been stacked away, and the davenports and lounge chairs set in a wide semicircle with the fireplace at its center. Firelight flickered over dark faces and light, a score of 'nationals' and an equal number of white Americans. There were Jimmie Tang and Jiro and Michi, Taro Okada, exchange student from Honolulu, and Käthe Mueller, exchange student from a German university, José Valerio, a Filipino, Cordelia Jacobs, an East Indian with chiseled brown face under waving black hair, some Mexican boys, and several sons and daughters of missionaries, looking more at home here than in other contacts on the campus. There were Miss Corinne, and Mrs. Phillips, the chief sponsor.

'They've certainly got the stuff for a good program,' Dusky commented, watching them drift in, while she and Mary Beth chatted intermittently with their neighbors.

But she and Mary Beth were not destined to hear that program. Into the broken hum of talk came, as once before it had come into the consciousness of the two girls, the doleful ululation of a siren.

This was not a fire siren, racing toward them with a rapidly rising shriek or racing away from them with a rapidly falling one. Stationary and implacable, its long scream rose and fell, rose and fell: oooooOOOOOooooo OOOOOoooooOOOOOooooo ——

Dusky turned unbelieving eyes on José Valerio, at her right. 'It couldn't be a frost signal!'

He ducked his head, smiling at her agreeably. 'Yess it could!' he assured her.

'But the boys aren't home! And the clouds ——'

'When clouds iss high and thin like this way,' he explained, still smiling pleasantly, 'they made out of ice and they let the ground get plenty cold all right.'

Dusky sprang up and crowded unceremoniously between the petrified Mary Beth and Jimmie Tang, sitting screwed around to talk to her. 'I don't know what we'll *do!*' Dusky exclaimed. 'We'll have to go to the grove this minute, and see what the thermometers say.'

With hurried excuses they edged past people and rushed downstairs and across campus to Lawrence, where they explained their predicament to Mrs. Forrester and signed out for an indefinite stay. Already they could hear the Paul Revere of the smudge-pots making the rounds of the dormitory, tapping at every door and calling, 'Shut your windows! They're going to smudge!'

Dusky wavered at the front door. 'Who on earth could help us?' she debated. 'Langston' — she sniffed the name away — 'but Laban might.'

'Laban!' Mary Beth's tone was eloquent.

'All the same, I'm going to phone over and see if he's at the dorm.' — Dusky whirled and ran to the telephone on the stairs.

'Belton? Will you buzz Laban Hitchcock? — He doesn't? — Well, will you please ask him to come over to the Day cottage whenever he comes in? — Oh, wait! Leave a note on his pincushion or whatever, saying to come to the cottage whenever he comes in. Mark it important. — No, whatever time he comes in. — Yes, I do too mean it: well, anyway up to one o'clock.'

The way to the Singing Wood seemed endless. Into the kitchen they came breathless, seized flashlights, ran to the nearest thermometer, standing on a post under its own small roof.

Thirty-two degrees!

'That isn't so bad,' Dusky said dubiously.

'Must we light the heaters?' asked Mary Beth. Well she remembered the long hard evening last year when they had kept the heaters going till the boys returned at midnight, and — having forgot to sign out — had been summoned before the Student Council next day.

Dusky considered. 'Do you know, Mary Beth, I have an idea! I'm going to turn water into the furrows!'

'But what —?'

'Anybody knows freezing water raises the temperature,' Dusky reasoned. 'Come on. Let's see if it's a day when we can *have* water.'

Aunt Phronsie was out for the evening and the cottage was very still. Even Pidge made no stir, his cage covered snugly with one of Grandma Wilson's famous blue-checked aprons. Dusky ran to Paul's chart on the kitchen wall: it *was* a day when they could have water.

Dusky dived into coveralls and galoshes, and Mary Beth followed her lead. Dusky seized a wrench from its place on the porch wall and Mary Beth grasped the flashlight, and they ran to open the valves that let the water into the furrows.

When the water was wriggling through the last zigzag, Dusky stumbled to the thermometer again. It registered thirty degrees.

'Let's get on some coats,' she shivered.

Even while they were bundling themselves in old wraps that hung behind the kitchen door, the siren sounded once more, a banshee wail through the dense dark. Again the girls dashed to the thermometer. The red column had slipped just below the thirty.

'We'll wait till it gets to twenty-eight, and then — we'll have to begin lighting up,' Dusky decided.

It was a hairsbreadth above the twenty-eight when a car came panting along the Zanja Road. Dusky and Mary Beth clasped each other and listened.

'It's not the Limb,' Dusky regretted, 'but it might be Laban.'

'And what earthly good would Laban be?' Mary Beth inquired.

Whoever it was, it was stopping. Feet pounded across the footbridge. Dusky turned the long beam of her flash-light on the approaching people. Its yellow circle picked out, not Laban's pale head but the shining eyes of Jimmie Tang and of Cordelia — Mexican faces behind them — Japanese faces —

'Michi say Paul and David not at home?' Jimmie wheezed, with a hurried bow. 'We come help with heaters. You got more overall, please?'

Dusky and Mary Beth rushed to and fro, handing out overalls, showing where the torches were kept, and the wrenches, and closing house windows and snatching down curtains. Jiro turned off the water, looking politely dumb-founded to find it trickling. Then he and Jimmie and the Mexican boys attacked the task of getting half the heaters lighted. Unless the frost was unusually severe only the alternate heaters need be used.

While the four girls stood and shivered and watched, joined by the returning Aunt Phronsie, the boys made a race of it — a race against the cold, a race against each other.

Starting at the head of a row, each snatched off a heater cap, opened the valve, lifted the torch — like a kerosene can with a long spout — lighted the burlap wick of the heater, dashed on to the third heater, lighted it.

Up roared the flame, two, three feet above the long stack, red and blue and terrifying. When a boy had lighted eight or ten, he dashed back to the first and adjusted it till the awful roar was a mild purr.

'To think,' Mary Beth boasted with a shudder, 'that I actually did that myself! Why, the thought frightens me to death!'

'Not much danger!' Dusky said, jiggling from one chilly foot to the other. 'Unless the screen's defective in the nozzle of the torch, and the flame gets back into the kerosene and gasoline. Don't they make a picture? — Confound Laban!' she added reflectively.

The boys made stumbling dashes along the rows as if they were runners in a clothespin relay race. Jiro flung his long hair back from his face, and his set grin, visible in the weird light, did not slacken, even when he slithered in the wet furrows, even when the caps, frozen on, resisted his wrench and bruised his hands, even when a sudden flare singed his eyelashes.

'I'm going to take a row myself,' Dusky declared. 'How would it be if the rest of you made coffee and raked up something to go with it?'

Soon her hands, too, were shaking with the exertion of opening those frozen caps, those frozen valves; soon they were scorched and blistered with adjusting them to lower the shooting flame; soon her feet were sore from striking against the furrows, her knees bruised from falling. Yet there was zest in the fight.

Before long all ten acres were lighted — Jiro the winner in the race — and the thermometers inspected. Twenty-eight degrees. They began again, lighting the remaining half of the heaters. When Aunt Phronsie and Mary Beth, Cordelia and Michi, came out with cups and sandwiches and a big pail of coffee, it was relief to sit on the adobe wall and sip the steaming hotness and eat.

This was the fairy scene that Dusky remembered from last year. As far as she could see in the deep darkness the fires glowed in converging lines, cutting leaf tunnels eerily green. The group of people, too, were picked out by that windward row of heaters: Mary Beth's blue-eyed fairness almost lost in a sweater of David's; Aunt Phronsie more sweetly vague than ever; Michi an Oriental elf with her tweed coat collar turned up around her sleek head; Cordelia, shadowy and glinting in the fitful light; short round Jimmie, short slim Jiro, Manuel, and José. Afterward, recalling the picture, Dusky was startled to think that they had not looked like a group of assorted 'foreigners,' but simply her friends, who had come generously to her aid. They were just 'folks.'

They had come to her help, and they stayed. The thermometer registered thirty now. By the position of Orion in the clearing sky it was well past midnight. A long watch lay ahead, for the most dangerous hours were those immediately before dawn.

'Aunt Phronsie and Mary Beth and I will walk home with Cordelia and Michi,' Dusky proposed.

Michi's small face flashed stubborn in the flare of the smudge-pots. 'Always I have wanted to stay like this,' she urged, 'and with Miss Smith here it is quite proper.'

'I'd love it, too,' Cordelia echoed.

So the boys carried planks from the storage sheds and made wabbly seats in the glow of the heaters. They sang and told stories. They talked of orange-growing.

'Why you don't plant those broadbeans and black-eyed peas between the rows for your cover crop?' Jimmie Tang questioned. 'Then the trees eat and so do you. Why you don't raise chickens on the piece of waste ground back there? Then you needn't buy so much fertilizer.'

They talked of other frosts; of classic freezes when even the trees had frozen.

'And always you pick and eat some of the orange,' Jiro instructed them, when the coffee had been sipped and the sandwiches devoured.

'I remember,' Dusky answered darkly; 'and then you get sick, because of the oil fumes and everything.'

They did pick oranges, and peel them and eat them. The boys' and Dusky's were black by the time they were peeled; and they were so cold as to set the teeth on edge. — And most of the boys, and Dusky, were sick. — And the constellations rolled slowly across the heavens and brought dawn.

When it was light, Dusky climbed groggily on the wall at a point where she could see something of the valley. Here and there the rows of cherry red fires dotted the dense brown smoke which filled the hollows and hung like torn chiffon from all the heights. Out of that dark fluff the sun rose red.

Wonderful that citrus growers had found a way to fight frost and grow tropical fruit above the tropics! Like trying to heat all outdoors, it seemed, until one understood about the 'ceiling' of warmer air some forty feet above the ground. Only that forty feet need be warmed, a layer at a time expanding and rising until little by little it is all brought past the danger point. Wonder to battle with winter for this summer fruit — and win!

From the beauty of the dawn she turned to her co-workers. The boys sprawled in a huddle of arms and legs on the planks, their faces uniformly black. She giggled at their minstrel show effect.

Mary Beth, yawning on the porch, stared from them to Dusky and laughed herself. 'You precisely match them!' she explained.

'Me? Really? I never thought of that,' said Dusky, spreading her sooty hands. 'Ma'Beth, isn't it funny that California tries to keep us from calling this "smudging"?'

XIX. ART AND ORANGES

THAT morning, with the oranges unquestionably saved, the group of friends went their several ways, too sleepy and sooty to wait for the breakfast Aunt Phronsie and Dusky wanted to prepare for them.

Dusky scrubbed herself with vigor, but her nails and the creases in her hands and all the corners of her face were dingy, 'like my bisque dolls when they hadn't been washed for a year,' she thought, inspecting herself. 'I'd have to bathe three times before I'd dare go to church.'

David and Paul came home late in the afternoon, and heard the story with consternation. 'This is the last time,' vowed Paul, 'I ever stay away after ten o'clock at night in winter. It's an awful risk.'

'As for me and my house,' David said, 'we're going to join the International Club.'

'They're good guys,' Paul agreed. 'I'll join, too, if there's an opening.'

'Well,' said Dusky, 'I always thought it was sort of dumb, but maybe we could ——'

'Put some life in it?' Paul guessed, grinning.

'Most clubs look dumb when observed from outside,' Mary Beth defended it.

The two girls were in bed at nine that night, and all the Sunday evening dates returning from town, all the clicking of high heels and thudding of low ones, all the soprano and baritone and bass laughter and good-nights could not keep them from deep sleep.

Dusky's dreams wove an irritating story. Someone was calling at the cottage door; tapping; pounding. 'Why doesn't he ring the bell?' she thought crossly. She was working the juice extractor at top speed, and she'd been pulling the left-over pulp from the skins and eating it, so that she tasted and smelled orange. — Bang, bang, bang! She thrust her head from under the covers and asked, 'Who is it?'

'It's me: Sally Lou.' — The door shoved open a crack. — 'Shut your windows in there.'

'What?' Dusky asked sleepily.

'They're smudging again!' Sally Lou said with unusual crispness.

'What?' Dusky repeated, eyes still closed.

'My goodness!' — Sally Lou ran in and banged the windows down.

Dusky lapsed deeper in her pillows and went on sleeping.

'It's good you didn't send Johnnie but two hundred dollars,' Mary Beth said soberly next morning, looking out at the gray haze that still floated across the campus.

'Yes. A couple of hundred dollars for just keeping the darling little oranges warm! A couple of hundred dollars gone like *that!*' Dusky's fingers, coming through the sleeves of a red wool dress, snapped expressively. 'Just because the fool thermometer took it into its head to go down a few degrees. My word! I remember carefree days when I loved to see that old red streak get shorter and shorter. Jumped up and down and yelled if it went below zero!'

'Money can be extremely annoying' — Mary Beth spoke absently, sewing up a hem-to-heel run with tiny stitches — 'If I ever get promoted to painting, I don't know how I'll manage. Doesn't it seem extravagant, how fast paint goes and how much it costs? Do you have to squeeze out such quantities, Dusky? And then have it dry up before you use it?'

'I have an idea,' Dusky murmured, banging her bed onto its hind legs and wheeling it into the closet. 'Why couldn't palettes be made of porcelain and each one have a little pan to fit it? Then you could put the palette in the pan and cover it with water and keep all those gobs of paint fresh till next time. It ought to save Laban enough to get a new car. — My word! What do you suppose happened to Laban last night?' she remembered indignantly.

Laban was taking his equipment from his locker with the speed of a slow-motion film when they reached art school.

'What time did you get in last night?' Dusky demanded.

He collapsed against the wall and blinked sleepily. 'About ten or twelve,' he mumbled through a yawn.

She stared at him. 'Didn't that what-you-may-call-him leave my message in your room?'

'Oh, sure. Sure. Good gosh, Dusky, you didn't expect me to come traipsing over in the cold dark night, did you? — What did you want, anyhow?'

Dusky breathed hard. 'I might have known it. If it hadn't been for Jimmie Tang and Jiro and those, we'd have lost our orange crop. No thanks to you we didn't.'

'Well, how was I to know? Besides, you've got all the Chinks and Wops on your staff — and Davey-boy; what more do you need?'

Simmering with wrath, Dusky watched him set himself going again. 'Laban, why can't you get a little pep? You could really do something, if ——'

'*I* like what I do,' he drawled, with a slighting glance at her portrait.

It was true that Laban's work 'had something.' It was also true that there were times when he worked steadily, unaware of anything around him. For a few minutes. Then he would drop his brush, cock on the back of his head a cotton cap lettered 'Brown's Best,' drag Mary Beth or Dorcas to her feet, and do a languid, falling-to-pieces Alice in Wonderland dance. Or else he would collapse on his shoulder blades, as now, and glance with nostrils dilated at the other canvases near him.

Sometimes his work was better than Dusky's, as Dusky's was better than the rest. As for Mary Beth, she was still drawing casts and still life at the end of the semester.

Today Professor Faunce stood and contemplated her drawing as if he hoped to find something thus far invisible. She went on self-consciously deepening a smooth patch of shadow, rubbing out a line and putting it back, restraining herself from looking at him.

He gave a short, explosive sigh and turned on his heel. 'You may as well try the portrait class,' he conceded. He might have been saying to himself, 'She won't draw casts any better if she draws them till Doom's Day.'

Mary Beth turned pink with pleasure, and Wing Lee, posing again, this time in a splendid embroidered robe, exuded benevolence and satisfaction without altering his pose by a hairsbreadth.

Professor Faunce stood long watching Laban. 'Man, you could do things,' he said shortly.

Behind Dusky, elbow in palm and chin in hand, he regarded her slapdash brush through narrowed eyes.

'Look where you're going before you start,' he advised. 'But I like the way you sling color.'

'Too smooth and hard,' he told Dorcas, 'like a lady in a fashion magazine, Miss — Miss — ' He seldom remembered names. His doing so was a mark of distinction for the one remembered.

'Is this an eye?' he demanded of Andrea, thrusting with his maulstick. 'Is this supposed to be a portrait of our friend Wing Lee?'

'I'm not interested in bourgeois likeness,' Andrea responded passionately. 'Mightn't you ask if some of Matisse's eyes are eyes?'

'Wait till you've grown Matisse's wings before you start sprouting his funny feathers,' Faunce admonished. 'It hurts nobody to learn to draw.'

When he had made the rounds he started to retreat, thankfully, to his office. In the doorway he stopped, fingering the crumpled bag of peppermints he was taking from his pocket.

'Remember the current Beaux-Arts problem,' he said, 'a design for a mural illustrating American education. This particular competition holds added interest. I have the pleasure of announcing that the University will consider any prize-winning — or mention-winning — entry for a mural in the downstairs hall, and eventually for the new arts building.' He opened the door and popped a peppermint into his mouth, simultaneously.

Jane and Dorian led a patter of applause. Professor Faunce wheeled, and his eyes slid ironically over them and rested on Laban and Dusky. He nudged his peppermint into his cheek.

'We'd like awfully well to have at least a mention,' he said. 'This department has been sending entries all year and has got nothing but stings.'

'Going to try, Laban?' Dusky inquired.

Laban regarded her coldly. 'Me, I'm going to let the reel earnest young things strive upward through the night. I like sleep.'

'Oh, you make me tired,' Dusky stormed. 'Here you haven't an earthly thing to do besides your classwork, and gobs of talent, and you won't even try. And look what I've got on my shoulders. But I'd feel like a fish if I didn't make a stab at this.'

Laban's eyes opened. 'My dear Walrus, which of us will get the commission for that mural, huh? I'm betting on me.'

The Beaux-Arts problems were announced from New York every month, and from art schools all over the country went work by students who had paid the fee. A first and second award were given, with medals, and a first and second mention, themselves high honor. Each month a few Highland students labored over the problems, but, as Professor Faunce said, they had drawn no awards, but only the red checks familiarly known as stings.

'I've got plenty to do,' Dusky grumbled on, 'I've even got to make up an extra lot of candied peel, though Aunt Phronsie does most of that. It's caught on at the Student Store and they're howling for more.'

For a variation she had tried candying orange halves and filling them with the crystallized strips. One of the other sororities had bought them for a banquet, adding cashew nuts and almonds and using them in place of ordinary nut cups.

Altogether, Dusky's days were one headlong dash upstairs and down, one hurried scrabbling over books, getting ready for the last quizzes of the semester, one feverish attention to her 'business,' trying to make it increase the payments to Johnnie after it has absorbed the porcelain burden of the refrigerator.

Next semester, though, was to be different. Next semester Dusky was going to conduct herself like an adequate adult whose goal was an education. She had the conference with Miss Corinne, and as a result her new schedule was so closely related that everything in it contributed to everything else, and all worked toward Mexico.

'Don't take any more courses from me,' Miss Corinne advised, above her arched fingertips. 'Your first two years carried a good deal of general background material; and you already had background. Now — specialize. Co-ordinate.'

Dusky sat and glowed at Miss Corinne. 'Spanish. Spanish history. Ethnology. I'll want it all. Miss

Corinne, why doesn't everyone specialize? Why don't we realize how — vital school can be to us when everything in it works together toward one end?'

Miss Corinne smiled, and Dusky felt as if she had been the typical Earnest Young Thing. 'The average student needs a great deal of literature and classical history to gain a background for life, Dusky. He doesn't understand allusions, and so he lacks the language of literature. He doesn't know the past, and so he can't understand the present. He becomes an ill-educated specialist. — But it's true that courses are too often chosen helterskelter, and then it's no wonder the poor infants study them in the same way. They relate to nothing vital.'

So for the first time Dusky found studies an end and a reward. She was not working for credits; she was not working to make good recitations or to pass examinations; she was working to learn things she wanted and needed. She no longer wished to crowd her books into the fringes of her days.

Yet such crowding was still often necessary. Though her business was well organized and running smoothly, it was always on hand — 'like washing dishes three times a day' — and, besides, it did suffer an occasional mishap. One morning, at six-thirty, she found that she was out of cartons; the box which she had supposed full was an empty one, set back in the pantry by mistake. Another morning the extractor broke.

Worse, there was Johnnie and the missing agreement of sale, which kept them constantly uncertain whether the grove was ever to be theirs. Paul and David, toiling at the spring tasks of moving the heaters out of the grove and cleaning them for storage, disking the ground with a hired team, working in fertilizer — Paul and David were tired and sometimes discouraged.

'It looks to me as if we were prize saps, Dusky,' Paul flared, ramming his fists into his overall pockets. 'What are we getting out of this, if that darn' Johnnie won't allow our claim? Room rent for Aunt Phronsie and Dave and me, and our board. Do you realize the first half of the taxes are due?'

'We can let them go till we have the deed to the property.'

'Until! Yeah! Until!'

'But, Paul, I can't believe that it won't really work out all right. Why, Grandpa Wilson meant it. You know he did. Where would be the justice? It would be so mean to jerk a grove right out of our fingers like that!'

'You think it's bound to come out right, like a fairy-tale?' Paul scoffed. 'It's time you quit being an adolescent, Dusky.'

'Can't you see she's worn out?' David interposed. 'You don't have to heckle her.'

David had the protective gentleness of strength. He was the only person who ever made Dusky feel small and petted — she who was usually so self-reliant and positive.

'Well, all this has nothing to do with Johnnie's lawyer's letter,' Paul countered.

'If you had let me send that first one I wrote him, telling just what had happened between the Wilsons and us,' Dusky mused — 'But by the time I'd got it toned down to suit you it sounded as if I were talking with flannel in my mouth. — And he comes back, cool as a cucumber, with *this*.'

For 'this' had been the most decisively disheartening letter of all. In it Johnnie's lawyer had acknowledged receipt of two hundred dollars; acknowledged it formally, but as a rental payment only and a partial one at that. Their claim of any right to an established twenty-acre grove on terms so slight as those they represented, he dismissed as child's nonsense.

XX. BEAUX ARTS

DUSKY refused to face the fact that the Singing Wood was slipping away from them. If they lost the Singing Wood, Dusky lost Mexico, even if the fellowship were awarded her; for Mexico meant expenses outside the provisions of the fellowship. But since nothing could be done at present about Johnnie and his lawyer and the missing bill of sale, Dusky hurled herself into the work of the semester, and especially into the Beaux-Arts problem, and tried to forget everything else.

Her temper frayed under the strain. 'I don't know how people can *sta-and* washing their stockings in the lavatory and draping them over other people's towel bars,' she murmured audibly.

'What on earth's eating you, Dusky?' Maxine inquired, hanging up another length of filmy wet chiffon. 'I've washed my stockings here for three years, practically. Everybody does.'

'*I* don't,' Dusky snapped.

At breakfast five minutes later she glared at Kate for leaning her knife and fork against the edge of her plate, and gloomily broke her bread into half-inch bits as a reproof to Kate for buttering a half slice at a time.

But almost more irritating than these suitemates was Mary Beth. Mary Beth's offense was her dismay at the untidiness of their room. For their room was absorbed, possessed by Dusky's Beaux-Arts problem.

Her huge drawing-board was propped up in the best light the South Suite could give. For days she had worked feverishly on the plan, making weird triangles and circles, horizontals and verticals, and laying them in in color, before she began the actual painting. Whenever the door was opened a sheaf of these sketches blew wildly round the floor. A glass of mauve paint water was always overturning on the abused rug. Rainbow-colored paint rags littered chairs and desks.

Dusky snatched the smallest interval of time to work on her design. She kept a shielding brown paper thumbtacked firmly over it whenever she left it.

'That's because I'm in no mood for foolishness,' she explained to her suitemates, who stood in a row surveying her work, 'and people always make the dumbest comments.'

'The hair of that end girl is so lovely.' — Kate spoke as if hypnotized.

'That's one of the dumb kind,' Dusky said shortly. 'You work yourself into a state of madness to develop an original idea and put it in a composition that has sweep and movement and still stays inside the canvas. You fight to find color that moves. And then some goof looks shocked and says, "You've done those eyelashes well, anyway." Or else, "How ex-*quis*-itely you've painted that hairpin!"'

'They really do talk that way in art school,' Mary Beth informed the others, 'about keeping the movement inside, and color marching. Only they never tell you how to do it.'

'Oh, well,' Kate said good-humoredly, 'it sounds fishy to me, but I know I'm more at home with cows than with pictures. I always supposed a picture was all right if it was pretty.'

'*Pretty!* Now, Maxine, it's time for you to say, "I don't know anything about art, but I know what I like!"'

Dusky spoke venomously, but she burst out laughing with the others.

'But do you realize,' she went on, 'that day after tomorrow spring vacation begins and tomorrow night's the limit for Beaux Arts? And there's loads more to do on this. It isn't much more than laid in. Oh, well, I can cut classes tomorrow and work like the dickens.'

Next morning she slipped softly into the dim gray kitchen and plugged in the juice extractor. Aunt Phronsie liked to sleep, and Dusky usually tapped at her door just in time for her to get breakfast for the boys, who did an hour's work in the grove before they were called. The deserted kitchen was ghostly and still.

Very still. No cheerful hum sounded from the extractor. Dusky reached up and jerked at the dangling chain of the electric light. Nothing happened. She ran into the sitting room and tried the hanging lamp. It, too, remained gloomy.

'Of — all — times — on — this — big — round — earth!' Dusky muttered, jerking the extractor cord out and plugging it in and staring at it scornfully. 'As if it wasn't enough to have to —!' She stretched up a long arm to pull down Grandma's reamer, pulled down a pitcher, too, and shoved the smashed pieces with a vindictive toe as she thumped the reamer onto the table and began to squeeze the innumerable oranges by hand.

Aunt Phronsie, roused by the crash, came padding down into the kitchen in bathrobe and slippers, and scurried to dress and help. Dusky slammed the teakettle over for coffee, and the boys, coming in from the grove, washed their hands and helped, with large spoons screwed round the orange halves instead of regular extractors. Dusky put the juice through a strainer while Aunt Phronsie squeezed, and Aunt Phronsie strained while Dusky squeezed, and Consuelo scurried over to Lawrence Hall only fifteen minutes late, her basket banging her knees as she ran. Dusky followed with another basket as soon as she could pour the remaining juice, with shaking hands, into the cartons.

Shaking hands! that was the unfortunate result of her frantic rush of screwing orange halves around the ridged glass peak. Shaking hands! when the design for the mural called for a steady brush. All day she worked, feeling like a frog in a well, climbing a little way toward completion, making a jerky line that must be washed out, slowly repairing the damage.

'You'll lie down!' Mary Beth urged maternally. 'Honey, it will really pay you to lie down.'

'A lot of good lying down would do me, all jittery like this.'

'Well, then, you'll take a bath,' Mary Beth compromised.

A bath and dinner did prove restful, and Dusky's spirits rose when she carried her painting over to Art School that evening. All the contestants were there, finishing and mounting their entries. Beaux-Arts entries would scarcely have seemed legal if they had been finished before midnight of the last day. On this occasion it was Dusky and Laban, Jane, Andrea, and Dorian who were *en charette.*

The deliciously bohemian expression had been borrowed from the student jargon of Paris, where Beaux-Arts problems were carried away in a literal cart — *en charette* — and the students, always late, followed their drawings onto the vehicle and completed them while rumbling over the cobblestones.

And the scene was somewhat bohemian, too. The five worked absorbedly, hair wild, and Professor Faunce prowled in and out of his office, sucking candies and looking at his watch; and a feathery acacia tree below the window drugged the air with golden sweetness.

With more than six months of school behind it, the studio was paintier and oilier than ever. Woe to girl or boy who was not well smocked: anything he sat on or brushed against would brand him.

Laban had worn the same smock all semester, till it had grown too heavy with oil and stiff with paint to serve any longer as protection. Thereupon he had amazed everyone by appearing in an old-style nightshirt of heavy muslin. It was cheaper, he explained, and cooler, and it covered his clothing more completely. Some older students had been shocked, but Professor Faunce had paid no attention; and presently Dorian and Andrea appeared in new nightshirts, also. The slit sides of Laban's flapped around the baggy knees of his trousers, but Andrea's and Dorian's came to their ankles. Dusky called them the Night Before Christmas.

The three painty nightshirts added grotesquerie to the picture tonight, as they bent absorbedly over final corrections or mountings. But Dusky did not notice the grotesque. She surveyed the four other paintings with swift eagerness. Jane's was entirely negligible: for all her large boyishness, Jane wielded a feeble brush. Dorian's and Andrea's were ambitiously modern; Dusky felt sure that neither had caught the deeper spirit of modernity, but only the startling aspects of its exterior. Laban's—Laban's was good work. Whether it was better than hers, Dusky could not be sure. It was a more conventional and less original conception, but for once he had worked long and hard, and it was adequately painted. Dusky looked with sinking heart at the faulty execution of her own. For an hour she worked, cleaning up lines, perfecting detail, before she began the preparation of her mounting.

Mounting required accuracy and steadiness more than artistry. With cramped fingers Dusky measured and drew guide-lines and cut with a sharp knife. When she fitted the mat over her picture she found the opening unaccountably too long.

Doggedly she started anew, measuring, checking, measuring again, cutting at length with a hand that ached as she pressed steadily on the rough back of the knife. — This time the opening was too short.

'My word!' Dusky commended it. 'I'm astonished that you weren't too long. I'll have you right in one jerk.' With tremulous care she cut two inches more, laid the mat over her drawing — and found that she should have cut only an inch and seven-eighths.

Gritting her teeth, she flung mat, knife, and ruler as hard as she could fling them, and then dashed down the back stairs, banging the door behind her.

The door opened again, and a head thrust itself cautiously into the dimness. 'Hey! Walrus!' Laban called in alarm.

'Oh, I'm not going to commit suicide or anything,' she reassured him. 'But my hands feel like two solid blisters. And they've got the ague besides. And I'm prickling all over. If I don't take time off before I try another mat, I'll — I'll pop.'

'Let's all,' Jane proposed, running her hands through her hair and lighting another cigarette.

They poured down the winding stairs and into the big kitchen, where Wing Lee sat nodding on a stool. 'Nonono!' he cackled, springing to his feet. 'Lookeesee: no studen' allow'.'

'Wing Lee, we're starved,' Dusky begged. 'Wasn't there a tea or anything?'

'Only three grains of corn, Mother, Only three grains of wheat,' Laban declaimed, 'I'll toil until the break of morn, But don't I got to eat?'

'Allee samee all gone!' Wing Lee insisted, darting this way and that and shooing them from his cupboards as if they had been a flock of marauding chickens.

'You'd have found us something if Mary Beth had been along,' Dusky reproached him.

In the end, Laban cranked his car and sped to an all-night lunch-counter, returning with hot tamales and a pail of coffee. This was one of Laban's gay and helpful evenings, after weeks of sulkiness.

They sat around the painty tables and ate, and Professor Faunce accepted their invitation and shared the feast, and twinkled at them, and rummaged through his unspeakable desk for one of his wrinkled paper bags of cone-shaped chocolates that tasted like glue. And they all felt fond of each other, as they had never done before and probably would never do again.

Laban had his design matted and under the press, and now he took Dusky's ruler from her hand, measured, drew swift precise lines, made swift precise cuts. The center dropped out, clean and beveled, and the rim fitted over Dusky's drawing without a hairsbreadth to spare. Dusky pasted it in place and put it in the press with Laban's.

'Professor Faunce will get them off,' Laban said. 'Put on your bunnet, Walrus, and I'll trundle you home.'

His car snuffled round the two sides of the campus under the bright stars. Dusky clambered out stiffly and blinked sleepy eyes up at Laban, thanking him. The shining round face of the chapel clock held its two hands to the right of the center. 'Five past one,' Dusky said, yawning, 'and I feel as if I hadn't slept for a week.'

She let herself in at the laundry door with the key Mrs. Forrester had given her, tapped at Mrs. Forrester's door to report, and stumbled off to bed. She felt let down. No juice business during the holidays. — Her regular classwork fairly well up, so that she could go exploring in collateral reading which she really — really! — wanted to do. — Her Beaux-Arts problem safely off.

But, oh, if she could have finished that painting as it deserved! If she could have given it her best, instead of being cluttered up with oranges!

Because, if the University should commission her to paint the mural, she would be so definitely singled out from the mass that the exchange fellowship would probably fall into her lap. Of course there was still Johnnie to prevent her accepting it.

But — Mexico! The Monastery of Tepozotlan — the Pyramids — Guadalupe Shrine — the Desert of the Lions —

XXI. FINER THAN ITSELF

THE campus was swept along on the flood tide of spring activities, but for Dusky, Spain, Mexico, and painting loomed so large that Junior Play, Basketball, Track, and Zanja Fiesta were thrust into the background of interest.

Spain — Mexico — colored every hour of her day. When Consuelo delivered the orange juice, Dusky tried her Spanish on the child, and Consuelo covered her giggles with a polite hand. Dusky tried new phrases on Carmelita, and Carmelita rolled, gurgling, on the Mexican blanket. Still, it was noticeable that they laughed less and answered more each week.

Through all Dusky's hours, too, the Beaux-Arts competition ran like a twanging taut cord.

On a day late in April the decision came. Again all the windows were wide to the heavy fragrance of orange blossoms, which fraternized pleasantly with the turpentine and oil inside. Mary Beth was drawing a prim head-and-shoulders portrait of the red-haired model; Dusky was laying in violent shadows; the nightshirted Laban was sitting on his shoulder-blades, gazing sleepily out of the window.

Professor Faunce emerged from his office and made a beeline for Laban's easel. There he stood, caressing his chin and studying the portrait, vigorously drawn, thinly covered with paint.

'Not much done since yesterday,' he observed.

'Meditatin',' Laban explained.

'I wish to glory something would stir you up,' the art teacher muttered. 'You could go a long way if you wanted to.'

Laban stifled a yawn. 'What's the good of going a long way?' he argued. 'I can get enough to eat and wear without going at all.'

Professor Faunce tapped an impatient foot.

'As for fame,' said Laban, 'what's fame? Pouff! Gone in a few thousand years at best. And what's a few thousand years?'

Silence.

'Why work yourself to a lather to have folks give teas and dinners for you when you hate teas and dinners? Mob you for your autograph till you get writer's cramp?'

'Have it your own way,' Professor Faunce conceded; 'but I wish somebody had walloped you when you were of a walloping age.

'Out of drawing, my dear young lady,' he told Mary Beth with hopeless patience. 'Eyes larger than mouth and whole triangle — eyes and mouth — skewhaw. — I've always thought,' he went on, turning back to Laban and Dusky, 'that you did the thinking, Hitchcock, and Dusky the working; for once you seem to have reversed the process.'

While Dusky sat transfixed with puzzlement and even Laban opened his eyes, Professor Faunce strolled into his office and came out with a pile of mounted paintings laid across his extended arms. He slid them onto the model's stand as she stretched her arms above her head and rose, stiffly, to take her period of rest. Easels scraped noisily as the students crowded around him.

'Ummm — Andrea Garramone' — The teacher read the signatures and looked vaguely for their owners — 'Jane Andrews; Dorian White.'

The nightshirted boys and the orange-smocked Jane retrieved their entries with a somewhat forced nonchalance, averting their eyes from the red crayon check marks in the mountings — the 'stings.'

'Laban Hitchcock, second mention,' the teacher went on crisply. 'This is the time you worked; but I must say I don't believe you thought as much as usual.'

'Mmm,' muttered Laban. 'Little you know!'

Dusky's heart had done a tail-dive. 'Congratulations, Laban,' she said.

'And — quite a coincidence when we've never drawn anything but stings before,' Professor Faunce continued — '*first* mention to Dusky Day. If you'd worked a little harder, you'd have made one of the awards,' he reproached her.

'Congrats, Walrus,' Laban said coolly, 'but don't throw up your cap and cheer yet. I'm still betting that the faculty will like mine best.'

The master nodded sharply and Dusky's heart, which had nosed up went into a spin. 'With two mentions, the faculty will have to choose which they want for their mural, and I shouldn't be willing to wager their choice would match the Beaux-Arts'. — Slick and conventional, yours is, Hitchcock,' he said with candor. 'It'll be just academic enough to suit 'em. How-come you did it that way?'

'Because it would just suit 'em,' Laban said smugly. 'How soon shall we know?'

'Faculty meeting tonight,' Professor Faunce answered.

The rest of that day, that night, were endless for Dusky. Breakfast next morning was savorless after a blessing that went on forever. Dusky's heart thudded and her mouth was as dry as blotting paper.

'Oh, Mary Beth, do for heaven's sake hurry!' she begged, when Mary Beth dressed with her usual deliberation. And, 'Mary Beth, couldn't you possibly run for once?' — when at length they were dashing across the quad.

'You certainly make me think of the Red Queen dragging Alice along till her toes trail in the wind!' Mary Beth gasped. 'And good gracious, honey, we have to go back to the dormitory!'

'Not on your life!' Dusky began; but her grim tones faltered when her eyes followed Mary Beth's dramatic finger. Dusky herself had left on her bright blue bedroom slippers.

When at last they did go charging up the long stairs, Professor Faunce's door was closed. Dusky diddled with her canvas, and Mary Beth mixed paints with care and doubt.

'If they'd only *tell* you!' she mourned. 'Dusky, does he mean you should always use purple for shadows? When they don't *look* purple? — Well, then, what should you use?'

Laban loitered in and slipped his indecorous smock over his head.

'Why so jittery, my Walrus?' he inquired.

'My word!'

'Oh — fate hanging by an eyelash. Shh! here he comes. But I've got it in the bag.'

Professor Faunce popped one of his chocolate cones into his mouth and rolled it under his tongue, scowling.

'I explained to them,' he said, 'something of the way in which Dusky's symbolical design was subordinated to mass and color, and its adaptation to the space. It seemed only fair to explain this, since only a small minority of the worthy faculty have turned their attention to painting.' He sighed. 'But they liked your clouds, Hitchcock, and the — I believe they called it the general fine mastery of your technique. — Trick work! — So you will receive a formal commission to paint the mural. The fee will, of course, be nominal. Materials, however, to be found by the University.'

Laban's face, which had emptied itself of expression,

suddenly brightened. 'I don't know a thing about mural technique,' he offered. 'Wouldn't do at all.'

'This isn't to be rigidly a mural, if you mean done in tempera and all that. Because it may be moved to the new arts building if there ever is one. — It will be painted on canvas and affixed to the wall afterward.'

Dusky moistened her dry lips. 'Think of using all the paint you want to, Laban,' she said, her voice creaking with effort. 'And the *best* paint!'

'Gosh darn it, Walrus,' he complained, 'why didn't you lick into it harder? Any dunce could see that this time you're miles ahead. And look at the work you'd have saved me. Sloshing paint over that gosh-awful stretch!'

'I licked into it as hard as I could. Under the circumstances. Those oranges ——'

'Sold your birthright for a mess of marmalade!' Laban moaned. 'I tell you I don't *want* to paint the blame thing.'

'And you just took it away from me for the fun of it,' Dusky fumed.

Because these were the first Beaux-Arts honors the department had won, Professor Faunce suggested that the National Art Fraternity mark the distinction by a tea, at which the two designs should be exhibited.

Accordingly, the big reception-room was adorned with Oriental rugs and batiks borrowed from faculty members, and Wing Lee outdid himself on his sandwiches and little cakes. Dorcas wove a quiet background of harmony at the piano, while Professor Faunce and Mr. Turner and another of the art teachers stood in a receiving line with Dusky and Laban, backed by their winning designs.

'Wear my blue and apricot mandarin coat, Dusky!' Mary Beth had begged, as the young people worked together in decorating the room. 'They'll expect you to look arty.'

'I despise artiness, and I don't believe in going around dishing out what people like,' Dusky flashed.

'And that,' drawled Laban, looking down from a step-ladder where he was perched, wreathing a chandelier with vines, 'is where you're going to stub your flippers many and many's the time, my Walrus. — Blue and apricot would be darn' becoming.'

'If anything's becoming,' Dusky reconsidered, 'I'll wear it. I've got the sniffliest kind of cold coming on, and colds make me look like an old maid aunt.'

She wadded her evening bag with handkerchiefs, and took a stiffer dose of cold medicine than was safe, but by the time the evening was half over she was croaking hoarsely. Everyone attended the reception, and everyone asked questions.

They did not ask so many questions of Laban. His design was a finely executed panorama of purple mountains and orange groves and academic buildings and classical figures. It was admired and passed by.

Dusky's painting, on the other hand, called forth silent stares, faint praise, startled query.

Against a blue background of mountain rose the white perfection of the chapel, of other Highland buildings. Huge before the hills a colossus loomed, straddling a building and dropping in at the roof a double handful of boys and girls, some struggling, some acquiescent. Out at the doorway and down the broad stair streamed the finished subjects, and the foreground thronged with them, all standardized as to outer covering of cap and gown, and many showing nothing more — college graduates and little else. Others indicated clearly their particular tendencies or callings: the artist, eyes turned back toward the peaks, palette in hand; the writer, making notes as he walked; the explorer, laced boots showing beneath scholastic robe, globe poised on hand.

That foreground was a splendid pattern of advancing color, a satisfying pattern of nicely filled space, as well as a conception of the college man and woman in modern life.

Not many of the onlookers were aware of the pattern of color and line, but they did seek — and find — other interesting features.

'Oh, good gracious!' Sally Lou shrieked. 'That third one from the right end — it's the image of Caro Felton. Isn't it? *You* look. — Dusky! Say, Dusky, is Caro supposed to be a society woman or something? Have you put in any of the rest of us?' 'Sure she has! The artist's Laban Hitchcock. And there's Dave Masterson in a surgeon's frock, with little Chinese kids tagging him. Dusky, am I anywhere?'

Dusky shook her head and watched the questioner's face lengthen.

'My word!' Dusky thought, 'Caro won't like herself, because I haven't prettied her up. And the ones that aren't there won't like that. I wish I'd never ——'

She heard David explaining to someone, 'No, they're not meant to be realistic likenesses. — No, they're painted that way intentionally. You've seen the reproductions of the great Mexican's murals — Diego Rivera's? Well, that's the way with these. Of course people that don't know about art ——'

Good old David!

'Gosh, Dusk,' Dorcas murmured, peering over her shoulder, 'that's good of Corinne, sitting on a knoll like a Sibyl or something, with her fingers together and that sort of ironic smile at the world. The giant's vaguely Prexy, isn't he? And ——'

Dusky sagged against a table. 'Everywud will have every *wud* of the figures tagged, whether I beant it or not,' she croaked. 'It looks as if I'd got byself in a bess.'

Dorcas wasn't listening. Her brows drew a shocked V below her brushed-back hair, and she tiptoed for a nearer look.

'Well, my goodness, Dusky!' she expostulated. 'If I look as skinny as that I'm going straight to Moulton's and get a milkshake!'

Nurse Morris came crisply through the throng, toeing out slightly in her capable white oxfords. 'You're making quite a sensation, Dusky,' she observed dryly. 'I don't know a thing about art, and I'm sure I can't see why you didn't do it more like your posters, but I suppose it's all right. There's a piece in the Los Angeles paper about it.'

Dusky looked at her between heavy lids. Nurse Morris frowned. 'I suppose you've been working day and night again,' she accused, 'and then you've caught some nasty flu germ. You've got brains, Dusky Day, but you haven't got as much sense as the Lord gave a soda cracker. Come on to the Infirmary.'

Dusky followed the imperative jerk of the white-capped head. 'It's dothing but a cold,' she mumbled thickly. 'I can't possibly stay in bed dow.'

'Examinations?' Nurse Morris tossed the question back over her shoulder.

'Do. Sorority beeting toborrow dight. Election.'

'H'mph,' said Nurse Morris.

Dusky's temperature being one hundred and two, Nurse Morris had the matter clinched. She did not even let Dusky go back to the dormitory.

Unwilling as she was to admit it, Dusky found the cool white infirmary bed deliciously restful. Giving way to necessity, she blinked heavy eyes at cool walls and orange curtains, stretched her fingers and toes to the very edges like a starfish, and slept.

Mary Beth did not wait for visiting hours next afternoon. Dusky, pulling open her eyes from an entrancing drowsiness, heard a soft 'Ssst!' from the nearest window, and looked into Mary Beth's wide eyes, set between clutching finger tips on the sill.

'Oh, honey, how are you?'

'Me? Grand!' Dusky lay blinking contentedly. 'But, Mary Beth, what are folks saying? About the mural?'

Mary Beth's eyes grew wider. 'Why, you scarcely hear anything else! Caro Felton's absolutely raving!'

'I'm sort of glad I'm in here.'

'Yes, they'll get over it in time,' Mary Beth said seriously. 'And some of them are seniors and won't be back anyhow. I like the picture of me, Dusky,' she added shyly, 'I really do. You've even got the little buns. But I don't see why you had to make Laban Hitchcock so good-looking. He really — Oh!' The round eyes had slid past Dusky, gone blank, abruptly disappeared. There was a gentle scrambling sound and the whitened finger tips disappeared, too.

The nurse's mouth was tightly disapproving. 'You may sit up, Dusky, and drink your orange juice.' She handed her the glass and snapped down the window shade.

'Orange juice!' mourned Dusky. 'I can't believe that I used to like orange juice.'

She could not throw it out of the window this time, for Nurse Morris's cool eyes watched the glass; even watched Dusky's throat as she swallowed. Dusky downed it all and flopped over on her face. This wasn't such a grand way to wind up her junior year: stirring up a hornets' nest without winning the commission, and then coming down with influenza. Everyone mad; scarcely anyone understanding the big thing she had attempted in color and composition; this evening sorority election, and she a pariah. And she had hoped — a little ——

It was half-past nine when Mary Beth visited her again, this time conventionally, by the hall.

'Well?' Dusky demanded. Her throat was still a little stiff and achy, but she was feeling quite herself again.

'Want to know whom we elected?' Mary Beth crowed, sitting on the very edge of the visitor's chair.

'Mmmmm.'

'They put me in as treasurer!'

'You can keep the money in your Satsuma bowl,' Dusky said. 'I'm glad, if you are, lamb.'

'For president,' Mary Beth gurgled, 'they elected — you, Dusky.'

Dusky sat straight up in bed and stared. 'But, Mary Beth! When they're so mad at me, and everything?'

Mary Beth giggled comfortably. 'Oh, they aren't so mad. I've learned something about human nature. They enjoy working themselves up. Even Caro Felton — she wouldn't have sputtered so if she hadn't really wanted people to notice. And any sorority would want *any*one for president who was being discussed from one end of the campus to the other, and getting into the Los Angeles papers, too. But — oh, I have to go. Sorority serenade tonight — remember?'

Dusky, sinking back into her pillow, thought with rare perception that her Omega sisters might be glad that she was not with them tonight. She was just beginning to realize that she always flatted.

The serenades were among the loveliest accents of the college year. She lay dreamily waiting to catch the far-off sound of voices. As yet she could hear only the subdued chatter of the 'out patients' in the lobby, the clear-cut clink of Nurse Morris's voice, the muted noises of the campus. Gradually these tapered into stillness. Through the window she could see a frail bright crescent of moon swung between dark spires of cypress. And then — voices bloomed on the night; singing voices that drew nearer; that curved around the side of the Infirmary. Dorcas's true alto, Sally Lou's fragile soprano, Jan's rich contralto, a murmurous accompaniment of other voices, an undertone of guitars.

Ah — lovely! Dusky was thankful that she lay alone in the dimness; that there was no one else on the girls' side, to rob the moment by a word. For once she need not pretend, even to herself, that the stars were not blurred; that there was no lump in her throat.

That was Sally Lou, who overate and was race-prejudiced; and Dorcas, whose tongue was acid; and Jan, whose soul seemed a fashion-book. But they were something more: fine, sweet, true, clear — and soaring high, high!

And that was college: bigger, finer, more soaring than any of its parts. — Finer than *itself!*

XXII. DISCORD!

SUMMER came. Paul and Dusky and Aunt Phronsie used the first two weeks of it to drive to Colorado in the Limb.

It was necessary to make the trip as cheaply as possible, and by carrying their own bedding they could save a dollar every night at the automobile camps where they stopped. So Paul and Dusky tied their bundle of bedding lumpily on the back, and David untied it and re-rolled it and wrapped it in black oilcloth and tied it on again. The travelers took a huge box of provisions, also, and cooking dishes and utensils. They forgot very little except cups, knives, a can-opener and dishtowels; toothbrushes and combs and respectable shoes.

They found the old brown house stretched asleep in the sun with the dandelions a trifle more luxuriant and the paint shabbier. Pendleton, the fox terrier, cavorted stiffly around them, whimpering with joy: he was a little more the stuffed sausage than when they had last seen him. Mother Day seemed a shade inkier and Father Day a shade paintier, but so engrossed in their son and daughter that the typewriter stayed under its oilcloth cover and the paint dried on the palettes during the four days of their stay.

'But why not all summer?' Father Day demanded, running both hands through his bush of black hair.

'Couldn't David and Mary Beth look after the grove?'

— Mother Day peered at them anxiously, her soft eyes magnified by thick lenses like her sister Phronsie's.

They explained that Dusky was going to finish out her Education units in summer school, so that she would be ready to teach art if the Mexican fellowship did not come her way, or if it came her way but was rendered useless by the loss of the orange grove.

They had still balked at admitting that the loss of the grove would mean the loss of Mexico for Dusky and the loss of other things for Paul and Mary Beth. Even now Dusky hurried away from the thought.

'At least we haven't heard anything more from Johnnie and his lawyer and no news is good news. — I want to get all the work I can in art school with Professor Faunce and with Mr. Turner. Mr. Turner has the composition courses. And I must take up Mexican history. And I want more biology, and anatomy to help with painting people. And Spanish. It makes me boil to think I ever took courses for credit, or because they were easy.'

'If we really get title to the grove,' Paul planned, 'you two could spend your winters out there and your summers here.'

'And live on orange blossoms and dew,' Father Day said dryly. 'We're still in our forties, my lad, and we'll have an appetite for beefsteak for a good while yet.'

So the three drove back with a feeling of being pulled both ways. They would have liked to take Pendleton. Dusky did take something almost as bulky: her own beloved typewriter.

She had won that typewriter as a prize for magazine subscriptions, when she was a sophomore in high school. It was a new machine, but old in design, its keyboard not standard, its gadgets superannuated. Nevertheless, Dusky had loved it fiercely and jealously: its nicely shaped composition keys, its moss-green enamel, its sturdy alignment. She had enrolled for typing the semester after she won it, and had perfected herself in the touch system, acquiring moderate speed and remarkable accuracy.

With Paul scoffing at the machine, as he had always done, and Dusky declaring that she wouldn't trade it for the latest noiseless model on the market, and Paul retorting that she certainly wouldn't get the chance, she tucked it up carefully in a corner of the back seat.

In the Singing Wood again, the two boys put up a tent for themselves, since the cottage would have split at the seams with all of them inside; and the summer work set in. Paul spent long days at the Citrus Experiment Station. He was fascinated by the work done there, and anxious about the scale in the Singing Wood. It had proved stubbornly resistant to fumigation and spraying, and promised still more trouble and expense.

David labored unremittingly at Paul's side, and Mary Beth learned to cook, and Dusky went to summer school and did practice teaching. She played with Carmelita, too, for the child ran away to the cottage so regularly that her appearance became a part of the day's schedule, and her little brown body in a sun suit Dusky made out of bandanna handkerchiefs a feature of the grove.

Dusky had said to Mama Vasquez, politely, 'I'd like to have Luisa spend some evenings with us this summer.'

Mama Vasquez had said to Dusky, politely, 'I'd like it, too, Mees Dosky, but it seem like that bad Luisa want nothing but dance and see show. I weesh she would have quiet time with you.'

Quiet times with her! Dusky knew the indignant astonishment of the unwilling patron whose object proves unwilling also.

Luisa did come once or twice, however; and in August she asked wistfully: 'You think I should go on at the packing-house, Dusky? I could easy get married, but I don't know. Or should I go through high school?'

Dusky voted for high school, and to her surprise, Luisa registered when the day came.

All in all, summer held no long luscious days of leisure; but it did hold comradeship, and evenings of fun, and mornings like the blue morning glories that flung their Madonna robe over the adobe wall.

And senior year began.

Suddenly the sleepy campus came awake. Parents' cars, suave and prosperous or earnest and shabby, purred or chugged along the driveways. Students' cars, smart and streamlined or rakishly crazy, flashed and banged around the curves. Taxis slid daringly in and out among them. All kinds of cars disgorged all kinds of luggage and all kinds of girls and boys. Grumbling draymen boosted huge trunks up dormitory stairs. Girls fell shrieking on each other's necks and boys pounded each other's backs. New students stood around contemplating the distance and pretending to feel perfectly at home. Dusky and Mary Beth, Maxine and Kate, took up their abode in the South Suite again.

Senior year would always stay in Dusky's memory as a succession of high lights on a richly woven background of hard work, in the classroom and out of it. It was like a memory book whose pages were of bright brocade, on which programs and place cards, newspaper clippings and blue books, stood out in high relief. And from page to page ran the strong motif of Mexican reds and blues, the hope that she would win the scholarship and that she could use it when won; the fear that she should not.

That hope and fear spurred her to keen endeavor in everything she did. She must make the most of all her courses; not only would they be of the greatest use to her if successful, but a good record in them would help her toward success. She must, besides, show efficiency in outside activities, since it was the rounded performance of the candidate that was watched. 'And one member of the committee in particular,' Miss Corinne warned, 'is an extremist in the matter of leadership and organization.' — Even the presidency of the sorority became important.

'I'm going to be a *methodical* president,' she vowed to Mary Beth, absent-mindedly scrubbing at a smear of paint on the hem of her dress. 'I'm going to be a model, even in stupid things like sewing on snaps. Have you noticed that all my snaps are on, and that I hemmed that new skirt instead of leaving it basted till it began to flop? — And I'm going to be the most efficient president ——'

'I'm going to be an efficient treasurer, too,' Mary Beth said meekly. She was sitting on her heels in front of the bookcase, counting the money in the lacquer box. The sorority receipts were in the Satsuma bowl; the Y funds in the cinnabar box; the Delta Alpha funds in the cloisonné box.

'It doesn't matter so much about that,' Dusky said flatly. 'If we can hold onto the Singing Wood I suppose your future is settled.'

Mary Beth turned deep rose color.

'I heard Paul saying the other day that he thought he could make a young orange tree bloom at any season by dumping a barrel of salt at its roots and keeping it dormant awhile. Don't tell me he was thinking of anything but a wedding under a blossoming orange tree. And the amount of paper he's been wasting on poems —!'

'It isn't wasted! They're the most wonderful — And you think being married isn't so important as going to Mexico?'

Dusky waved the complaint aside. 'Well, anybody can be married. And Paul won't give a snap whether you keep books properly or count on your fingers like Dora-the-Child-Wife. But I have to make an impression on the committee, and I don't even know who they are. I daren't lose a trick. Even our sorority faculty sponsor might be one in disguise. So things have got to move like clockwork. Did you ever see a better rush season?'

Rush season had been successful. Beaning had gone through with little friction. Bids had been accepted by eight of the ten favored rushees.

'And now,' Dusky continued, stooping over Mary Beth and automatically pushing her waves into a different contour, then inspecting her through narrowed eyes, as if she were a picture in process of being painted, 'I must go down and get the pledge pins out of the box where all that stuff is stored away. Come on, Ma'Beth, it'll be sort of fun to see the robes and things.'

Mary Beth patted her hair back into place, locked the lacquer box and dropped its key in with the sorority funds, and followed Dusky down to the basement trunk-room.

It was as orderly as such a room could be, but the trunks were piled ceiling high, and interspersed with boxes and bundles. One little group of boxes had been left by girls who expected to return after vacation but did not — boxes that had waited pathetically through years. Other boxes were the property of sororities, and were pompous with padlocks.

Dusky reached outside the door and snapped on the light which hung, a naked bulb, in the center.

'Sally Lou said she'd take me down and show me where it was, but she never did get around to it. It's got Omega Phi on the front right-hand corner of the cover, she said, in black paint. My word! I hope it isn't way back under a heap of others.'

They picked their way among the trunks and chests, inspecting front right-hand corners.

'This one hasn't any mark — nor padlock, either.'

'Here's a padlocked one — but it's Kappa Gamma.'

'This one has a shiny black top — like a coffin.'

'Coffins are mostly gray and shirred, like an old lady's best dress,' Dusky instructed absently. 'It looks as if we'd have to get someone to help us lift that wardrobe trunk off the two boxes in the corner. Why would anyone need a trunk like a — like a private car?'

'Jan, of course. — Maybe there's some boy waiting for a girl in the parlor,' Mary Beth suggested. 'Someone that would lift.'

They went up to see, and found Langston Trevor trying their own buzzer.

'I can't possibly go anywhere,' Dusky announced, with her customary diplomacy. 'But I'm glad to see you all the same.'

Langston Trevor cocked one eyebrow and drew down the other. 'I'm trying to look pepped up by the end of your sentence and smashed down by the beginning,' he said.

'We need trunks lifted,' Dusky said, disdaining his humor.

He raised both eyebrows. 'I never saw such a girl,' he grumbled. 'Here I come to ask her to go to the Nu Delt Formal at Arrowhead, and she says, "Heave us a trunk, my good man." All right. Lead the way.'

He clattered down after them, with an effect of tap-dancing, stood in the doorway surveying his task, and then, standing well away from the boxes, maneuvered the big shiny black trunk to the floor. Dusky knelt on it at once, peering at the corner of the upper box. 'Oh, shucks,' she mourned. 'Langston, will you please move this one, too? The one under it has to be the right one, because we've looked at absolutely all the rest.'

Langston, his jaw squared, tugged the top one off on its edge, laying bare the bottom one. He drew an immaculate silk handkerchief from the pocket of his immaculate white linen coat and wiped his neck carefully, but Dusky paid no attention. She was staring in blank consternation at the corner of that last box. It carried the stark letters, JUNE GOULD.

'And who is June Gould?' she asked resentfully. 'I guess you'll just have to put them all back, Langston.'

While he banged them back, and flicked a shadow of dust from the heavy white linen of his trousers, and dusted his hands, Dusky considered the room. 'We really have examined every single box, haven't we, Ma'Beth? Do you suppose we'd better start all over again?'

'N-o, no,' Langston Trevor informed her. 'There is such a thing as too much. Besides, you may not have noticed that you have a caller, Miss Day?'

'We'll have to order new pledge pins from L.A., because we simply can't wait any longer for these,' Dusky murmured.

Langston Trevor reached around the door jamb and turned out the light. He held the door for the girls to pass. Dusky caught the glint in his eye as the light snapped out. Well, that was rather fun: he wasn't used to being treated lightly by girls.

'Oh, yes, I did notice you were here, Langston. We'd have had to telephone for a man if you hadn't been. But I've got an assignment on Mexico that's a mile long. Sorry.'

'In my old man's day they said, "Here's your hat. What's your hurry?" — But if I might be so blunt, did you also notice that I asked you for a date? Nu Delt Formal. Arrowhead Lake.'

Dusky chuckled. He was like a jazz band. 'Why, thanks,' she accepted, 'if I haven't a date for that night. I'll have to look at my date book. Shall I let you know tomorrow?'

'I'll wait,' Langston Trevor said grimly, and arranged himself against the living-room fireplace.

Dusky was still chuckling when she came back into her room again after telling Langston that she had the evening free. 'It will be fun to show him there's one girl who doesn't think he's a tin god on wheels,' she told a sober Mary Beth.

'It might be fun for David to take Kate Oliver to

Gamma Chi Formal, too,' Mary Beth said stiffly. 'The poor girl gets so few invitations. And they really would make a handsome couple.'

'But just now,' Dusky said hastily, 'I must write that order for the pledge pins. And a letter to Sally Lou, asking her if she had that box moved or something. Funny that all the officers were seniors, and all gone. Fine business if we came up to initiation without the regalia — and me the model president.'

The pledges were models, too, and worked off their pledge duty with precision. They had been waiting expectantly, hopefully, reproachfully, for their initiation, before word came from Sally Lou, in Yemassee, South Carolina.

'Air mail doesn't seem to help a bit, Dusky,' she wrote. 'But surely by this time you've found the box, for we never did move it. Likely you've been looking right at it all the while. It's funny, like you say, about all last semester's officers being gone.

'As I remember it, that box stood kind of alone, to the right of the door as you went in. Only I forgot to say that we spilled shoe blacking on it, and so we painted the whole top black to make it look neat.'

'All that fuss for nothing!' Dusky cried gayly, bringing armfuls of regalia up to their room. 'No harm done, though, except an extra outlay for pledge pins; and they'd need them in a year or two anyway, pledges lose so many.'

'I'd call Langston Trevor a lot of harm,' Mary Beth murmured. 'And having to get a new evening gown for his old Formal.'

'I never did!' Dusky cried. 'I got it in Denver at the midsummer sales and you know it.'

Dusky had found the frock on a rack of left-overs marked down from thirty-nine-fifty to four-ninety-five. It was there because it had been made for a tall woman, and in a style not attractive to the masses. Dusky loved it: an archaic robe of rough white crepe, heavy and glossless, with a girdle of brilliants and a square neck and sleeves that pointed down over the hands and a slinky little train that snapped out of the way for dancing. It needed cleaning, and a few lost brilliants had to be replaced by ten-cent-store beads; but when it had been thus renovated, it made Dusky look like a mediaeval princess. Mary Beth's mandarin coat made a gorgeous wrap for it, though Mary Beth lent it with obvious reluctance. Dusky only wished that Caro Felton might see her; but Caro Felton, having been graduated last June, was out of reach.

The dinner-dance was all that Dusky had hoped. Some of the world's most courted movie stars added luster to the lounge; Langston's classy favors were clips with the Nu Delt insignia; and Langston carried a fluent line of small talk.

By the time they had driven home again, pausing on the brow of a hill to look down into the little city's sea of stars, Dusky had learned much about Langston. She had learned much, too, about the sophisticated girl he met in New York, and the beautiful girl he met in New Orleans, and the smart girl he met in San Francisco. They had all been superlative girls, and they had all — Langston tried of course to conceal the fact — liked Langston Trevor. Inconsolably.

'And that is that,' Dusky observed, whirling to get the effect of her dress again while Mary Beth sat up in bed and hugged her knees and disapprovingly admired. 'But it *is* fun to be foolish once in a while, and let a boy be extravagant without minding. I do get tired of always pinch-pinch-pinching while I'm young.'

'You sound like Meg or someone in *Little Women*,' Mary Beth said coldly, 'but you certainly don't look it. Funny kind of pinching they would have thought it, going to a dinner-dance at Lake Arrowhead, in clothes like that, and an *orchid.* I suppose you'll be asking Langston Trevor to the Omega Formal.'

'Well, no, because I'd naturally ask David. But that doesn't mean, you little prickly pear, that I've *got* to ask David. I don't know that there's a law. If David felt half as bad about it as you do ——'

She skinned off the archaic gown with difficulty, and struggled and gasped inside it while she tried to undo the loops and buttons that fastened the sleeves from wrists to elbows. Having escaped, worn and breathless, she only snorted when Mary Beth said:

'He does too feel half as bad about it as I do. You don't know David. And you'll go to the Omega Formal with Langston Trevor.'

Dusky made a great clatter in the closet with the coat-hangers that crowded the transverse bar. 'If there is any one thing in all this universe that is haunted by evil spirits, it's a wire dress-hanger,' she said airily. 'You can't tell me that they don't hook each other on purpose, and slide their dresses and coats off onto the floor, and tangle themselves with every other hanger in the closet.'

'You will,' Mary Beth repeated in a small soft monotone. 'And there David keeps on not knowing that there's another girl on the campus. Beautiful girls. Sweet girls. And he just stumbles over them as if they were — as if they were rice straw, while he's tagging after you.'

Dusky snapped off the light and jumped into bed.

XXIII. FUMES

David and Paul were having as busy an autumn as the girls. David's pre-medic course was heavy, and Paul, majoring in biology because it fitted his plans for orange-growing, had two long laboratory periods. Their only extra-curricular activities were the International Club and the Singing Wood.

David clung to the grove. Though he was close-mouthed about his need for money, Paul and Dusky understood that earning his board and room had become a necessity. The usual fall work was heavy enough for the two of them: plowing the ground between the trees; planting vetch as a winter cover crop; irrigating because the winter rains had not begun; picking the last of the Valencias.

But the regular work was not all. It was to discuss the extra work that Paul called a conference. He summoned Dusky, because she was his partner, and David, because success was important to him, too, and Aunt Phronsie and Mary Beth, because they belonged to the group. The five sat in the sunny court in the shade of the chinaberry — thinning with another autumn — and talked of scale and how to fight it.

The citricola scale had succumbed before a thousand-dollar fumigation, but citricola was not their only enemy.

'We've got yellow scale, too,' Paul groaned, 'and that means fumigate again. Fumigate for Johnnie, maybe; not even for ourselves.'

'But what else is there to do?' Dusky asked. 'Unless

we simply throw up the whole thing. And we can't do that, as long as there's the ghost of a chance. It means too much.'

'Easy to say.' — Paul stared up between the clots of mistletoe — 'But the cost is terrific.'

'Why does everybody have to hold you up?' Dusky cried.

'Well, it isn't just that. Fumigating equipment is expensive, and so's the hydrocyanic acid; and there's the high wages they pay the fellows that work the guns — do the actual fumigating,' Paul said.

'High wages?' inquired David, his eyes glowing and his big hands flexing. 'Because of the danger?'

'Oh, there isn't such a lot of danger if a fellow's got a lick of sense.' Paul winked warningly at David.

'Danger?' Dusky asked. 'What kind of danger?'

'Well, of course there's always some risk when you go fooling with poison gas. — But I've been thinking I might make up some of this confounded extra expense by hiring out to a fumigating crew awhile. They work at night, you know.'

'Oh, but you oughtn't to take on anything more,' Dusky objected.

'It's getting sort of serious, Sis, if we have any idea of holding on to the grove. I doubt if we'll net anything beyond living expenses, what with this scale. And at that' — he laughed ruefully — 'Aunt Phronsie's been at her wits' end to keep us filled up.'

'If it hadn't been for Jimmie Tang's broadbeans ——' Aunt Phronsie admitted.

'But if we don't make some sort of payment,' Paul went on, 'Johnnie's pretty sure to come down on us and turn us out.'

'I've continued to hope,' Aunt Phronsie said slowly, 'that if we held on Johnnie might come across that paper of his father's; or that we might find it ourselves; and that the University might really want a few acres of the grove at a good price ——'

'Fat chance that things would come out so pat,' said Paul. 'And as for our finding the contract, haven't we all been over the house steen times? — Anyhow, we can't bank on bubbles. I think I'll hire out to Bob Thompson's father's fumigating outfit.'

'If you do, I do,' David said.

'To take care of me, I suppose?' Paul bristled at the idea.

David shook his head, his jaw tight. 'It's got nothing to do with you. I want some of that good money. — I guess it's the first time in my life I've thought much about — just money.' He looked thoughtfully at Dusky, and she felt herself reddening uncomfortably.

'I wish you wouldn't, either of you,' she said. 'I think it's silly to run such a risk.'

'Oh, Sis, we're not kids,' Paul retorted.

David said nothing at all, and Mary Beth only bit her lip. Both boys hired out to Bob Thompson's father's crew next day.

After a few nights Dusky and Mary Beth and Aunt Phronsie wound up the Limb and rolled loftily out to the grove where the Thompson crew was working. It was several miles from town, and the Limb's headlights bored uncanny tunnels through the darkness of the shallow canyons, the hollow roads, which intervened.

The grove was a large one, stretching into black mystery, only its nearer trees picked out in gray and unnatural green by the lights. One of the workers, sketchily garbed, came up to the car to ask what was wanted, cupped his hands at his mouth, and bawled, 'Hey, Dave! Paul!' Paul, as sketchily garbed as he, sprinted along a black aisle, his blank face filling with pleasure as he saw the tall Limb.

'Drive up a little closer and I'll show you where I'm

working,' he told the girls, and jumped to the running-board on Mary Beth's side, reaching a hand through the window to hold to the top of the car, and telling Dusky where to go bumping slowly between the trees, and where to stop.

They watched a shapeless mass of canvas become a tent enclosing a whole tree. They watched Paul insert a pump under the tent's edge and turn it on, carefully gauging its force. An hour, he said, should be enough to reach every leaf, every twig, and destroy every bloodsucking mite, in spite of its secure little shell.

'Dave's working a pump down this row a ways,' Paul called back over his shoulder. 'Dave! Hi, Dave! You all right?'

Dusky turned off the ignition and walked a few yards down the tree aisle where Paul had pointed. Softly she whistled the Omega call and listened for the Gamma Chi answer. She heard nothing but the soft rustle of leaves, the whoosh of pumps, the shouts of men at a little distance. She was about to turn back when she saw ahead of her a lantern standing on the ground and near it a large bundle lying against a tented tree. Uneasily she hurried forward. Reaching it, she saw that it was what she had feared: David.

There was no time to lose. She felt her own head whirling: the gas fumes were too strong for delay. She tugged at David's head and shoulders, dragging them away from the tent: tugged and jerked at him, his inert body pulled at by the roughness of the ground. Only when she had got him well away did she turn to whistle a call for help, and then she found that no whistle would come from her dry lips. Running feebly and calling as one does in a dream, she stumbled between the trees to Paul and the others.

At once all the hurry and bustle of the grove was centered on David's unconscious body. Bottles of ammonia jostled each other as the men crowded around him.—

'Here, you guys!' Paul begged, 'one at a time!' He pressed the salts to David's nose. Someone else flung cold water in his face. Still he remained white, bloodless. Still the breath came hard through blue lips.

'Best get him to the hospital,' the foreman of the gang advised, shouldering his way into the anxious cluster.

They lifted the inert body into the back seat of the Limb, and Mary Beth sat on the floor with the salts pressed against his nose. Paul rode the running-board, Aunt Phronsie clutching nervously at a strap of his overalls. Again they tunneled their way through darkness. Dusky peered ahead to ease the Limb over the bumps, and Paul warned her of others she could not see.

Within twenty minutes they had drawn up before the Infirmary, minutes that seemed hours, stretching out as if in a vacuum.

Nurse Morris shooed some of her young men patients ahead of her to carry David in. At sight of his ghastly face she pursed her lips and lifted her eyebrows and clicked, 'That nasty, wicked poison. I suppose he chanced it for the money. — Would he like to go home in a box?' — It was her ultimate threat.

While the doctor worked over David, Aunt Phronsie and Dusky and Mary Beth waited in the office. Nurse Morris, closing the door on the last of her throats and fingers and athlete's feet, and finding that the doctor did not need her, seated herself with companionable intent. She rocked slowly, her eyes fixed in a ghostly stare on the wall between Dusky and Mary Beth, her scoured hands coming up at intervals to pat a yawn.

After a while the doctor and his assistant came out, nodding brisk reassurance.

'Fine, husky fellow,' the doctor told them jovially. 'He'll be fit as a fiddle. Matter of a few days. Week or so, maybe.'

Nurse Morris rose with alacrity. 'So you better all go

and tuck yourselves in your little beds' — she shuddered the words through yawns — 'because all David needs tonight is sleep.'

Dusky came to see him next day, and found him pale but comfortingly normal. He cleared his throat hesitantly.

'I was planning to send you roses, Dusky,' he said, 'to wear to your sorority Formal, you know. I'm awfully sorry this had to happen. Miss Morris says I can't be around in time for the doings, either.'

'My word, no!' Dusky said hastily.

David looked at her soberly. 'Of course you'll have to go yourself, being president. And if you want to ask someone else ——'

'You know I wouldn't, if you were able, David. But it will be a good thing to get the obligation out of the way.'

'Yes, fine,' he agreed. 'And can you imagine Trevor's letting it rest there? Of course you're referring to Trevor.'

'But, David, you suggested yourself ——' Dusky carefully dissected a sleeping hibiscus she had brought him.

He stared soberly through the window.

'Well, you needn't act as if ——' Dusky could not finish. She jumped up and strode from the room, her nose in the air and her throat smarting. Goodness knows she wouldn't have had him risk a gassing, not for all the roses and gay good times in the world. She wasn't any such silly heartless thing as that. Mary Beth should have had better sense than to repeat her idle chatter.

In spite of all that, and of the ache that persisted, the Omega Formal was full of gleam and glamour. Dusky had to wear the same dress again, but she had devised a Juliet cap of rhinestones out of which her black hair curled quaintly.

This Formal was held at a hotel fifty miles from Green Valley, on a cliff that overlooked the booming breakers of the Pacific — a magnificent setting. This time, too, Langston's debonair line surpassed itself, and his grin was so boyishly ingenuous — and his chestnut hair so appealingly wavy! — that Dusky found herself excusing him the number and vanity of his girl reminiscences. She tried to forget David, stretched in an infirmary bed, with Nurse Morris giving him orange juice; and she succeeded so well, at least on the surface, that Mary Beth crept into bed that night without even a good-night for her.

SHE TRIED TO FORGET DAVID, STRETCHED IN AN INFIRMARY BED, WITH NURSE MORRIS GIVING HIM ORANGE JUICE

XXIV. NOEL

David made a good recovery, and was soon in his classes again. As he grew better, Mary Beth's manner toward Dusky grew softer, but the old warm harmony was gone from the South Suite.

And the Singing Wood was in as bad a plight as before. David's recovery did not mean immediate strength for his work in the grove. Paul would have to hire someone in his friend's place, and at cash wages rather than board and room. This extra outlay would consume Paul's earnings with the fumigating crew — and there they were.

Dusky told Laban about it as they painted one morning.

'Tough luck, Walrus. — Masterson was sort of a sap to go in for a risky job like fumigating. Paul, too,' he said candidly.

'*That's* helpful of you!' Dusky snapped.

'Well, gosh, I'm sorry and all that; but I don't know what there is I can *do* about it.'

His long pale face was so helplessly doleful that Dusky could only laugh abruptly. 'No, of course you don't — White Knight,' she responded ambiguously.

Michi had been listening with alternating smile and frown. 'David would be likely to help again in a few weeks, wouldn't he?' she asked, peering past Laban.

'Oh, yes, in a few weeks he would.'

'The doctor says he *thinks* so,' Mary Beth put in, with a hostile glance at Laban.

There the topic was left. But that night Paul whistled

below Dusky's window, and she ran downstairs and out to the shadow where he waited. He was keeping well hidden, because of his working clothes, but Dusky did not need to see his face to sense the smile there.

'Say, Dusk, what do you suppose? We don't have to hire a hand. A gang from the International Club came over this evening.'

'You mean they're going to ——?'

'Yeah: to divide up the time till Dave gets going again, and take his work in the grove. Not for money. Just for friendship.'

A round dozen of the boys had volunteered, and they worked in twos, so that each had given three or four evenings or Saturday mornings by the time David was able to undertake the task again. By that time, too, the winter rains had set in and ended the need for irrigation; the five hundred heaters stood in place, filled and ready for any frosts that might come; the last of the Valencias had been picked.

Autumn rushed by, carrying the Highland team to victory over Citrus and a wild jubilee, during which the freshmen were permitted, by old tradition, to order upper classmen off the quad. And Christmas bore down upon Highland.

Before the campus was deserted for the holidays, the Singing Wood gave a Christmas party. It was a dinner party for the International Club, a thank-you for help in time of need. The International Club accepted, with the proviso that each national group be allowed to bring a national dish for the dinner.

The night was fine, and a full moon — or full enough for all practical purposes — was rising above the orange trees as the guests assembled. Dusky had devised extension tables of planks and sawhorses painted Mexican blue, and these had been set up in the patio. The outdoor fireplace was blazing and the blue tables were drawn as close to it as tables and benches for forty could be drawn. Miniature Christmas trees rose from mounds of oranges on the tables. Moonlight and firelight together made strange pictures of the scene, moonlight painting cool shadows on the brick paving and firelight sending other shadows to dance and gesticulate against the walls.

The air was cool enough so that the hot food sent up clouds of steam; cool enough so that the fire was welcome and the smell of food enticing.

Such loads of food! Taro Okada came bearing a plate as broad as a washtub, laid out with wafer-thin slices of fish. Jimmie Tang had fat almond cakes, each wrapped in tissue because of its fragility. The Mexican boys brought two kettles of brown beans, hotly seasoned, and tortillas to eat with them. Cordelia had been busy in the cottage kitchen, producing a pan of hominy spoon bread for each table. The Indian boys had been uncertain what to contribute, but a Sioux youth had written his sister for advice, and Mary Beth helped him work out the sister's instructions. They had mixed biscuit dough, and at dinner time they heated fat in an iron kettle hung on a crane in the fireplace, and fried the bread after the others were seated, serving it, crisp and crackling, direct from kettle to table. Some of the other nationalities, who could not devise a way to reproduce their characteristic foods, had joined forces with two Armenian lads and provided a *pilau* of rice and mutton and strange herbs.

'Food for a hundred,' Dusky said with conviction. She was trying to find room for her great wooden bowls of salad. It was chicken salad, compounded of chicken and veal and hard-boiled eggs and savory mayonnaise and sharp cress, and it reposed, cool and luscious, on crisp curled lettuce leaves. 'Enough for a hundred! What under the sun shall we do with what's left?'

'It has been well said,' Jimmie Tang answered her, his eyes twinkling, '"The wise host does not order his table cleared until the guests have departed." Also, "Good comrades and the tingle of winter make sharp sauce for the rice."'

Jimmie's maxims proved true. Everyone, of course, must sample every dish. Even that pre-Raphaelite angel, Mrs. Phillips, ate with a human relish. Dusky had seated her at Aunt Phronsie's right, at the head of one of the tables, and could see her plate clearly. It filled and emptied, filled and emptied again.

When the play of knives and forks began to lag, Paul and Dusky made 'cowboy coffee' in a huge kettle in the fireplace. They started it with cold water and as soon as it began to boil added a dozen crushed eggs, washed shells and all.

They beguiled the time of the coffee-making by singing in grotesque duet — Dusky flatting freely and happily — 'Oh, bury me not on the lone prairee!' When that had dissolved in choking laughter on Dusky's part, everyone swung into a favorite of a past year — 'Oh, give me a home, Where the buffalos roam —' while the dessert was being served. The dessert was orange ice from the monstrous refrigerator, and the sugary Chinese almond cakes, whose deliciousness melted in the mouth, and the cowboy coffee, clear and strong.

When they had really eaten all they could, Paul and David heaped more wood on the fire, and they sat around the depleted tables and sang. Dusky contemplated the blaze and sparkle with dreamy content. It didn't cost anything! The boys piled the accumulation of brush trimmed from the trees each year in the waste acre at the back of the grove, and this gave the fuel for their occasional open fires.

Finally, they lifted tables and benches to one side and Käthe Mueller taught them a square dance from her own country; and they danced the Virginia Reel, with the parlor window open and someone pumping out the tunes on the wheezy old organ which Paul had found in a secondhand store.

The moon sailed across the sky; and an occasional mocking bird piped sleepily from the grove; and the young people piled on more wood and told stories, and ate what remained on the tables, and sang a Christmas carol and dispersed, still singing.

Mrs. Phillips lingered.

'There was something lovely and friendly about this dinner, Miss Day,' she said. 'I can't quite put my finger on the difference. Some attempts at race friendship are so — silly, I'm afraid. Artificial. This was real; it was —— Listen!'

Along the dark Zanja, high and sweet above the night winds, came the retreating voices of the guests, in harmony,

'The first Noël
The angels did sing!'

XXV. MEXICAN MOTIF

DUSKY breathed freer after the holidays when her successor as sorority president had been inducted. But a dozen other responsibilities crowded in to take the place of the surrendered one.

She was appointed member of a committee to choose the senior gift to the school. She was elected art editor of the *Annual* — at Highland a senior publication. She was made chairman of the committee for the Zanja Fiesta, crowning festivity of the school year.

She considered this packed program one February day, facing Mary Beth across their desk. 'I could use every minute for these outside things, and still not have any too much time for them. But I won't let my studies go.'

'Possibly you should discontinue your juice business,' said Mary Beth.

'No, we need money too badly.' Dusky sucked in her cheeks and frowned. 'That old Johnnie's always hanging over us. Like a thundercloud. We couldn't send but two hundred dollars again this time, and we only did that by squeezing every penny. — Anyway, the juice runs like clockwork: I'm so used to it that it doesn't complicate things much. No, I simply have to use all my minutes, and con-cen-trate.'

It was easier to concentrate, now that most of her activities swung on a common pivot. Her mind steeped in Mexican history and art, her plans shaping for a Spanish fiesta, it was natural to think of a Mexican motif for the *Annual*.

She spent hours poring over piles of other *Annuals*, working out a broad general plan, making sketches, forming a dummy of the book, with title page, decorations, end papers. Laban, her most capable committeeman, helped her when he was in the mood.

Block prints seemed especially suitable to the plan, and here Mary Beth proved an unexpected aid. Once the drawing was made — Dusky and Michi making a good half of them and Laban an inspired few — Mary Beth could trace it accurately on the linoleum block, and cut it as finely as she had traced it.

Many hours the four worked together amid the rich incense of the painty studio. Laban tied himself in knots above a table. Mary Beth, a little too silent, bent close over her tracing and cutting, cheeks flushed, mouth a pink bud. Michi hooked her small heels over a chair rung and sat very straight. Michi had slipped unnoticeably into the place left empty when Dorcas was graduated.

'This is another of the things that is going — going — gone!' Michi murmured wistfully, as they all worked at top speed to finish their plates on time. 'And it's been such fun.'

Fun, Dusky thought to herself; but more fun if Mary Beth hadn't been so gently subdued, as one who says, 'I'll be loyal to you and yours, whatever you are to me and mine!' And if Michi's enjoyment hadn't been almost too intense, as if the end of everything were upon her and she must be happy while she could. And if even Laban had not had blackly melancholy moods, alternating with sulky moods, alternating with gay moods!

'Going — going — gone!' he echoed now, in an undertone that reached only Dusky's ears. 'I'll miss you, my annoyin' Walrus.'

'Yes; like a mosquito,' Dusky said uncomfortably, and blotted a border line with a jerk of her ruler. 'My aunt! Don't let's get sentimental. I always blot things.'

She wielded an ink eraser vigorously, put in another line, stood back and squinted, and then spatted the drawing down with the others. 'Whoosh!' she sighed, putting her hair back with both hands and leaving black streaks across her cheeks.

Laban looked up at her, solemnly added two lines to his own drawing, and held it out for her to see. 'The tail-piece,' he explained.

She knitted surprised brows. The group showed a Walrus, a White Knight, a White Queen, a kimonoed Japanese, all bowing, hand in hand. 'Good-bye!' was the caption in Spanish.

'It mixes the motif,' Dusky objected.

'I want it in,' said Laban.

'It's sort of — personal.'

'I want it in,' Laban insisted.

'That Walrus has a nice inky face, just like you, Dusky,' Michi observed with a giggle.

Dusky rubbed at her cheeks with a handkerchief already inky. 'I inherited it,' she said. 'It's practically a birth-mark.'

All this while the fiesta had been unrolling before Dusky's mind in vivid, broken pantomime. It had danced across the pages of Mexican history; it had shaped itself in the motif of the *Annual*. Much of the pageant she could see, but she could not hear it, nor put it into words. For the music she had a brilliant music major as a committee chairman, with the facilities of the music department behind her. For the words, she had Paul.

Together the brother and sister snatched hours to huddle before a smouldering fire in the court, planning the pageant. She showed him her crayon sketches and told him what she had in mind; he stared at the sketches, stared into the fire, nodded, made notes in his pocket note-book between tag ends of verses scribbled there.

Together they and the Limb went to Los Angeles for

two week ends, and dug into the historical department of the public library with hungry zeal.

'But one of the things I'm learning,' Dusky told Paul as they rolled home in their high chariot, under budding magnolias and rattling palms, 'is to let other people do their share of the work.'

She had a committee on costume, working from her sketches and from library plates. She had a committee on music, since without music the pageant would be dead. She had a committee for the street fair which was to climax the evening. She had Paul to write the script. She had the dramatics director, who first doubted, then conceded, then promoted. And she had herself, buzzing here, buzzing there, checking up, overseeing.

She could not have accomplished what she did if her work had not been so interwoven. Even Carmelita, who still popped up in the South Suite sometimes, though she was six now, and in school — even Carmelita seemed a part of the pattern, so that Dusky found it as hard as ever to send her home.

'Here's a magazine you can color, Caramel,' she told her one afternoon. 'Yes, use those paints in the little black box. — Yes, yes, there are brushes: lots of brushes; and when you've colored your ladies you can cut them out. But don't bother Dusky. Dusky's got all this to learn before dinner, and you mustn't say a word to her: not — a — single — word!'

For an hour the room was a quiet backwater in the dormitory's current of noise and gaiety. Dusky kept up her usual murmurous sputter of protest against this and that in the text, but it was no more than an accent to the stillness. When Mary Beth came in, Dusky looked up, lips moving, and flipped a hand in greeting. Mary Beth smiled and stood watching Carmelita.

'Why, Carmelita,' Dusky heard her sudden soft little voice, 'did Dusky say you could ——?'

'Use my good paints? Yes, I did,' Dusky interposed. 'Just so long as she'd let me alone.'

'Your good paints *and* brushes,' Mary Beth said briefly, and laid two long-handled ones on Dusky's desk.

Dusky's chair went backward with a bang. 'My word!' she cried hoarsely. 'My *word!*'

Carmelita scrambled to her feet, both hands full of daubed paper ladies. 'There wasn't no leetle brosh!' she shrilled. 'Nassy old beeg broshes!'

'Two dollars! — Three dollars!' Dusky groaned. 'And I've nursed them as if they were babies. Carmelita! you —' She brandished the ruined brushes, and Carmelita, panic-stricken, ducked past Mary Beth and out at the door, squeaking loudly as she went.

Dusky pelted down the stairs after her.

'*Qué peste eres!* — You little pest!' she was calling breathlessly. '*Espérante un momentito y verás que te daré una paliza que* — Just wait half a minute and I'll give you the best paddling ——'

'*Lo hice sin pensar*, Dosky! I didn't mean to, Dosky!' Carmelita was pleading, as Dusky bore down on her. '*Lo siento muchísimo y ahorraré.* I am so, so sorry. *Todos mes centavitos y te compraré unos nuevos, y* —— All my pennies I shall save and buy you new ones, and ——'

Finding escape impossible, the child turned and flung herself upon her pursuer, as one who seeks the center of the storm. Clambering up Dusky, monkeywise, she buried her face in the girl's neck and clung there, whimpering little endearments. Dusky sat down abruptly on the stairs and began to laugh.

'You are the naughtiest little Caramel that ever was — *Nunca jamás ha habido una Carmelita tan mala como tu*,' she scolded gently, 'and Dusky will have to go without sugar in her tea for a year and a half.'

'Dosky, my lovely lady!' Carmelita cooed engagingly, nuzzling a silky black head against her friend. 'Carmelita give Dosky sugar.'

Dusky looked over the child's curls into the laughing eyes of Mrs. Forrester, the coolly amused ones of Miss Corinne. She set Carmelita on her feet and gave her a small spank.

'Take your dollies home now,' she told her, 'and mind you never cut Dusky's paint brushes again!—*fijate bien, no vuelvas nunca a cortar los penceles de Dusky!*'

'I practice my Spanish on her,' Dusky explained to the listening women.

'And so fluently!' Miss Corinne praised her. 'Spanish is a dark secret to me.'

Dusky gave devout thanks for her ignorance.

XXVI. THE SENIOR GIFT

THOUGH even the monkey Carmelita could be endured because she matched the Mexican motif, matters that did not match annoyed Dusky like broken threads in a tapestry: Langston Trevor's committee for the selection and purchase of the senior gift, for instance.

It was a stupid committee, anyway, Dusky thought: Langston and Dusky, and Jan, who could think of nothing but her costume for the fiesta, her gown for the final sorority party, and the new spring suit her mother had promised to send her from New York.

The student body had decided on a marble bench for the campus, and the committee had now to choose the style. Langston, sliding as much work as possible from his fine shoulders, suggested that they each send for a catalogue.

When the catalogues came, he called a conference, to take place in a window seat in Lawrence Hall. As Dusky ran downstairs at the hour of the conference, she reminded herself of a number of things; she reminded herself that, although she must run from this meeting to another with the street fair committee, and though she must squeeze in two hours of solid study on Mexico before she went to bed, besides an hour in biology lab — *still*, this was itself an obligation and must be disposed of in due order. Her hard-won patience furrowed her brow and tightened her lips, but Langston did not notice the forbidding manner, and Jan had not even appeared.

Langston was not at all hurried. He told Dusky — looking at her provocatively between thick lashes — that hard work was becoming to her and even paint looked all right — 'blue paint. On your nose.' He asked her if she was going with him to the Student Mix, just dawning on the calendar; and he asked it sunnily, certain that she could not refuse.

'Oh, here's Jan!' Dusky cried, astonishing Jan by the warmth of her greeting.

Jan said, 'Please do tell me you like this little old dress. I know it's awful, but I just saw it in Davis's window and I hadn't a rag fit to wear.'

Dusky said, 'Awful, my word!' and ruffled the pages of her catalogue suggestively.

Langston said, 'Dusky, you're so businesslike! You got something good?'

Dusky lifted her eyes briefly to his lazy gray ones and opened to a page with a turned-back corner. 'I like this,' she replied, 'and this. Nice lines; and they don't go badly with the campus architecture.'

'Neat,' Langston patronized without enthusiasm.

Jan nodded, frowning anxiously at four polished finger nails, and said, 'Why, anything that suits you two is all right with me.'

'But I've got something to show you that's going to make you sit up and take notice,' Langston announced. 'Look at this one!'

He flung open a folio of heavy polished paper and put a finger on the photograph of a bench. He drew back expectantly, his eyes on Dusky.

'Anything that suits you ——' Jan murmured.

'You — you mean you like this one?' — Dusky hesitated, suspicious.

'I figure it's about the neatest little number you'll find anywhere.' He turned the page toward himself and gloated.

Dusky jerked it back and stared. The carving was a rococo riot of grapes and leaves. A semblance of rough bark showed between.

'I suspect there's a cupid on each side,' Dusky hissed.

'Why, I don't think it needs cupids. Just enough as it is. And appropriate to a fruit country.'

'Let's — let's submit it to the student body,' Dusky choked. 'I'm overdue at a meeting now.'

If she lingered she'd find herself saying something snippy, and she was trying to get over the habit. But for anyone — a senior in college — to be so dumb! So cocksure and wrong-headed! And without a notion in the world that she, an art major, might know some things he didn't! She dashed out of the hall and toward the library and the other committee meeting.

'What's the rush, Dusky?' — Langston was at her elbow, catalogues under arm. 'About the Mix. Shall I come for you at eight?'

He stopped where the curved walk, all laced with palm shadows, met the library walk. Dusky, poised for flight, stared at him.

'About eight?' he repeated, his smile ingratiating.

My word! she was thinking, nobody ever made me so mad in all my life! So sure of himself! Why did I ever think he *had* something? All that talk about other girls, too! Pouff, Langston Trevor!

'No,' she said distinctly, 'you needn't call for me. I'm probably going with someone else. He hasn't asked me yet, but if he doesn't, that's all right, too.'

Langston's lip dropped. He stood agape, catalogues still gripped under arm, while Dusky whirled and ran into the library.

When Dusky had slapped her books shut that night and was brushing her hair, she began to laugh. 'That Langston Trevor! I never saw anything so funny. — But I don't know why it made me so mad to have him choose that awful bench. It still does.'

'It's because you liked him a little bit and thought you might like him more,' Mary Beth guessed wisely.

'It was because he didn't recognize that I, Dusky Day, could instruct his ignorance about art,' Dusky contradicted.

The explosion had echoes. Langston never spoke to Dusky again; and at the next meeting of the student body, where his report was to have been made, his resignation as committee chairman was read in its place.

Unexpected business affairs, it said, were calling him home at once. 'And flunking too many courses might have something to do with it,' the class president commented, *sotto voce*. He looked oddly, nevertheless, at Dusky.

'It is quite possible,' Mary Beth whispered, 'that Langston Trevor had been boasting that he had taken you away from — from David. I've heard that boys do boast.'

Dusky automatically stepped into the chairmanship and added Laban Hitchcock to the committee. Laban agreed with Dusky as to one of the dignified designs she had chosen, the order straightway went in to the company, and the incident seemed closed. — Never before had Dusky so appreciated Laban. Agreement in taste, she observed to Mary Beth, was one of the most important requirements for friendship.

The incident, however, was not closed. In mid-April, when Dusky was using every moment to gather notes for her long term paper in Mexican History, and reorganizing a fiesta committee that had flown violently to pieces, she received a letter from a garden furniture company in Los Angeles. The letter was addressed to Langston Trevor, Chairman Gift Committee, and had been re-addressed to her. It said that they had the bench, Sylvan Design, ready for the inscription, and would the chairman kindly forward data at once?

'My word!' Dusky remonstrated, thrusting the letter at

Laban in art class. 'Surely Lang couldn't have fired the order in without anyone's confirming it. What do I do about it, Laban? If there's anything I hate and despise, it's writing business letters.'

Laban folded the crackling sheet and poked it into his pocket. 'I'll tend to this,' he promised, with one of his infrequent paternal gestures.

Dusky promptly dropped the letter out of her crowded mind. Until another followed it.

That next letter brought her to a sharp halt. She tore it open on the steps of the Administration Building and read it as she walked toward Lawrence Hall. Her halt was so sudden that Mary Beth and Kate Oliver crashed into her from behind and sent two books and a roll of sketches and a handbag flying in all directions.

'Look at this!' she scolded, ignoring her scattered belongings. 'They're off their heads! They threaten to bring suit!'

'Bring suit? Who?' Kate Oliver jerked her head this way and that, trying to focus on the wildly waving letter.

'This idiotic garden furniture manufacturer. They say they'll have to bring suit against the committee chairman if that order isn't completed and the money sent! — My word, they don't seem to have paid a lick of attention to Laban's letter.'

'Laban!' — Mary Beth's gentle voice scorned him — 'Quite likely Laban never gave the matter another thought. You might as well count on quicksilver.'

'What on earth am I to do now?' Dusky stood staring blankly while a trickling stream of students divided on the reef of the three girls and flowed together when it had passed them.

'Why don't you ask Paul?' Mary Beth queried, with sublime faith in masculine wisdom.

'Paul?' Dusky's voice was astonished. 'David might help me out, though.'

XXVII. ZANJA FIESTA

As April's parade of flowers and lush green hurried past in a bright blur, Dusky's tasks continued to fit into one another like a picture-puzzle. For her term paper in Mexican history she had chosen the Mexican influence on California's development; thus her copious reading for the fiesta contributed to the paper and the reading for the paper to the fiesta. She had painted painstaking pictures of many of the scenes in the pageant, using them to work out composition problems in the class in illustrating. So, art and fiesta also exchanged contributions.

Not until May did the fiesta take place. Always it was a time of anxiety, since in May the weather had not settled into its summer procession of sunny days and starry nights, and rain often drove the program and the audience into the large gymnasium.

Dusky and her committee of committees had loads of palm and pepper branches ready for such a shift, so that the gymnasium could be made to simulate an outdoor scene if it became necessary. The luxuriant subtropical growth kept Green Valley busy trimming the trees along its avenues, and it was easy to secure a foundation of opulent trimmings.

At the best, however, an indoor fiesta lost half its charm, and Dusky was keyed up in an intense hope that it would not rain, an intense will that it should not. When at last she and Aunt Phronsie were seated in the topmost row of seats in the bowl, she felt as if she had been directly responsible for holding the weather bureau steady. The evening was cloudless and gentle as only Southern California evenings can be.

The bowl was brimmed with spectators, and cars were lined up along the other bank of the Zanja, when the harpists, the violinists, the pianist on the stage, struck the opening chords, which were taken up and prolonged by flutes and a trumpet in the darkness at the stream's edge.

Into the radiance of the spotlights paced brown-robed friars with high-held banners, and a richly gowned prelate on a white mule. — Dusky had insisted on the white mule, and he had finally been attained by combining a spray-gun, kalsomine, and a dun-gray animal. — Gayly caparisoned horses followed, carrying Spanish señoritas in mantillas and flowing skirts, and grandees with bell trousers and embroidered jackets and scarlet sashes. Behind the riders trudged other friars and Mexican peons and Indians in garments of hide. When the whole group were centered in the light, the music crashed command, the tableau was still, and a hidden voice declaimed Paul's lines, beginning:

> 'From far the friars came, their sandaled feet
> Bleeding on flinty stones and angry briar,
> Seeking the lost and nurturing the found.
> Hot flamed their zeal and high their courage blazed,
> And burned a path through forest and through waste.'

The leading padres grounded their banners, the Indian men plied their rude picks — rib bones of cattle — the Indian women scooped imaginary earth into their bowl-shaped baskets. Another crash of music, and they rested from their labors, all eyes turned toward the darkness.

Dusky sat poised ready to give prearranged signals with her strong flashlight, ready to run at need. She was only dimly aware of the audience; brimmed bowl, still cars. The only vivid thing in the world was the group there on the bank, glowing with light. She strained forward, holding her breath. Would the water come through exactly on time? It had been held back by the irrigation gates along its course, until signals had flashed for the opening of one gate after another, until — How *long!* Dusky dug her nails into her palms. What an endless minute!

A shout from Indians and peons let Dusky back into her seat. The horses curvetted and pranced at the clamor, and Mexican dons held fast and waved their flat hats. Into the light sparkled the water, creeping along the emptied stream bed.

The prelate made the sign of the cross; the people knelt; two Indians brought the friars two small orange trees, precociously gilded with large yellow fruits. Solemnly the friars set them on the banks of the living waters.

Again the tableau held, while the hidden voice declaimed:

> 'A gentle folk, they wrought as they were bid.
> They delved and spun, they hewed and baked and pruned;
> And, following the brown-robed friars' word,
> They brought adown the hills the sparkling flood
> Which made our Eldorado.'

The procession resumed its course, across the stage of the Greek theater, down, and out into the dark again. And again the swinging rhythm of Paul's verse rang out across the audience.

The stage had been set like an open market, with booths encircling it and displays spread on the floor. Now a multicolored throng of Mexican figures lounged into place among the wares, and two hidalgos, behind the footlights at each side, posed indolently and strummed steel guitars.

> 'Proud names, high hearts, the heritage of Spain,
> In beauty that leaps onward through the years' —

so went the poem. Into the center sprang a boy and girl in Mexican garb, whirling and posturing through a lively

Mexican dance. It ended amid the strains of a Spanish song sung by the people of the market-place, who stood, arms akimbo, and sang and shouted their approval.

Tall eucalyptus trees — pale trunked and lofty crowned — made a wall behind the theater, their high foliage lost in the dark sky. Now they flashed out under flooding colored lights, trees of light, ethereal rose and sapphire and gold like San Berdoo at sunset, weirdly exquisite against the black night. Stage and background became as unreal as a dream, and the actors were part of the fantasy. Chinese, Filipinos, East Indians — all the races who had helped create the state — took their place in the swirling color. They danced, they sang, they formed stately tableaux, and all were held in a shifting unity by Paul's rhythmic verse.

It was the final number, the Japanese, that thrilled Dusky with delighted anticipation, and her heart sank when a girl in front of her, straining her eyes to make out the printed program, said: 'Michi? Michi Nasaki? I heard they took Michi to the Infirmary after the pageant began.'

'My word!' Dusky murmured to Aunt Phronsie. 'If Michi's out, the thing falls sort of flat. She was the loveliest ——'

Michi had worked out her own dance, with the help of a Japanese woman whom she had found in one of the citrus groves near Green Valley. This woman could play the proper Japanese music on the proper Japanese samisen, an instrument exotic in shape and sound.

'There's the samisen,' Dusky whispered distractedly. 'Do you suppose —? But it *is* Michi!'

Dressed in a straight plum-colored kimono with chrysanthemums blazing across its rich darkness, Michi minced out before the footlights and danced to the strange barbaric music. The footlights had been dimmed, and the floodlights, and the spot was held on the one small figure, bowing and rising, lifting and arching its hands in exquisite line and perfect rhythm. The dance was a fluid picture, painted with motion. Every attitude was beauty, and Michi moved through one after another in a rapt silence that was like a trance.

When she had sunk to the floor, a small bright petal broken by beauty, another crashing chord brought all the actors with a simultaneous rush to the stage. They pirouetted and stepped and curtseyed in a folk dance that was an adaptation of the Virginia Reel.

Few of the onlookers guessed that it was not a part of the act, when David, a Mexican peon, lifted in his arms a slight bundle of colored silks and carried it into the wings. Dusky, who had felt her whole body twanging like violin strings when Michi fell, blessed David for his quickness of thought. It was strange how finely he seemed keyed to the needs of other people.

After the final dance the vendors began to call their wares. A gypsy fortune-teller, a flower-seller, a sweets-seller, ran down through the audience, inviting it up into the market-place. The evening broke into a froth of fun and buying. The Mexican border was not many miles away, and all sorts of knickknacks had been brought across for the occasion, and were spread in tempting confusion: carved and painted wood, tooled leather, blue glass, small Chimayas. There was a chile stand, too, and hot tamales steaming from a quaint cart, and *dulces* alluringly shaped.

Mary Beth, a blonde Chinese maiden, and Paul, a Spanish don, beckoned Dusky from the stage. Dusky, who had sat as if rooted, sprang up and reached back a hand for Aunt Phronsie.

'Run along, child!' Aunt Phronsie ordered. 'I'll roam where I please. You forget me and have a good time. It's been beautiful.'

Dusky smiled at her and went with long steps down the bowl and across to the market-place. Laban materialized as she went, and loped along beside her. 'An oyster, Walrus?' he invited. 'Or tortillas and sich?'

'I don't know whether I can eat a thing.' — Dusky shook her head, blinking, and smiled absently at someone who plucked at her sleeve to congratulate her — 'I feel all bubbly inside.'

'A tamale will soon settle *that*,' said Laban.

'But I must find David and see how Michi is!' — While Laban ordered steaming dishes of very hot Spanish food, she peered this way and that through the weaving crowd. No David.

'No,' coldly answered Mary Beth, who was managing to eat a fat tamale out of its dripping husks with delicate propriety. 'I haven't seen him since he carried Michi out.'

'Oh, he's prob'ly round with some señorita or other,' Laban comforted her, waving a tortilla vaguely at the throng. 'What would you like for a souvenir, Walrus? A painted chopping bowl? Or a carved egg beater doodad? Or a set of those horsehair baskets the size of acorns?'

'Not any,' Dusky refused. 'I hate and despise the painted chopping bowls. What should I do with one?'

Her eyes continued to roam the crowd as she ate. Maxine scampered past, eating lusciously from the tray of dulces she had for sale; Jan pirouetted in and out, whirling her gay Spanish skirts to the admiration of attendant youths. But there was no David. Dusky felt chilly, and the iridescent gaiety of the evening flattened. A raindrop spattered on her nose.

Few had noticed the clouds that rolled across stars and moon, and the sharp pelt of rain set the merrymakers shrieking. Canopies were hastily put up over the booths and the buyers huddled under them, jammed together with scarcely elbow room but still buying and eating.

Coming now, the rain was not a calamity. The market was almost emptied of its goods, and the shower was a period at the end of a full paragraph; — or perhaps a dash. Couples went scurrying across the campus, the boys' coats thrown over the girls' gay costumes. Laban and Dusky, with their easy, long-legged canter, outdistanced most of them and soon stood damp and breathless in the entry of the Infirmary.

'Thanks, Laban; here's your coat. I'll run in and see Michi, and then it's only a step over to Lawrence.'

'I'll wait. Maybe Miss Morris has a fire.'

'Oh, run along!' said Dusky. 'Good-night.'

'Well, then you have to lug your souvenir home,' he said, handing her the large object that had been tucked under his arm.

It was one of the painted wooden bowls. 'Well — thank you!' Dusky murmured, and went into the office, giggling.

Nurse Morris, sitting alone by her radio, said, No, certainly Dusky couldn't see Michi tonight. No, not for a half of a half of a minute. Michi had had a bromide and was sleeping like a little Jap doll. Yes, Michi had been stark staring mad to get up out of bed and dance, but she wasn't going to die of it this time.

Dusky stood on one damp foot and scribbled a note of affectionate thanks, and Miss Morris took it, severely, with the tips of her fingers. Dusky dashed through the rain again, and up onto the porch of her dormitory. All the dormitory porches were gay with color under the lights, and Spanish dons thrummed guitars on the railings, screwing their necks to avoid the spattering rain.

In the Lawrence lobby Miss Corinne, umbrella in hand, was taking leave of Mrs. Forrester. 'Dusky, it was the loveliest fiesta I ever saw in any school!' Mrs. Forrester cried, holding out both hands in one of the spontaneous gestures that so charmingly accented her dignity.

'How does it feel to see the child of your brain make so brilliant a début?' asked Miss Corinne. Even in the half-light of the entry Dusky could see Miss Corinne's usual half-mocking scrutiny, as of one withdrawn, watching the world with a smile.

'So much of it was other people's,' Dusky deprecated. 'Wasn't Michi marvelous? And sick, too.'

'A tubercular tendency, Miss Morris says. It's most unfortunate. But, Dusky, will it keep you awake if I say that the other members of the Mexican fellowship committee were as favorably impressed as I?'

Dusky wetted dry lips. 'The other members': that meant that Miss Corinne was one.

'The chairman observed to me that few gestures could be more effective in promoting race friendship and appreciation than your full-colored picture. — Because it was a picture of the contribution of many races to the whole that is California, a whole which could not have been without them. He felt that the mind which wrought it, though obviously immature, was worthy of nurture.'

Dusky, feeling immature indeed, shifted boyishly from one damp foot to the other, eyes on Miss Corinne.

'We must not be too sanguine, though,' Miss Corinne warned. 'There are some flaws on the record ——'

'*Not* the bench and the lawsuit?' Dusky gasped. 'David has fixed that. They couldn't sue when I'm not of age. And it was only partly my fault.'

Miss Corinne laughed. 'No, though it sounds interesting. I must hear more about it. — No; another of the members is a stickler for the scholastic. She's a sworn foe of the interference of outside activities in the classroom work. So she holds any scholastic deficiency against you.'

'That term paper?' Dusky breathed.

'That term paper. It *is* overdue.'

'Professor Sands gave me till Wednesday morning.'

'And you think you can have it completed and in his hands by that time?'

'I know I can. There was never any question of it. And Aunt Phronsie has even taken over my orange juice for the week to make it easier. — It's a little like Christmas shopping, Miss Corinne. You know the folks that have their presents bought and wrapped and the cards on them before Thanksgiving? My word, don't they miss a lot of fun? Well, when you've really worked as hard as I have this year, there's something thrilling about getting in all out of breath, just before the bell rings.'

Miss Corinne's lips curved understandingly. 'Well, be sure it's before the bell rings, my dear!'

Slowly Dusky climbed the stairs to her room, absently waving an answer to calls from girls and boys. She was very tired; and, of course, she was very happy; so happy that she found herself weeping into her pillow. Where *had* David gone?

XXVIII. THE OLIVER

FRIARS and Temecula Indians, hidalgos and señoritas, whirled and stamped through Dusky's dreams all night, hot with lights and excitement, while she herself tried endlessly to go somewhere, and was unable to find her shoes — her gloves — her hat.

She waked in the morning tired and tumbled. 'My word!' she told Mary Beth, 'I feel as if I'd swallowed the camel in the Bible — or was it a whale? I ought to plunge into my term paper and work with all my might, but I simply can't settle down till I've seen Michi.'

Michi was propped up among the pillows, a little too much color in her lips and cheeks. Dusky perched on the foot of her bed and gazed at her.

'Did you ever think you might be a great dancer, Michi Nasaki?' she asked. 'I mean it. You're wonderful.'

Michi shook a languid head. 'There are many things I really wish to do,' she said. 'But it doesn't matter. I'll not get to do them.'

'You mean — your health?'

'Oh, no, that isn't so bad: I'm much better than I used to be. But what's the use? My parents will send me back to Japan, now I am through college.'

'But won't you like that? I'd give my boots.'

'Yes, if it were only for a visit. But they send me to marry. Someone I do not know. And settle there — in a foreign country.' Michi's voice quickened, and her flush grew brighter — 'You *know* I'm American, Dusky! In everything except the face I wear, I am. To go away ——'

She broke off, and her lips parted in a forced smile. Dusky staring at her with new vision, thought that, inside, Michi was crying just as Dusky might cry. It was only her Japanese smile that hid her American tears. She put out a quick hand, but Michi averted her eyes from it, still smiling.

'Miss Morris says I shall be dressed in a few days if I keep very still now,' she went on, turning the subject in her quick, bright little voice. 'I can study for the Comprehensive, too, if I rest a great deal between.'

Troubled, Dusky made notes of the books Michi needed, covertly watching the smooth little face as she did so. With all her vaunted lack of race prejudice, she had never sensed the feeling that could lie beneath the suave Japanese finish, the light manner.

'Michi,' she said abruptly, 'we're going to get caught up in a whirl now — those frightful Comprehensive Exams and all — But I do want another real visit before Commencement. Things will let up during Senior Week. Will you run away with me then? Come over to the cottage and the Singing Wood, and have a picnic lunch together?'

'That Singing Wood!' Michi murmured. 'I love that Singing Wood. I shall be glad to come.'

Back in her room, Dusky put aside the thought of Michi, swept away all the usual Saturday occupations, and plunged into a sea of notes.

'I should think you would have kept a notebook,' Mary Beth commiserated. The waste-paper effect overflowed Dusky's half of the desk and flooded her own tidy rectangle.

'Notebook? I've three notebooks!' Dusky waved a blue one, with girls' heads sketched all over it, a brown-covered one marked 'Lombard High School' and a paper-covered one. 'These papers are extra.' She shuffled a double handful despairingly. 'It's going to be worse than I thought, getting them sorted and organized and the thing written and typed. It's so awful to get started. I'd rather clean a dresser drawer, even, than start a paper. — It's too near lunch time, now,' she decided with relief.

Climbing slowly back to her room after lunch, however, she resigned herself to her fate. All afternoon she read notes, some of them with considerable difficulty because they had been penciled on scraps of paper, abbreviated to the quick.

'What could I mean by "See Cor. Ex. for Era-reac"?' she pondered. 'It's so strange how you always think notes are going to be as plain when you come to use them as they were when you made them.'

She clipped them together with a general title fastened to each swatch; and she made an outline of her paper, knitting her brows as she clicked it out on her typewriter; and she numbered the swatches and the entries in her three notebooks, according to the outline numbers.

She reached that stage on Monday evening just before dinner, and jumped up so suddenly as almost to overturn the desk and Mary Beth. Mary Beth had early learned to cover her ears when studying, to shut out Dusky's incorrigible current of comment. She uncovered them now and raised mild eyes.

Dusky stretched joyously, while Mary Beth's puzzled gaze sought the ragged notes and the outline for explanation.

'The hard part is all done!' Dusky informed her. 'From now on it's easy sailing. I'm going to take a bath and enjoy my dinner with a clear conscience.'

She did enjoy it, relishing the gay confusion of the room, a sea of braids and curls and demurely brushed wings cresting the summer colors; relishing the chatter that called for Mrs. Randall's monitory bell; relishing even the fact that none of them relished the cereal custard that was dessert.

At seven she had immersed herself again, ticking out the first draft of her paper with flying fingers.

'*Will* it keep you awake, Mary Beth?'

'I'll put cotton in my ears. You'd better close the transom. Windows, too, or Mrs. Forrester might hear that Oliver.'

'That Oliver's no noisier than lots of others, and it's ——'

But Mary Beth had buried her head in her pillow.

Dusky wound a wet towel around her head and went ticking on through the night, until her old typewriter ribbon was so frayed that it tangled in the mechanism, and so dim that THE END was a whisper, scarcely intelligible.

When she clicked off her light and threw open the windows, the sky was paling with dawn. Dusky leaned both hands on the sill and took deep breaths of the cool freshness. The campus was intensely still, stirred only by the little breeze that is the waking breath of day.

She must get as much sleep as she could, for the last hard pull was ahead. She shucked her bathrobe off onto the floor, dived into her bed, and was asleep.

As on some other strenuous mornings, Mary Beth let her sleep past the breakfast bell, waking her only when she brought her a bacon-and-egg sandwich and an apple, stealthily removed from the breakfast table. Dusky ate and bathed and dressed with one eye on the thick stack of yellow paper that held the rough draft of her theme: one eye and a vigorous red pencil, with which she added commas and semicolons and slashed out cumbersome phrases.

Fogged with Mexico, she went to art class, the yellow sheaf under her arm.

'Going downtown today, Laban?' she asked.

'Could. Want to go along?'

She shook her head. 'Mind getting me a new typewriter ribbon? Mine is run ragged. No one but me could read it.'

'Oh, sure. Any special kind?'

'Oliver. No. 9. All black. Say it after me, Laban.'

'Oliver. No. 9. All black,' he repeated, cocking his Brown's Best cap over his ear.

'Here's the dollar. Sometimes you're worth a cent and a half,' Dusky assured him.

'Here's the dollar. Sometimes you're worth a cent and a half,' he parroted; 'but usually you're in the red,' he added.

Dusky turned a disdainful shoulder.

The day sped by on the wings of art classes, history, Spanish, biology lab, Dusky making sharp red corrections on the yellow sheaf which was her constant companion. Day sped, and evening.

'But, Dusky, haven't you even begun typing it?' Mary Beth cried. 'Why — you can't possibly have it ready tomorrow morning. Is there some way we can help?'

'You can go to bed,' Dusky advised. 'And I can, too, possibly have it ready. There aren't but fifty pages, and I can do a page in four or five minutes. I'm *good.* That's only about four hours. — Now, hush, Ma'Beth, don't you know it makes things harder to think they're so hard? — I've got to concentrate on a better conclusion — a sort of smashing one. Then I can copy.'

Mary Beth sighed. 'I can anyway take your wastebasket to the incinerator,' she said, 'so you'll have room for all those wads of waste paper.'

She gathered up the yellow wads that had already overflowed and were blowing round the room, carried the basket out, and was soon back, cuddled down in bed in her kitten fashion. Still Dusky was murmuring phrases, writing in sentences, crossing out words.

The little clock had ticked its way to twelve when she flung out her arms, yawned, and reached for the paper-wrapped parcel in which Laban had brought her new typewriter ribbon. She scooped it out of the wrapping. Cheerfully the round tin box announced itself, 'Underwood, Black Record.'

Dusky gasped. 'Oh, if I could just wring his neck!' she hissed through gritted teeth. 'If I could only just *once* wring his neck! Why did I ever count on him, anyway?'

She yanked the tinfoil from the ribbon and inspected the spool, smelling keenly of ink.

'It won't work on the Oliver, not in ten thousand years it won't. I'll have to put back that old rag and do the best I can. Probably lose the Mexican fellowship, and all because of Laban.' She slapped the loose billows of paper on her desk with a practiced palm, stooped and rummaged under the yellow paper wads in the basket, sat back with a bang. 'Mary Beth burned it up!'

Mary Beth stirred uneasily and made little kitten noises in her sleep. Dusky nibbled her fingers and thought wildly.

'I can't possibly do it by longhand. — I *won't* lose my chance of Mexico!' — It was as if she said, 'my chance of heaven.' She slipped out of her shoes and padded across the room to the door, opened it and looked up and down the hall. No lighted transoms or under-door slivers of brightness tonight. 'Let's see: Jan has a typewriter. And Phyllis. And the Lancaster twins.'

Down gray hall and gray stairs she stole, her flashlight darting discreet glances before her. Softly she tapped at Jan's door; turned the knob, hairbreadth by hairbreadth; slipped in, feeling like a burglar after the family silver; turned the flash on Jan's desk and sent it creeping softly up to the typewriter. It *would* have a cretonne cover piped with rose, Jan's typewriter!

Heart thudding, she lugged it out, with an awkward

thrust of the knee at the unlatched door; shifted it to her right arm and closed the door with her left; crept up the stairs to her room.

Safe inside, she felt like a scout who has escaped the forest and reached the stockade. She set Jan's machine on the desk from which she had lifted her own, snatched off the rosy cover, and heaved a deep sigh. The ribbon looked passably new.

Her fingers pranced confidently across the keys — went on prancing, automatically, after the confidence had gone. The paper showed a medley of letters, one on top of another. The machine moved like a horse that paws the ground without advancing.

For ten minutes — fifteen — Dusky worked with the mechanism, and then she gave it up, covered the useless machine, set it with a thump on the floor beside her Oliver, and started grimly down the stairs.

At the door of the end room, the twins', she tapped, while her heart pounded. When there was no reply, she tried the knob. The door was locked.

Along the hall she scurried to Phyllis's room. It, too, was locked. With her hand on the knob she stood wondering whether to risk rousing Mrs. Forrester by a louder tap. She did not wonder long: a businesslike click of a switch flooded the whole long corridor with light, and Mrs. Forrester approached her down its length, an avenging goddess in a white flannel robe, her hair a nimbus of silvery curls.

She stood before Dusky, her lips severe.

'Dusky Day,' she said, 'I hope you are sick.'

Dusky gasped.

'It would be the only excuse' — Mrs. Forrester turned her wrist, showing the dial — 'After one o'clock.'

'Mrs. Forrester,' Dusky said faintly, 'there didn't seem to be anything else to do. They sent the wrong typewriter ribbon. Phyllis has a machine, but her door's locked.'

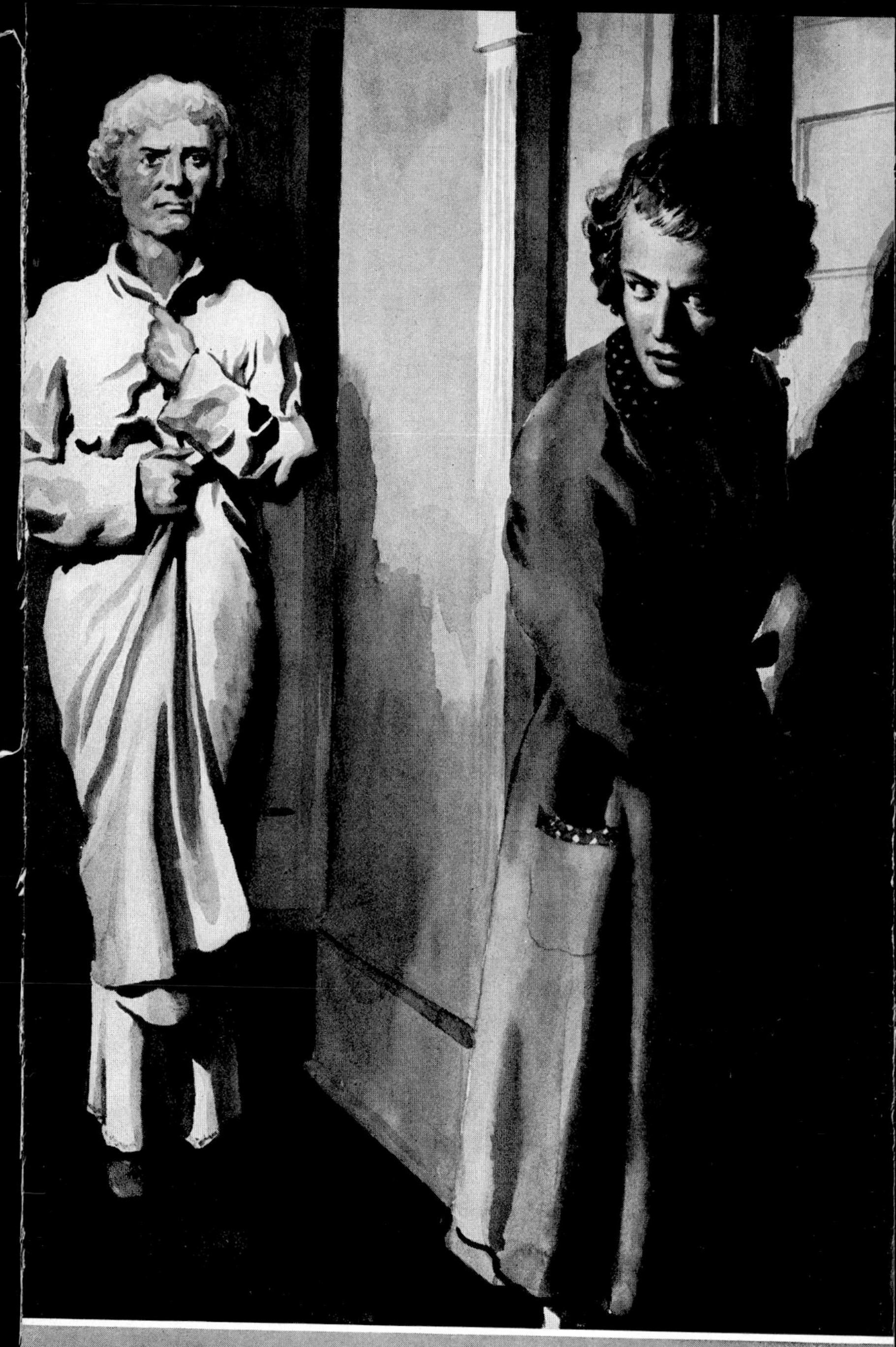

MRS. FORRESTER APPROACHED HER DOWN ITS LENGTH, AN AVENGING GODDESS IN A WHITE FLANNEL ROBE

It seemed as well to suppress the abduction of Jan's Underwood for the moment.

'But — a typewriter at this hour of the night?' — Mrs. Forrester's eyebrows went up.

'A typewriter's the only way I can possibly get my term paper in by tomorrow morning at nine. *You* know, Mrs. Forrester: unless that paper's in, my Mexican fellowship is out. — Why, Mrs. Forrester, I thought you had a typewriter!'

'I lent it to one of the boys last week. I've all the supplies, but no machine. Besides, this escapade is scarcely excusable, Dusky, even for a term paper. A term paper, by the way, which should have been in some time ago. — What is it now?' she broke off, amusement getting the better of severity.

Dusky, apparently not hearing the menace of her words, was poised for speech.

'*All* the supplies, Mrs. Forrester?' she asked eagerly.

'Oh, but not a ribbon, Dusky.'

If Mrs. Forrester expected Dusky to wilt at that exception, she was surprised by the girl's jubilant answer:

'No, but that's all right! Oh, that's perfectly all right!'

XXIX. TASTE

WHEN Mary Beth uttered her kittenlike waking yawn that Wednesday morning, Dusky was going over the last of her fifty typewritten pages with careful ink eraser and pen.

'Loduska Day! you never worked all night?' Mary Beth demanded, coming to a sitting position in the middle of the yawn, and staring round-eyed at Dusky.

'Didn't I though?' Dusky smiled at her from beneath the enormous turban, wet towel, dry towel, that she assumed at such times.

Mary Beth pattered over to her and looked at the thick pile of typed pages.

'Why are you correcting your carbon copy so well?' she inquired. 'Nicely enough for the original. It *is* the carbon, isn't it?'

'It's the carbon, and it better *had* look nice,' Dusky declared inelegantly. 'Here's the original' — she shoved a few limp yellow pages at Mary Beth — 'and if ever I was thankful I'd learned touch typing —!'

Mary Beth stared with puzzled eyes: at the limp yellow pages, inkless, but perforated with innumerable minute holes; at the typewriter on the desk.

'It hasn't any ribbon in.' She said it with a question mark.

'No, darn you and Laban, it hasn't. He got the wrong kind of new one and you helpfully burned up the old one.

So I had to go it blind. Oh, look here!' — Mary Beth still gazed, uncomprehending — 'The keys will print on the carbon paper even if there isn't any ribbon in. So you get a carbon copy even if there isn't anything but a blank sheet on top.'

She inserted a sandwich — yellow paper, carbon sheet, white paper — in the machine, and typed the title of the paper and her name, while Mary Beth watched the keys, fascinated, as they swung up and struck the yellow sheet, and dropped back without leaving a mark on the yellow. Dusky took out the sandwich, peeled the carbon from the white paper, and exhibited the clear black carbon lettering.

'The idea just flashed on me like that!' she said.

So the term paper went in, just under the tape; and at the end of the week came an official communication from the University, notifying Miss Loduska Day that she had been appointed a fellow at the University of Mexico for the following year.

The letter was in the D rack in Lawrence Hall after breakfast, and Dusky walked on air to art school, floated up the stairs, got out her palette, and squirted extra large caterpillars of paint all around the edge, and then sat gazing ecstatically out of the window. She was not aware of Laban until he had leaned over and made passes in front of her nose with a paintbrush. She smiled gently and moved a little away.

Laban tapped her knees sharply with a ruler.

'Ouch! My word!' she protested, coming out of her dream.

Laban regarded her intently. 'The reflexes *seem* normal,' he opined gravely. 'She may come out of it with a fair measure of sanity, if put in a padded cell at once. But, my poor Walrus, what happened?'

Remembering the typewriter ribbon, Dusky came to life and snorted, 'No thanks to you!' But she was too happy to nurse her wrath. She shoved the letter toward him.

'Say!' he cried, jarred out of his languor, 'Dusky, that's great stuff! Art, I suppose, and other things?'

She nodded. 'And archaeology — think of the field work! — and lots of Spanish — and for lighter courses, folk lore and folk dancing and handcrafts ——' She stopped suddenly — 'Only I may not be able to go after all,' she ended flatly. 'That *would* be a joke.'

'Oh, you'll go. — You've been working toward it these two years, haven't you?'

'Sort of.'

He narrowed his intensely clear pale eyes and his face tightened. 'I'd like to go to Mexico myself. — You — Dusky, you wouldn't want to make it a kind of jolly old partnership? You and me?'

Dusky was suddenly all awake, as if she had been doused with cold water. Her eyes flew around the room — no one near enough to overhear them.

'Why — why, Laban!' she stammered.

'Look how we like the same things, Dusky!' he urged. 'Look what a keen time we'd have, drifting on where we pleased, and liking the world, and ——'

Thoughts and feelings were flickering across Dusky's mind like the flicker and dazzle of sunshine on forest leaves.

'Oh, Laban,' she said, shaking her head, 'you've been such fun, but I — I —— No, I don't feel that way about ——'

'About me.' Laban finished her sentence, his voice flattening. 'I don't suppose anyone would. — But, Dusky!' — the voice rose angrily — 'that great ox of a Masterson — why, he wouldn't see things your way at all. I thought you'd finally had sense enough to see that he wasn't your kind. You haven't been around with him much lately, and I've seen that little suitemate of yours —

the dimply one — making up to him — Anyway, your tastes and his ——'

A rush of anger made Dusky dizzy. 'Maxine is engaged to a boy in Paris and David never would give a snap for her anyway. And his tastes and mine are very much alike, really.' — She spoke stiffly, absurdly. — 'As for drifting, neither of us would be satisfied to drift, no matter how much fun it might seem.'

As soon as she had spoken, the stiffness went limp. It was true that she and David had spent little time together lately; she had been too busy to realize how little. Now she ached with loneliness. Laban's face looked as lonely as she felt. He was quicksilver, maybe, but ——

'Oh, Laban, you know I think you're wonderful! You won't mind much?'

'Not me, my dear Walrus!' Laban had recaptured his drawl, though he was still white. 'One thing about me, my dear: I don't care about anything, much or long.' But he swung toward her for an instant before he bent to his work. 'With that black lie, my dear Walrus, we will consider the matter forever closed.'

Dusky puttered blindly at her canvas. The Mexican fellowship — the Singing Wood — Laban — David ——

David, who had been always there, these four years, and who was gone when she became aware how much he mattered. For he mattered a lot. She could see him more plainly now, with her eyes closed because of their wetness, than she had ever seen him with them open. So big — and strong — and sure! Fun, too. And understanding. Such an ease about being with David; such a certainty that he would always be the same. Weren't girls the silly nuts, never seeing what was right before them? Until it was too late?

Mary Beth cleared her throat, softly. 'May I go with you to the cottage,' she asked, 'when you show them your fellowship letter?'

Dusky's eyes opened, wet lashes clinging together. This was the old Mary Beth, the constraint of past months melted. 'My word, yes,' Dusky said huskily.

They hurried over together while Aunt Phronsie and the boys were still at the table, that evening. Wordlessly Dusky thrust the letter into her aunt's hands, and Aunt Phronsie, adjusting her glasses, read it aloud.

'You deserve it, Dusky,' David said soberly. 'You'll go on and make a name for yourself.'

'When she — well, I couldn't help hearing — when she rejected Laban this morning,' Mary Beth said in one rush of determined disclosure — 'she told him that you and she —— '

Dusky, her face horrified, clapped a hand over Mary Beth's reckless mouth. She was hot with shame. Didn't Mary Beth realize that people sometimes changed? And David — he had changed.

'Did you, Dusky?' he demanded. 'Dusky, will Mexico keep you — keep you out of mischief for a few years?' he added shyly. 'Medical school and an interneship — it seems like forever. But, afterward, wouldn't China be a great place for a painter?'

'Why, David!' Mary Beth protested in a small shocked voice, 'you ought to have taken her out in the moonlight somewhere!'

Dusky was looking strangely at David. What she said seemed to have no connection with what had gone before. 'Wait a minute, David, I want to ask you something. About a matter of taste.'

She ran into the sitting-room and brought the bundle of garden furniture catalogues she had left in the secretary. 'Tell me,' she begged breathlessly, 'which of these designs would you have chosen, David?'

David's jaw tightened. Slowly he turned the pages, inspected the designs that had been checked.

'I don't know what it's all about, because the bench has

been ordered and delivered, of course. But I'll try to play the game.' He flipped the pages back to the rococo bench Langston had chosen and looked at it a long time with his steady eyes. 'I must say this one appeals to me,' he acknowledged, 'but I'm beginning to get a glimmering that it may not be the finest. I still think it's pretty, though,' he said with dogged honesty, while Dusky fidgeted and bit back protests. 'Now this one we did get' — he riffled the pages of another catalogue till he came to the chaste design — 'it did seem to me it was pretty plain. For the money and all. But I was sure it must be right if you chose it.'

Dusky was still looking at him, at the way his wheat-colored hair flopped over his square forehead; at the troubled sincerity of his wide-set eyes; at the firmness of his jaw. Inside her brain she was laughing at herself and at this test of hers. Because, if David had chosen the plain bench, she would have accepted the choice as a Sign; but when he chose the terrible one — it didn't matter. Because David was more than taste; much more.

'Good gracious, Dusky, what's all this folderol?' Paul asked.

'Folderol's right,' Dusky admitted gaily. 'Nothing to it. Or scarcely anything. — David, do you *want* to walk out in the moonlight?'

'I think it would be lovely, but wait till I put on my shawl,' Aunt Phronsie said. 'It's cool for the end of May.'

Mary Beth got up from her chair and made a flustered little clatter among the dishes. 'Let's — let's do up the dishes first,' she proposed. 'You and Paul and I — Aunt Phronsie.'

But the week, like the day, held shadows.

'Confound Johnnie!' Dusky cried tempestuously, when Paul telephoned her. 'He might have held off till Commencement was over, when he'd waited this long.'

For Johnnie had written, with complete finality, that in the absence of any documents regarding a sale agreement, he found it necessary to terminate the present lease, and require Paul and Dusky to vacate the premises before the first of September.

XXX. COMMENCEMENT

Dusky and Paul had often declared that they wished Johnnie would decide one way or the other, because anything was better than uncertainty. They discovered their mistake.

'It was something, just to hope that the grove might be ours — and Mexico,' Dusky said disconsolately. 'And I really never stopped hoping it, and believing it, too.'

'I suppose you may have guessed,' Paul said truculently, 'why Mary Beth and I feel so especially low about it. I know we haven't acted that way, but we ——'

'Whoops!' Dusky hooted. 'Did you really think we might have guessed? — I will admit, though,' she conceded, laughing at Mary Beth's startled face, 'that Mary Beth hasn't acted like a lot of the nitwits on this campus. There's something in being brought up in China, maybe.'

'Well,' Paul observed with a brotherly glare, '"if the lady is through; if she is quite through," I will conclude that it would have been a shade too perfect — Mary Beth and I and ——'

'The Singing Wood,' grieved Mary Beth.

'And my year in Mexico,' Dusky added, 'and then I could have settled down with you for a little while and painted and illustrated till I got a start, and ——'

As matters developed, the cottage in Singing Wood would have had to be of rubber to accommodate all the clan members who wished to take shelter there. Mr. and Mrs. Day were as instantly charmed with grove and house as any of the rest had been.

It was a great day for Paul and Dusky when their parents arrived. Dusky's heart gave a leap of joy when, waiting aloft in the Limb, she saw them clambering from the big blue-and-white bus. Her mother's hat rose jauntily from the top of her unfashionable coil of hair, and a half-smile of expectancy parted her lips. Mr. Day, peering over his shoulder for his children, absent-mindedly assisted her.

Proudly Paul and Dusky drove them through the pretty little town, whose wealth and culture sat serenely in earthly paradises on its encircling hills. Proudly they brought the Limb to a stop before the Singing Wood, where Aunt Phronsie waited at the gate.

'It's more heavenly lovely than I even supposed,' Mrs. Day murmured, gazing out of the window into the green while Dusky took off her hat and wiped a smudge from her cheek.

'May I pick some oranges and eat them?' Mr. Day demanded boyishly. 'Say, Mother, look at the court these young sprigs have fixed up! — Now a studio, Dusky, for you and me ——'

'Don't forget the court's Johnnie's,' Dusky said.

'It would have been too perfect,' Mrs. Day murmured.

'H'mph! Perfect!' Paul gallantly contested the point. 'She doesn't know how fiendishly hot it gets in summer, does she, Dusk? And she isn't acquainted with our little friend the citricola scale and her expensive progeny.'

Dusky followed his lead. 'Nor with orchard-heating and the nice black smudge it spreads.'

'Nor the gosh-awful low price of oranges the past few years!' Paul chanted.

'Nor the way you have to keep replacing old trees.'

'Nor the cost of an ordinary thing like fertilizing.'

'Oh, Paul,' Dusky interrupted, 'did you know Jimmie

Tang's uncle really wants to put a model poultry farm on that waste two-acre strip? He and Wing Lee want to pool their resources and buy two thousand of those great big Petaluma Leghorn hens. They've got it all figured out that it would practically supply the whole nitrogen requirement for ten acres, and they'd swap the fertilizer for the use of the land.'

'Wing Lee?' Paul asked.

Dusky giggled. 'He wants to be our house boy. Imagine! — a house boy! He's tired of teas and artistic ladies and gentlemen.'

'Well, they'll have to see Johnnie about it,' Paul remembered dourly.

Mrs. Day had continued to smile benignly and wander around the house, looking long from each window. 'Too perfect,' she reiterated, as if she had heard nothing of the brave duet and its denouement. 'Dad and I could have spent our winters here, when we were old, and our summers in Colorado.'

Dad was looking quizzically from his son to his daughter. 'Well, if you've lost the grove, what have you gained, these past four years, you children? Besides learning to say secret'ry and portr'it. I didn't know how constantly those words occurred in the vocabulary: Great Caesar's Ghost! it's full of secret'ry, diction'ry, portr'it, dec'rative —— But have you got anything else that you didn't have when you left Lombard High, son?'

'Gosh, yes, I've got Mary Beth!' his son grinned. Mary Beth smiled shyly from the kitchen door.

Mr. Day nodded, his eyes satisfied with Mary Beth. — 'And what about you, tomboy?' he asked Dusky.

'Snaps!' Dusky said triumphantly. 'I've learned to sew on snaps! Look!' She opened the single fastener her thin dress carried — under its belt button — and stared blankly as one side of it came loose in her fingers.

'I told you darning cotton wasn't the right kind to use!' Mary Beth reminded her; and everyone laughed.

'Do you suppose all my improvement is like that?' Dusky moaned. 'I still get mad and make other folks mad. And I was going to do things about race friendship, and I don't know what to do — not as much as when I started, even. All I know is that I, personally, can be friends with Cordelia and Michi and Luisa; and that the same things hurt us all. And that — that the Singing Wood sings to every one of them.'

'That's a lot to learn, Dusky,' her father said after a pause. 'I guess you're right, and there's a lot under the words, too: the Singing Wood sings to us all.'

'And now Ma'Beth and I have got to make a dash for the dorm and get ready for the class day shindig,' Dusky said uncomfortably.

There was not even leisure for the sense of flatness that often dulls life's most eagerly expected moments. This was Monday and Commencement was Wednesday, and life had no time to flatten out.

Of course Mr. and Mrs. Day must visit art school and meet Professor Faunce and Mr. Turner and Laban and Andrea and Jane. They must see the studio, though it did not look like itself, with everyone emptying lockers and tying up disorderly bundles of paintings and drawings, and dumping disorderly litter on the model's stand to be burned. They must go down into the kitchen and get acquainted with Wing Lee. They must see Dusky's mural design, which Professor Faunce had had her execute for the studio, as an exercise in tempera.

Because Professor Faunce was at his side, Mr. Day assumed a critical air as he stood back from that mural. He shoved his hands deep in his pockets and chewed his lips and nodded.

'Not so bad,' he observed to Professor Faunce, 'for a young painter. — Now that way she's got of carrying the color through — Rather gone on Rivera, isn't she? But she'll work through that. She has a streak of independence, so I don't worry about her following anyone too long.'

Mrs. Day smiled with indulgent vagueness. 'Very nice,' she said; 'very nice. — And I never saw your father so bursting with pride.'

That evening there was a reception at the president's house. Dusky helped her mother dress for the occasion. She straightened her belt, and lent her a pair of chiffon hose in place of the heavy silk ones she had felt perfectly suitable. She unpinned the flower from the shoulder of her mother's dark blue crepe dress, and ripped off the fall of lace from its neck. Mrs. Day had a half-mechanical way of pinning pieces of lace where there seemed to her a lack.

'See, dear,' Mrs. Day said with mild pride, 'you always wanted me to use rouge, and I finally bought some. But lipstick — no. I can imagine being chronically flushed, but not with the fever which would explain those lips.'

Laughing, Dusky wheeled her toward the light and smoothed in the edges of the powder on the angle of the jaw, and wiped off the vehement rouge and delicately dabbed on a little of her own softer color. Finally, she anchored Mrs. Day's loose coil of hair more firmly and pulled her hat down with both hands. 'Just jerk it down whenever you remember it, Mom,' she urged.

'Yes, only I never do seem to remember it, dear.'

'Anyway, you look lovely, darling!' Dusky told her with unwonted feeling.

'But so many of the mothers are as young-looking and fashionable as their girls.'

'I wouldn't have any of those ordinary parents,' Dusky assured her.

She was genuinely proud of her serene mother, that night, proud of her father, with his strongly chiseled dark face and his mop of iron gray hair.

Tuesday was the day that had been set for Michi's lunch and visit.

'You don't mind?' Dusky asked her family. 'Something's wrong with Michi. I can't seem to get back of the surface and help, but — well, I want to stand by.'

They all had luncheon in the court. Michi fascinated Mother and Father Day: a brittle bit of painted porcelain with a quick smile that flashed between expressionless intervals.

After luncheon, the senior Days and Aunt Phronsie took the Limb and fared forth to see some of the surrounding country, and Michi and Dusky wandered through the grove and back to the stillness of the cottage. Dusky firmly seated Michi in the biggest chair and pushed a footstool before it for her feet.

'Such a sweet little place,' said Michi. 'Will you leave it at once, after Commencement?'

'We can't. There's irrigating; and the Valencias to pick. Especially irrigating. I'd love to leave it all and let it go to ruin, only, of course, you can't let trees die. Grandma Wilson used to say they were like children, crying when you neglected them.'

'It is not the trees alone that you consider,' Michi said wisely, 'it is those old people whom you love and revere. Very like the Japanese. — Of course,' she went on, smiling into Dusky's astonished face, 'the way in which you speak to your parents, you and Paul, is on the surface disgraceful. But under the surface I see the good strong feeling.' Suddenly she sighed heavily.

'Michi, what is it?' Dusky coaxed. 'You spoke of going back to Japan. Of not wanting to.'

Michi's transparent little hands clenched. 'Not want to? It is death to me. As I said to you, I am American, except this yellow skin, these slanting eyes. I shall not fit Japan. And they treat women so differently there. But the worst is marrying someone I do not know. — You have your boy who is a comrade — you and Mary Beth both. You have chosen. Well, we chose, too; but to what end?'

She turned her head and closed her eyes.

Dusky stirred unhappily. 'What do you mean, Michi?'

For a minute Michi lay still, and then she spoke, low and evenly, her face still turned from Dusky. 'Jiro and I.' She pulled a locket from her dress, slipped the chain over her head, passed it, opened, to Dusky. The picture showed a smiling Japanese face, the mask face that had always seemed to Dusky so cool and unfeeling.

'Jiro and I, we were born in houses side by side in Los Angeles. Together we went to school, to high school. Always we liked each other. Always since we were high school seniors we have planned marriage and our own home as soon as Jiro should be through the university. Behind our faces both of us are all American. Both of us are Christians. But our parents are Buddhist; and —' her voice dropped heavily, tragically — 'all four parents have only us two children.'

'But what of that?' Dusky asked, looking from the smiling boy face to the small mask of pain opposite her.

'What of that? Everything. Don't you understand? Jiro and I are both only children!' She sat straight in the chair, eyes fixed on Dusky. 'No, you do not understand. We know so little of each other. It is like this: since I am their only child, my parents must adopt my husband, when I marry, so that they shall have descendants to worship at their ancestral tablets. Otherwise, for them, blank hopelessness. But Jiro's parents, also, since he is their only child, cannot permit that he be adopted, for then it would be they who would have no descendants. It seems bitter fate that we should have set our hearts on marriage with one another.'

Dusky studied the face in the locket indignantly. 'But will this Jiro stand for anything like that?'

'It would break our parents' hearts,' Michi argued. 'They see only darkness forever, if we marry each other. Better break our hearts than theirs. — I have made Jiro promise that he will not — take his own life as he has tried to do. For Buddhist that is honorable, but not for Christian. And for me it would be the final sorrow. — Can you see, Dusky? Life holds little understanding from white people, in this country, and little opportunity; and in Japan only a foreign land where we do not fit.'

Dusky sat shocked and still. So griefs like this hid behind these smooth faces.

'But, Michi!' she expostulated, 'it isn't right. I *know* it would be better to marry Jiro. Promise me, anyway, that you won't let them send you away without talking to — to your minister. Without talking to me, too, Michi!'

She was kneeling beside the other girl, now, holding on with all the force of her will. Michi smiled faintly.

'You really care. As if I hadn't the yellow mask. Well, then — I promise.'

There was no time for more. The Limb came limping back, driven by a display of motor temperament. It behaved well for its own, but it was crotchety under a new hand.

When Michi had gone, Dusky came back into the sitting-room and sat down silently among her family. Briefly she told them Michi's story.

'It seems to me,' she said thoughtfully, 'that age must earn that reverence, if it is to be worth anything. Like all of you — and like Grandpa and Grandma Wilson. Do you know what Michi thinks? That our reverence for Grandpa and Grandma is why we do our best for the grove, even when we have lost it.'

'They must have been dear old people,' Mrs. Day said. 'You've certainly kept the dear feeling of them in this little house.'

'I rarely come in,' Aunt Phronsie assented, wiping her glasses, 'without seeing old Mr. Wilson in that big chair in the window.'

'The time I remember best,' Dusky went on, reminiscently, 'was one evening — oh, three years ago, I guess. I didn't know Grandpa had been hurt. Of course we weren't such close friends yet. And I found Grandma, the poor old blessed, sitting there in his chair, all alone, rocking and crying.'

Dusky sniffed and shook her head sharply, daring the tears. 'It was then she said that about the orange trees being like neglected children. And she sat staring at the calendar and wiping her eyes and whimpering like a child herself, because she didn't know how to manage.'

Dusky's eyes went to the calendar beside the secretary, and all the other eyes mechanically followed.

'Anybody could see you had a sort of Buddhist reverence for age, to keep that atrocious calendar,' Mr. Day said with feigned brusqueness. 'You don't have to tell us it's the same one. Otherwise you wouldn't have let it stay two minutes.'

Dusky nodded. She walked over to the calendar and patted it. 'See,' she said, 'this is the way they kept tab on the grove, writing their little reminders on the margin of the pad. Blessed old funny spelling! — Look: "Fumagate for scale. — Iragate. — Time to prune. —— Remember to replant along South End." And here' — she turned the pages that had been clipped back all these months — 'in Grandma's writing, "Set the Old Red Hen," and "Wrote Johnnie," and "Duskey brought Candey."'

Mrs. Day squirmed out of the old deep chair and came to look. 'Phronsie,' she asked, 'do you remember? Grandmother Smith used to write things like that on the edges of the old almanac that hung from the clock shelf. Like a diary, a little.'

Aunt Phronsie nodded. 'The almanac that always had a Shakespeare play in it.'

Dusky turned another leaf. 'March, two years ago: here's a regular screed. "This day have sold ——"'

She stopped, her mouth open for the next word, and swallowed.

'Why do you open and close your mouth so oddly?' her mother asked interestedly.

Dusky leaned up against the secretary, laughing and crying together. 'Because — because this *isn't* Johnnie's Singing Wood!'

Mr. Day strode over to the calendar. 'What's all this? What's all this?' he blustered, stooping to read:

> This day have sold — to Paul and Dusky Day — the grove and cottage — and all therein contained — for consideration of — Two Hundred Dollars Down — and what they can a year — till price of Twenty Thousand Dollars be paid. Rec'd of Paul and Dusky Two Hundred Dollars.
>
> Signed, Abijah Wilson — Martha P. Wilson.

Across the quadrangle that night they marched, all in the new young dignity of flowing gowns and mortarboards. Dusky and Paul marched together because they followed one another in the alphabet. Behind them, when Dusky glanced back, she could see David's high-held head and seeking eyes. She knew that Mary Beth walked beside him, too, although her wide eyes and fair hair did not appear above the rhythmically swaying black shoulders.

Off at one side the keenest sickle of a new moon hung between the black columns of two cypresses, against the primrose sky that Dusky loved. Before them the chapel was set white against the dark loom of San Berdoo. — This was nothing but Commencement, Dusky warned herself, trying to recapture her old nonchalance.

This was *Commencement!* Dusky answered herself, and her heart felt as shining as the sickle moon. Commencement. Beginning.

On into the cloisters that ran the length of the chapel, slowly they marched to the great throb of the organ. Dusky glanced aside at the audience thronging the body of the building. She couldn't find Mom and Dad and Aunt Phronsie; but she found five dark, eager faces — Cordelia's family; she found Wing Lee; she found Papa and Mama Vasquez, and Luisa, heavily curled. Carmelita, sitting eagerly forward, waved excitedly.

Dusky waved at the little girl, and smiled serenely at Paul's shocked whisper. Then she looked ahead at the vested à cappella choir in the loft; at the president waiting on the rostrum. Up the steps slowly, slowly. — Mustn't trip. — Mustn't get there too soon or too late.

Dizzily before Dusky's eyes the president's face smiled: the president's hand came up to lift the tassel of her mortarboard and draw it to the other side of the cap.

'Loduska Day, Bachelor of Arts!' said the president.

Commencement! Life had commenced. Life was well on its splendid way.

THE END